"If you're thinking Stephanie Plum in *My Big Fat Greek Wedding*, you're not far off." —*Mystery Scene* on *Dirty Laundry*

"Sexy, suspenseful, and flat-out hilarious: that's my kind of book. I loved *Sofie Metropolis*!"

—Karen Robards, *New York Times* bestselling author

"So you say that your Stephanie Plum novels aren't coming fast enough? Well, this saucy plum of a PI will do just fine in between those. You're going to love *Dirty Laundry*." —*Queens Tribune*

"Sexy and provocative. Sofie Metropolis, PI, is Everywoman . . . and a whole lot more!"—Carly Phillips, *New York Times* bestselling author

"Sexy, exciting, laugh-out-loud fun. If you love *My Big Fat Greek Wedding* and Stephanie Plum, this is definitely the series for you!"

—Christine Feehan, *New York Times* bestselling author

"Smart, snappy, and so original you won't be able to put it down." —Lori Foster, *New York Times* bestselling author, on *Sofie Metropolis*

"Sofie Metropolis is the Greek Nancy Drew and makes me wanna be both when (and if) I grow up." —Jill Conner Browne, *New York Times* bestselling author and *The* Sweet Potato Queen

"Snappy dialogue and offbeat characters ensure a great time!" —*Romantic Times BOOKreviews* on *Dirty Laundry*

"I swear that the Sofie Metropolis series by Tori Carrington is getting better and better. If you haven't picked up the first two in the series, what are you waiting for? For a laugh-filled, enjoyable time wrapped around a superb mystery, don't miss the continuing adventures of Sofie Metropolis in *Foul Play*." —*Romance Reviews Today*

"This fast-paced book captures the colorful Greek community of Astoria, where Sofie navigates between the expectations of her Greek upbringing and the desires of her heart to be an independent and strong woman." —*Greek Circle* magazine on *Dirty Laundry*

FORGE NOVELS BY TORI CARRINGTON

Sofie Metropolis
Dirty Laundry
Foul Play

Foul Play

A Sofie Metropolis Novel

TORI CARRINGTON

TOR®

A TOM DOHERTY ASSOCIATES BOOK
NEW YORK

This is a work of fiction. All of the characters, organizations, and events portrayed in this novel are either products of the author's imagination or are used fictitiously.

FOUL PLAY: A SOFIE METROPOLIS NOVEL

Copyright © 2007 by Lori and Tony Karayianni

All rights reserved, including the right to reproduce this book, or portions thereof, in any form.

A Tor Book
Published by Tom Doherty Associates, LLC
175 Fifth Avenue
New York, NY 10010

www.tor.com

Tor® is a registered trademark of Tom Doherty Associates, LLC.

ISBN-13: 978-0-7653-5678-9
ISBN-10: 0-7653-5678-3

First Edition: June 2007
First Mass Market Edition: April 2008

Printed in the United States of America

0 9 8 7 6 5 4 3 2 1

As always,
for our remarkable sons Tony and Tim.
με αγαπη.

ACKNOWLEDGMENTS

Our standard response to the question "How do you two work together?" is "Very carefully." (The old joke of how porcupines procreate comes to mind.) But in reality, after writing together for over twenty years, our collaboration is second nature. Neither of us has written separately, and although occasionally we both threaten to break off from the whole—usually when one of us doesn't get his or her way and "compromise" becomes a difficult word to swallow—we can't imagine writing any other way. And we're thankful to the following people for making our lives, and thus our writing experiences, that much richer and more fulfilling:

Our two adult sons, Tony and Tim, sports heroes and enthusiasts. We tease that since we have two sons, we had to create a daughter in Sofie. What we don't say is that walking in Sofie's shoes helps us remember what it was like to be in our mid-twenties. The experience has made us recall how challenging that period in life is . . . and recognize how damn well you both are doing. You make us proud.

The extraordinary Robert Gottlieb, whom we're honored to call agent and friend and fellow blues and barbecue lover, and everyone else who works behind the scenes at Trident Media Group, including Holly Henderson Root and Amy Pyle. Thank you for covering the business angle of our lives with brilliant aplomb so we may focus on the creative end.

Melissa Ann and Jacqueline Singer, dear friends and Mets fans whose Queens roots go deep and whose love of the team and the borough is full and lush. This book wouldn't have been possible without you both.

Additionally, Linda Quinton, Tom Doherty, Elena Stokes, Anna Genoese, Alexis Saarela, and everyone at Tom Doherty Associates. We didn't think it was possible for anyone to love our girl as much as we do. You all prove us wrong every day. Thank you!

Mystery Writers of America, P.I. Writers of America, Orange County Chapter of RWA, Columbus Fiction Writers, Maumee Valley RWA, Romance Writers of America, NINC, and the Authors Guild are but a few of the writers groups that keep us plugged into the industry and connected to fellow writers. SquawkRadio.com and Writerspace.com and ToriCarringtonFriendsyahoogroups.com are places where we can put our feet up and chat with friends near and far. And, last but certainly not least, to our XromX pals: We love ya, man!

The many booksellers and fellow readers at Borders, Barnes & Noble, Joseph Beth's, and the countless indies—including but certainly not limited to Mystery Lovers Bookshop in Oakmont, Pennsylvania, Foul Play Books in Westerville, Ohio, Books & Co. in Dayton, Ohio, Black Orchid Mystery Bookstore in Manhattan, Don's Books in Kokomo, Indiana, Paperback Outlet in Warren, Michigan, Chester County Book and Music Company, West Chester, Pennsylvania—not to mention the libraries and librarians, we've encountered and continue to encounter in our travels. Thank you for making it a pleasure to emerge from our cave to mingle with the natives . . . even if it means we have to actually get dressed in order to do so. (Check out our travel blog at www.sofiemetro.com for an ongoing list and photos.)

Members of the Greek- and Cypriot-American community—including Toledo's own Holy Trinity Orthodox Church, *Greek Circle* magazine, and AHEPA, to name but a few—for cheering us on and making us feel we're in the company of family whenever we meet during our travels. *Zeto E Ellas!*

New York's Amazing Mets . . . you guys rock!

And, finally, we would be remiss if we didn't also thank the residents, past and present, of Astoria, Queens. Your cards, letters, and e-mails thrill us beyond words. We'll be thinking of each and every one of you the next time we're enjoying a frappé at a café on Broadway or Ditmars. Long live New York!

FOUL PLAY

Prologue

"OH, COME ON, UMP! YOU need a good referral to an optician? My five-year-old niece could call a pitch better than you."

Yes, there were definite advantages to having a primo theater-style seat in the Home Plate Club Gold rows at Shea Stadium. First on that list was that you had a direct line to the umpire when he made an asinine call like the one he just made against Mets player Carlos Beltran, who'd struck out for the second time that day. No thanks to the umpire's questionable vision. I didn't consider myself an expert when it came to baseball, but even I knew that last pitch was a ball.

I sat down heavily in my cushioned chair, ignoring my new hire Eugene Waters where he grinned at me from the neighboring seat, his single gold tooth glinting in the afternoon sun. Probably he was amused by my display of baseball Tourette's. Actually, you could call it sports Tourette's, because either I was not interested in sports at all, or I was in the whole way till the end, uncomely commentary included. And my interest usually coincided with a winning streak, which was definitely what the Mets were riding.

It was the bottom of the eighth and the Mets were down a run against the Florida Marlins. While there were plenty of diehard baseball fans in New York, sunny day fans like me probably outnumbered them five-to-one. And were probably five times as loud.

Hey, my team was only a game out of first place in the final month-long run toward the play-offs. I figured I was entitled.

"Who knew you were capable?" Eugene said, shaking his head.

"Oh, shut up, Waters." I crossed my arms over my Amazing Mets T-shirt after I tugged down the rim of my Mets cap, hiding from not only Eugene, but from the others in the exclusive seats around me.

On any other day I might use my workplace superiority over Eugene and issue a threat. But the truth was, if not for him, I wouldn't be sitting where I was, watching a great game at Shea Stadium on a warm day in early September. While I still wasn't clear on what Waters' connection to the Queens team was— and wasn't all that sure I wanted to know considering the other details I had on him, including illicit drugs of the weed variety and pink robes with feather cuffs—I'd leapt at the opportunity to attend the game when he offered.

Even if it meant going to the game with him.

But how a guy who couldn't make his rent had access to the most exclusive seats in Shea Stadium was beyond mind-boggling.

Hi. My name is Sofie Metropolis and I'm a private investigator and Mets fan. Neither title has been easy to bear lately. The first because I still found a lot of my cases in my newish job tedious rather than darkly exciting, as I thought they would be—although things might be improving. The latter because, well, if you're up on your baseball, the Mets have had their ups and downs over the past decade. In fact, there were long stretches when my Mets T-shirts had been relegated to night-shirt material because wearing them in public might elicit teasing from Yankees fans.

But the tide had begun turning in their favor over the past couple of years. And then some.

And hopefully that tide would soon begin to do the same in the other area of my life.

Oh, don't get me wrong. There have been a few interesting happenings in my job since I first hired on at my uncle Spyros' agency six months ago. But those were momentary blips, and although they resulted in shooting one of my clients in the knee and purchasing myself a pair of cement overshoes I'd been fitted for on Hell Gate Bridge, well, the rest of my experiences were boring by comparison. Cheating spouse cases and missing pets mostly, with a few workers' compensation and commercial background checks thrown in to mix things up a bit.

If I had my way, my workdays would more resemble a Humphrey Bogart movie. At the very least, an episode of the *Rockford Files*. But as I was coming to learn, many things were prone not to go my way. Including my almost-wedding six months ago, and the fact that I hadn't seen man-of-mystery bounty hunter Jake Porter in at least four weeks, much less slept with him like I wanted.

More important, at the moment, this ball game wasn't going the way I'd like. But at least I was there, while the majority of my fellow Queens residents were at home watching the game on TV.

I looked at Waters, who had just taken a bite of a hot dog, a thick smear of mustard standing out on his dark brown skin.

Okay, maybe it wasn't all that.

"What?" he asked when he caught me staring.

I ignored a waiter that tended to the Gold and Silver

sections—a waiter at a ball game, go figure—and handed Waters my own napkin and pointed to the general area of his unshaven chin.

I turned my attention back to the field to find Beltran walking back to the dugout and Reni Venezuela stepping up to the plate. I was immediately on my feet as his music cue blasted over the speakers and his clip ran on the Diamond Vision display screen alongside his stats and picture. I clapped in time with the beat.

"Go Reni! Knock it out of the park!" I cheered, my voice lost in a sea of the tens of thousands of others.

Ah, yes, Reni Venezuela. The Mets' latest midseason acquisition and former Long Island Islanders closing pitcher. It wasn't just that he was a pitcher; it was that he was a damn good ambidextrous pitcher. In baseball you heard of switch hitters, but this was the first time—that I knew of anyway (recall my sunny day fan status)—I'd heard of a switch pitcher, although I understand that there was one that played for the Expos back in the nineties. Reni was equally good pitching with his left arm as his right. And he was to credit for the Mets' turn of good fortune this year.

And that wasn't saying anything about his dreamy good looks. Lately it was all I could do to keep the agency's office manager Rosie Rodriguez from swooning whenever his name was brought up or was mentioned on the portable radio she kept on her desk to follow the team's games. I imagined the endorsement contracts Reni was accumulating—that put him on billboards and posters everywhere advertising sports drinks and even underwear—especially affected her. Along with every other living, breathing female in the tristate area.

Not that Rosie thought she stood a chance with him, even if they were to cross paths (a long shot to be sure since she'd never been to a game). The Venezuela native was happily married to an Astoria girl and they had two great kids.

Just about perfect, if you were into jocks. Which I, most assuredly, had never been. But Reni had a pretty good shot at changing all that.

If he'd just hit the damn ball.

"Strike two!"

"Swing the goddamn bat already!" I shouted, not at all amused by my own behavior. One minute I was cheering him on, the next I was dissing him.

Welcome to my life. If I could just make up my mind on myriad topics I'd probably have an easier time of it.

"Strike three, you're out!"

A stream of profanity that not even I knew I possessed, and probably hadn't said in the whole of my life, exited my mouth, shocking both me and Waters, who'd added more mustard to the smear already on his chin. He sat gaping at me in a way that revealed he didn't chew his food particularly well.

The ump I had been taunting for the past hour and a half turned toward me. He lifted his protective mask and stalked toward me until only the fence behind home plate separated us.

"You're out of here!"

TWENTY MINUTES LATER WATERS GLARED at me where we'd both been escorted to Gate C.

"What?" I grumbled.

We'd listened as the best part of the game played out during our expulsion, the Mets coming back in the bottom of the ninth to pull the game out 7–5. One game closer to the play-offs.

And I was standing in the parking lot with an unhappy Waters.

"I'm not sure you deserve to meet Venezuela," he said.

"Hey, I figure I'm due. What? I did what all good fans do."

"Get kicked out of the game?"

"No, support my guys."

"Support like that gives all New Yorkers a bad name."

"Are you going to take me back in or not?"

"Not." He sighed heavily. "Oh, all right. Come on."

I followed him toward the press gate that lay between Gates B and C.

My cell phone vibrated in my pocket for the fifth time since my mug had been featured on the Diamond Vision display screen, larger than life and the zit on my chin twice as ugly. Given the phone attention I was getting, probably the image had gone live to TV as well. Ugh.

I slid the cell out of my pocket and saw Rosie's name featured. I answered.

"Oh my God, girl. What the hell do you think you're doing?" she asked.

I looked away from where Waters still glared at me as we walked. Not that I was intimidated. He was a couple of inches shorter than me, and at least thirty pounds lighter, making him look smaller yet. I could take him out with a carefully aimed glare, so long as there were no doors around for him to slam in my face.

"Are you calling for anything work-related?" I asked.

"No, I'm calling to ask why you made such a fool out of yourself on national TV."

It wouldn't be the first time I'd looked stupid on national TV. I swear, sometimes I thought I could still feel bug legs stuck between my teeth after that stunt on a reality show designed to gross people out. Mostly, it served to gross me out.

"If this doesn't have anything to do with work, then I'll talk to you later."

I rang off and checked the display to see who else had called. Three messages from my mother, Thalia Metropolis, one from my grandfather who was probably watching the game at his café on Broadway along with half the Greek-American community (well, at least those over sixty), and another from Jake Porter.

My heart did a funny little pretzel move in my chest as I checked to see if he'd left a message. He hadn't. My thumb hovered over the call button, and then I shoved the phone back into my pocket instead. If he wanted to talk to me, he'd just have to call again.

Of course, my nonchalant attitude had nothing to do with the effect Porter's having called had on me. I hadn't seen him for over a month. Not by choice, but rather we seemed to have reached an impasse of sorts. Namely, one or the other of us seemed to back off whenever things started getting hot and heavy. Including me, which amused me not at all since I'd tried so hard to back him into my king-sized bed. A piece of furniture he didn't appear to want to go anywhere near. Not because the bed was rumored to have been made special by one of my aunt Sotiria's casket makers, but because of the towering pile of unopened wedding gifts that sat stacked against the wall right next to it.

He thought the presents meant I wasn't over my last relationship. What my ex Thomas-the-Horny-Toad-Chalikis had to do with our indulging in a one-night stand was beyond me, but hey, there you had it. The full lowdown on my sex life. Or, rather, my unwelcome celibacy.

Waters flashed the same credentials he'd used to get into the stadium two hours ago to the guard posted at the press gate and then motioned for me to precede with him back inside the stadium.

"Where did you get access like this?" I asked as he directed me toward an elevator.

"Don't ask, don't tell." His gold tooth glinted at me.

"That's the military's motto. You're not in the military. Besides, I asked."

"And I'm not going to tell."

I gave him an eye roll as the elevator took us to the press level.

"We're going to miss them," I said, taking in the reporters milling around us.

"No we won't."

He led me in a maze-like route, through rows and aisles, down stairs, flashing his ID to another set of security guards, finally leading me into another area that looked like it might be . . .

I froze, suddenly incapable of movement. "Is that the Mets locker room?"

I peeked around the shoulders of others gathered and stared at a door in the middle of a wide, long hall. I looked to my left.

"Oh my God, are the field and the dugout that way?"

A guy wearing a ratty plaid blazer and a striped shirt stared at me. A card pinned to his breast pocket identified him as press.

While my words just identified me as not belonging to the press.

Another guy tried to elbow his way around me.

"Hey, person standing here," I said.

He eyed me even as Waters yanked me back to let the guy pass. "You think you can keep your mouth shut for five minutes?" he whispered.

"Hey, yo. Isn't that the broad that got booted from the game?" another reporter said a few people down.

Crap.

"Yeah, it is. The idiot who was bad-mouthing the ump."

I couldn't resist. "He's the one who should've gotten kicked out. My grandmother could have made better calls than he did."

"Our team won. Remember? Shut up," Waters said in a fierce whisper.

"What? Are they going to stone me?"

I raised my brows in challenge. I didn't think I had to remind him of my Greek heritage and the fact that my ancestors had practically invented stoning. And that it would take far more than the threat of a few rocks to get me to back down from any opinion.

Of course, I would have to pick here and now to stand my ground when throughout my life I hadn't exactly been a pillar.

Thankfully neither of us had to face that particular test because the players began to exit and the reporters' attention switched from me to them.

"Here he comes," Waters said.

"He" was Reni Venezuela, the star of the game, and the brightest rising star on the Mets' horizon. And with fellow teammates like Rodriguez, Hernandez, Reyes, and Wright, well, that was saying a lot.

I stared at the hunk of a man. To be fair, Porter had already claimed the top spot on my personal list when it came to mouth-watering, but Reni . . . mmm. At about six one, all lean, hard muscle, and with the chiseled features of an Aztec god, the saliva collecting in the back of my throat was worthy of note.

"Reni," Waters called.

The yummy pitcher finished talking to a FOX television reporter and then came over to us.

"Eugene," he said, giving Waters a hearty handshake and a big grin that spoke of a very good dentist. He'd apparently showered and had changed into a snug black T-shirt and jeans. My gaze was drawn to his large hands and whip-taut arms. I'd known he had a tattoo on his right forearm, but seeing the ten-inch black scorpion up close and personal seemed almost too intimate to me in that one moment.

"I want you to meet my new boss," Waters said, "Sofie Metropolis."

Reni squinted at me as he nodded. "You're the one who got kicked out of the game, no?" he asked with a sexy, thick accent.

"Yes," I said, surprised to find myself a little breathless.

Before I knew it, the players began to move on down the hall, propelling Reni with them.

"Good to see you, Eugene," Reni called.

I watched as a beautiful woman I smelled before I saw advanced on the bunch, throwing herself into Reni's arms. "Good game, Poppy!" she said.

"The wife," Waters pointed out unnecessarily. "Astoria girl."

I nodded. We Queens natives are proud of our own. Working as an accountant in a firm that was connected in some roundabout way with Trump was enough to get you a mention in the local papers. Being married to the hottest new pitcher for the Mets landed you on the front page.

Waters began to lead me back the way we'd come, having to physically pull me as I gaped at where Pedro Martinez was giving a television interview.

Once we were finally outside the stadium, with me suffering from more than a small dose of shock and awe, Waters said, "So, ejection aside, does this make up for my losing that summons and put me on the fast track to full PI?"

I considered him for a long moment, blinking away images of Reni and Martinez and exchanging them for Waters' scruffily familiar face. He'd only been serving papers for the agency for a few weeks. And there was that summons-losing incident to think about (I still thought he'd done it on purpose because he was friends with the guy).

"I don't know that we're there yet," I said, wondering if he could get me into the next home game. "But you're getting closer."

I'd always wondered what it would feel like to be the boss. And even though my uncle Spyros Metropolis was the licensed private investigator in charge, in his long absence I was the closest thing the agency had to a boss. At least one that spoke.

I smiled, deciding I liked it. . . .

One

Two weeks and one day later . . .

SUNDAY DINNER AT THE METROPOLISES' was always a big event, even without Diamond Vision. Forget that there were usually at least seven present at a table that was piled high with all sorts of great Greek delicacies, and that the longtime feud between my father and my maternal grandfather, Kosmos, periodically erupted into an almost food fight. This was the day when opinions were aired in an open environment where, yes, you might be judged, but you were always accepted. The exception being politics. Long ago, my mother Thalia had banned the discussion of any type of politics while there was still food on the table.

Of course, when coffee was served afterward, I imagined that a stoplight was hanging from the ceiling—instead of a chandelier—and it turned green, and everyone revved his or her engines.

Debating politics was as much a part of being Greek as stories about mythological gods doing strange things to swans. And there were usually as many opinions as there were gods, all different from the ones next to them, yet attached to the same family tree.

I'd once read somewhere that consistency was the one true sign of an intellectual. If that were the case then I'd pretty much say we all fell on the dumb side. One of my mother's maxims was that if you didn't have anything nice to say, then you shouldn't say anything at all. And my father always added that the one speaking the loudest was generally the one that had the least to say.

Welcome to dinner at my family's house.

As I sat at the dining room table sipping my post-dinner frappé, feeling sated and watching the goings-on around me, I recognized that I was in more of a thoughtful mood as of late. Where I might jump into the conversation right there, to contest my brother's take on the latest political scandal, or there, where my father spoke on the viability of a female candidate for president, I instead stayed quiet.

The truth was, lately I'd become aware of a slight shift in our family dynamic. Oh, nothing drastic. We were still the same loving, sarcastic bunch, each of us easily giving as good as we got. And the changes went beyond the new fondness I'd witnessed between my mother and father ever since he'd surprised her with a thirtieth wedding anniversary party. (A really nice surprise for both of us, since Thalia had thought her husband was carrying on an affair and had half-convinced me of the same. Okay, she'd flat out convinced me. But in this case I'd never been happier to discover I was wrong.) The change also transcended Efi's recent participation in the dialogue when she usually sat back with her skinny arms crossed over a chest bearing a T-shirt with some sort of crude or offensive saying or another. (Today it was YES, I'M A BITCH, JUST NOT YOURS!) And even my maternal grandfather and father seemed capable of trading words without either one of them lunging across the table at each other.

Then again, maybe my family hadn't changed. Maybe I had.

Someone said something along the lines of, "So what do you think, Sofie?"

I blinked as they all looked at me while my mother poured glasses of cold water and handed them out, perfect with the kumquat preserves she'd spooned onto tiny plates.

"How about those Mets?" I said.

Okay, so I hadn't been paying attention. In all honesty, I'd much rather give my realization more attention than what it took to accept a water glass from my mother and pass it down. But obviously that wasn't going to happen. At least not now when I had a family with which to engage in conversation.

"World Series, all the way," my younger brother Kosmos said.

"Baseball." My grandpa Kosmos *tsk*ed. "When is America going to get with the world program and make soccer its national sport? World Series. Outside of the Americas, who plays baseball?"

"Japan," Efi offered.

"And when was the last time you saw them play in the World Series?" my grandfather asked. "Give me a good soccer game any day."

My grandpa Kosmos had recently taken to watching soccer games on a Spanish-only station, even though he didn't speak a word of the language. My mother said it was because he liked the way the commentators yelled "Goal!" when the teams scored. I'd watched a match with him last weekend and quickly understood that soccer language was pretty universal. Foul, corner, penalty, they were close enough even in Greek for a non-Greek to be able to follow the game. Besides, all you did was sit around and wait for the goals to be made anyway.

At any rate, I was glad that everyone seemed to have forgotten about my momentary blip on the baseball radar screen two weeks ago. Finally. I swear, for at least a week I'd gotten nailed by at least five people a day who'd seen me and either made a snarky comment or openly laughed at me. Not the makings of a good day any way you looked at it.

"Is that another tattoo?" my mother asked my sister, segueing into the "what were you thinking" segment of Sunday after-dinner discussions.

Efi considered her upper arm, which bore a yin-yang type of symbol. "No."

"I don't know why you want to go and mark up your body like that." Thalia shook her head. "It's a sin."

"Actually," I said casually, "I was thinking about getting a tattoo myself. What do you think, Efi?"

My sister's face lit up like Times Square at night.

Of course, I was merely trying to deflect my mother's attention. I liked that Efi was participating in after-dinner conversation and not going upstairs to lock herself in her room.

While every now and again I wished I were more like my little sister, the Sofie jury was still out on the tattoo issue. I loved to look at Efi's. But would I feel the same with the ink on my skin? Hell, I changed my mind on which pair of jeans was my favorite from day to day. What would I do with a permanent tattoo? Especially at this time in my life when it seemed everything was in a state of flux?

"I got the court notice yesterday."

Grandpa Kosmos' words stopped all conversation. Partly because he was off topic. Mostly because we all immediately knew what he was talking about but had conveniently relegated the reality to the edges of our collective conscience.

Correction: The fact that my ex-fiancé was pressing criminal assault charges against my sixty-pushing-seventy grandfather for having busted his nose was something I went out of my way not to think about. Otherwise I was afraid of what I might do. Particularly in light of the new bond I was forming with my Glock.

Of course, we'd all known that we'd have to face this sooner or later. You know the saying, "We'll cross that bridge when we come to it"? Well, we were now standing staring at the bridge and had to decide who was going to take the first step.

The way I saw it, Grandpa Kosmos was completely justified in socking Thomas Chalikis—more than even I was, maybe. He'd given the lousy skirt-chaser my late maternal grand-mother's ring so he could propose to me. And after I'd decided I wasn't too keen on the idea of nooky roulette—meaning I didn't want to be left wondering which one of my friends my spouse was showing little Thomas to now—and Jake Porter had rescued the mangled ring from my garbage disposal, I'd found out that the diamond wasn't a diamond at all, but high quality CZ—cubic zirconia. Meaning that somewhere between the time Grandpa Kosmos had given my ex my grandmother's ring and Thomas had it reset to propose to me, the diamond had been switched out.

All things considered, the question should be whether I would sue Thomas for the cost of the missing diamond, rather than whether my grandfather should be facing criminal charges for hitting a man a third his age.

"I can't believe that no good, lying, cheating, son of a bitch is getting away with this," Efi said.

Normally my mother would cuff the back of her head or my father might glare at my sister to get her to apologize for her crass words.

Now we were all in agreement.

"When's the date?" I asked, barely able to swallow the big sip of frappé I'd just sucked into my mouth.

"A week and a half from now. Wednesday at ten in the morning."

A week and a few days. Good. That gave me some time to work with.

Although what work, exactly, I was going to do remained undetermined.

I could always take a cue from Tony DiPiazza and fit Thomas-the-Toad-Chalikis with a pair of cement overshoes and push him into the East River from Hell Gate Bridge.

But since getting Thomas to come anywhere near me, much less on top of a bridge, was out of the question, I'd probably have to get far more inventive.

ONE OF THE ADVANTAGES OF being a private detective was that you set your own hours. There was no time clock, no boss breathing down the back of your neck questioning your tactics or your work ethic. Of course, it also helped that my uncle Spyros was the SPYROS METROPOLIS, PRIVATE INVESTIGATOR that was stenciled in gold letters on the front window of the small office on Steinway, wedged between a Thai restaurant and a fish store. And that for the past few months he'd been an absent boss, on an extended vacation in Greece. When I first hired on six months ago Spyros agreed to give me a regular weekly salary until—when and if—I started pulling in commissions greater than that amount.

And I was proud to say that I'd recently passed that important benchmark. Which meant my uncle and I were due for a conversation. An exchange of words that couldn't take place unless I could get him on the phone in Greece, which I appeared completely incapable of doing no matter my growing proficiency at my job. So I had to wait until he called the agency, something he did every few days or so around the same time in the early afternoon.

Since the office manager Rosie Rodriquez held down the proverbial fort at the agency, my being there on any kind of regular basis wasn't required beyond the increase-in-income quest and to fill out paperwork for the cases I worked on, much of which I could also do and did while working other boring cases, mostly of the cheating spouse variety. The spitfire Puerto Rican was more than capable of taking care of anything else that came the agency's way.

Or in this instance, came in through the door.

I walked into the agency after a fifty-something man who was wearing a neat orange Polo shirt and Dockers. Rosie opened her mouth to say something to me and I made a cutting motion across my throat indicating I didn't want the guy to know I worked there. She made a face that looked altogether too cute on her.

"Hello," she said, probably more polite to the customer than she normally would have been given that I'd thrown her off her game. "How can I help you today?"

I sat down in one of the two chairs against the front windows put there for people to cool their heels or find out their spouses were knocking boots with everything this side of the East River. I picked up a month-old tabloid Rosie must have brought in and stared at the cover story: ALIENS AMONG US.

Story of my life.

"I need to hire someone to find my dog," the man said.

I gave an eye roll and then lifted the paper to cover my face before Rosie could bestow one of her own puppy-dog looks on me and convince me to take on another missing pet case. The last one had netted me a urine stain from a hamster on my favorite T-shirt and had marked the official end to my pet detecting days.

"I'm sorry, sir," Rosie said, getting up from her chair and coming to stand beside me. She shifted in a way that knocked the paper right out of my hands. "But our agents are really busy and aren't currently taking on new clients right now."

I picked up the paper and managed to partially swat her with it before pretending to read it again.

The man sighed, looking a bit too much like my father for comfort. "You're the fifth place I've been to. Hey, I'd probably refuse the case, too, if our roles were reversed. But Tiffany is my wife's eight-year-old toy poodle and, well, she's literally worried herself sick over her disappearance."

I forced myself to read the tabloid cover story. "A farmer outside Harrisburg, Pennsylvania, reports that the flying saucer landed in his soybean field, where it remained parked for two hours before taking off again. Afterward he discovered that at least an acre of his field had been harvested."

So aliens liked soybeans. As far as I was concerned they could have them.

"I'm sorry to hear that, Mr. . . ."

"Kaufman. Albert Kaufman."

She'd named him. Damn. The first rule in keeping things casual and by extension at a distance was not to name an individual. That's why I referred to most of the cheating spouses I followed by their last names. Helped me keep things in perspective.

But now the man in front of me was Albert instead of a guy who'd missed his tee time and had nothing better to do than hire someone to look for his wife's froufrou pet.

"Mr. Kaufman, why don't I take down your contact information and check to see if one of our agents might have time to look into the situation for you?"

I rustled the paper loudly and then turned the page to follow the alien story while Rosie ignored me and took Albert's information.

Finally, he was gone. I lowered the paper to find Rosie standing in front of me, chewing her gum a mile a minute and making her dimples pop, her arms crossed under her very generous chest.

"You coulda at least talked to the guy."

I put the paper down. "Have you spotted any alien spaceships lately? According to *The Tattler*, there appears to be a lot of them."

"That's not the only thing there's a lot of lately." Rosie sat back down in front of her ancient computer while I searched the top of my paper-covered desk for something interesting. "I swear, we're getting at least two missing pet case requests a day. Must be the weather or somethin'."

"Must be." I picked up a package that was big enough to hold a violin and shook it. "What's this?"

"I dunno. What do I look like to you, your secretary?" Her fingers hit the keys harder than was necessary, indicating she was a tad upset. "You know, you could take one or two of those cases, already. I mean, we're talking about people's pets, their babies."

"Babies with teeth and the ability to use them."

I peeled away the plain paper wrapping that bore only my name and address and then opened the lid of the box. The smell of something rotting made me cringe away. Rosie was immediately next to me, looking over my shoulder.

"Oh, no. Somebody sent you dead roses." She reached around to pick the smeared card out of the decaying stems. "Thanks a lot for ending my marriage," she read.

She tossed the card back into the box and I closed it and then stuffed it into my garbage can.

"Oh no you didn't." Rosie stared at me. "You need to take

that out to the back Dumpster on account of them stinking up the place."

I gave her an eye roll. "I don't plan on being here long anyway. You don't want to smell them, you take them to the Dumpster."

I found it odd that we were both acting nonchalant about the delivery. Truth was, receiving the dead roses creeped me out. And told me that a caught spouse was focusing his or her attention on me rather than accepting responsibility for the fact that they'd screwed up their marriage by engaging in a round of tube snake boogie with someone not their spouse.

"Uncle Spyros get a lot of roses?" I asked Rosie.

"No. He gets death threats."

Yikes.

And here I thought cheating spouse cases were routine and boring. And they were. Up and until the client received the pictures of their significant other's extracurricular activities and then introduced the now insignificant other to the meaning of the word "consequences."

"You dig up anything on the Hanson case yet?"

"Not anything interesting." She hit a key several times, and then made a go at singeing the brows from my forehead with inventive profanity. "Damn thing, always freezing up on me. Now I gotta go and reboot again."

"Probably if you had a new computer you could dig up something on the Hanson case."

"Probably I could. And probably I could use this one to hit your uncle over the head with because I've been asking for a new computer and he still hasn't gotten me one. Holy shit."

I put down the message slips and looked up to find her staring through the front window.

"Now that's something you don't see every day on Steinway," she whispered.

Outside, a bright yellow customized Hummer the size of a city block rolled up, apparently somebody's idea of a limo. We both watched as the black-clothed driver got out and walked up to the agency door.

"Now what kind of trouble have you gotten me into?" Rosie whispered, looking in her drawer, probably for her mace or holy water, depending on what she feared was the source for the Hummer visit.

Me? My mind flashed to Tony DiPiazza and those cement boots he'd fitted me for. Then again, this limo wasn't Tony's style. And he was in Italy anyway and would be for a good long time to come.

Thank God.

"Ms. Metropolis?" the granite-looking driver said, taking off his hat.

"That would be her," Rosie said, pointing a red talon in my direction.

"My employer would like to speak to you."

"Send him in."

"In private."

I looked around. "This is about as private as it gets."

"In the car."

"Oh."

I exchanged glances with Rosie who was trying to inconspicuously shake her head.

But curiosity had gotten the better of this particular cat and I followed the guy out so he could hold open the back door of the Hummer for me.

Two

HOLY SHIT WAS RIGHT. AS my eyes adjusted to the interior of the limo, I thought the thing must be as big as my entire apartment. Okay, I might be exaggerating, but not by much. Big, black leather seats lined the vehicle's walls, mirrors and crystal chandeliers were attached to the ceiling, and the big-screen TV and computer station at the end next to what looked like a full bar made me want to ask when I could move in.

"Ms. Metropolis?" a female voice asked.

Okay, so the employer wasn't a male. I blinked a woman about my age into focus. She was vaguely familiar. Latina. Very beautiful. And with the money to make herself look even more attractive.

"Do I know you?"

"No, you don't. But I know you." She pushed a button, opening her window a bit to let some daylight in, then leaned forward, throwing her features into relief.

If I didn't know better, I'd say that she was Mets pitcher Reni Venezuela's wife.

"I'm Gisela Venezuela," she said.

In honor of holy shits, I didn't think one more was out of line.

I extended my hand and shook her smaller one. "Nice to meet you. How 'bout those Mets, huh?"

"Screw the Mets." She sat back and pushed a button. The car began to move.

I looked around, not sure how I felt about her response or the fact that the car was moving. As big as this thing was, it couldn't possibly be safe to move around in. And the Hummer's relationship to the military didn't sit well with me, no matter the custom interior decor job.

"Where you taking me?"

"John's just going to drive us around a bit. It's not a good idea for me to be seen sitting outside a PI's office for too long. Something to drink?"

I thought about the frappé I'd been just about to make myself inside the agency, and refused.

As the car turned off Steinway onto Broadway, she relaxed noticeably. She must have been serious about not wanting to be seen outside the agency.

Then why not call?

I shifted on the leather seat. Whenever I was this eager to find something out, it usually led to something bad.

"I want to hire you," Gisela said.

I blinked at her. "Me? You can easily afford the best agencies in the city. Why me?"

She took off her hat and almost immediately she looked more like me. Or, rather, Rosie. "Because you're a fellow Astorian, like me. A homegirl." She waved her hand. "I don't want somebody who's going to pat my hand, empty my purse, and tell me not to worry my pretty little head about nothing. I want the truth."

I stopped short of offering my hand for a high five and saying, "Damn straight."

Instead, I asked, "What truth?"

"I want you to follow my husband."

I sighed, leaning against the seat. Probably because I wouldn't know the feel of one like it again anytime soon.

Another cheating spouse case. No matter how much I could probably charge, or the fact that Gisela and I were "homegirls," I didn't much like the thought of getting the money shot on the Mets pitcher. Especially not the red-hot Reni who was steadily driving my team toward the pennant.

If my current reluctance also had a little something to do with my flower delivery, I wasn't going to admit it.

Allowing that a regular Joe could send an unspoken threat via roses, what would someone of Reni's caliber send me? A rattlesnake?

She held out an envelope.

"Gisela, I'm sorry, but if you think your husband's having an affair, why don't you just ask him?" I suggested, the same way I did whenever a new cheating spouse case walked through the agency doors and I didn't want to take it.

Why couldn't I be the one to get the missing museum icon case? Or the missing person who'd end up being the victim of a serial killer I could catch? Hell, I'd even settle for a low-end embezzlement case if I had to. Just so I didn't have to witness another couple going at it full coital when my own sex life had basically been in the crapper for the past six months.

I opened the envelope to find a neat stack of brand-new thousand dollar bills inside. Double whoa.

"Having an affair?" Gisela did a head thing that bespoke her great offense at the suggestion. "My Reni would never do that. Not to me. I'd have his member bronzed and framed and would hang it next to all his damn trophies."

I closed the envelope before I dropped drool inside it and then started stuffing it into my back pocket, changing my mind midway and sticking it inside the front waist of my jeans instead and covering it with my shirt. "So why do you want me to follow him then?"

She looked a little awkward. Funny that a minute ago she'd been so talkative and now appeared not to know how to express herself. "I want you to follow him because . . ." She trailed off and then heaved a sigh and looked at me almost defiantly. "I want you to follow him because ever since he got back from playing in Pittsburgh, he's not the same guy."

"Like how?"

"Like . . . like. He forgot which side of the bed he likes to sleep on. Where his clothes are. That I don't like him leaving the seat up." She gestured with her hands. "Those kind of things. He looks like my husband. Talks like my husband. Plays baseball like my husband. But it's like somebody else in a Reni suit."

I thought of the aliens article I'd read in the tabloid earlier, and then remembered a scene from the movie *Men in Black,* the first one. Maybe aliens were harvesting more than soybeans.

I snorted just short of a laugh, then covered it with a cough when Gisela glared at me.

Denial. Reni Venezuela's recent successes apparently had gone to his head and he was reacting with his other one. Happened all the time, if the divorce rate among professional sports players—or any celebrity of any level—was anything to go by.

And in this case, I thought it was.

I mean, here he'd gone from the barrios of Venezuela to playing Major League Baseball.

What guy wouldn't get a swollen head—pardon the pun—in the same situation? After all, wasn't it ex-Mets pitcher Kris Benson's wife who had threatened to "do" the whole team if she caught him cheating? Of course, she was an ex-stripper and the couple had been caught getting a little too friendly in stadium parking lots, but that was something I preferred not to think about just now.

I pretended to take Gisela seriously and jotted down some notes in my ever-present pocket pad. Cheating spouse case. Simple as that.

But as I asked Gisela to give me Reni's Social Security number, his credit card accounts, and additional information, I had the sinking sensation that dead roses were going to be the least of my worries when Gisela found out her husband was cheating.

I'd have to work on my "make him pay by buying you the biggest diamond on earth" speech now and hope that Reni's affair or affairs were of the temporary variety. Because I had the feeling that if there was a serious other woman involved, this case might graduate from simple cheating spouse to first-degree murder.

SOMEONE AT THE WOODHAVEN FIRING range had the Mets game on. The team was down by one in the bottom of the fifth. I squinted through the plastic safety goggles and aimed my Glock at the target I'd positioned twenty feet away. I braced myself against the kick and squeezed off a round, then another two in quick succession. One hit the target dead on, the other two spit holes around about where the paper enemy's ears would be.

I pulled the headphones from my own ears.

"Going to get yourself a rep as a Van Gogh shooter," a female voice said from the booth next to mine.

I listened as the Mets made a tying run and leaned back to see who had spoken to me.

"Pamela?" I said, watching as the pretty blonde took aim at

her own target and emptied two bullets directly into the head of the paper target, two others into the left chest. Whoa. Pamela Coe was one of our process servers. All right, she was my uncle Spyros' best process server, with nearly a one hundred percent success rate. And recently I'd been throwing some of the more pedestrian cheating spouse cases her way, which I'd thought was a good idea at the time. Until the other servers started making noises about taking on more interesting cases.

"Hey," Pamela said, moving her right headphone from her ear and then popping the clip on her Beretta to replace it with a fresh one. "When did you start shooting?"

I made a face, just then linking her Van Gogh reference to my questionable aim. Okay, so the last time I'd shot a gun I'd shot Greek-wannabe-Italian goon Panayiotis Rokkos in the ear (I'd been hoping for a more serious shot). Then shot him in the other ear the next day (an accident—I swear).

I shrugged, realizing Pamela was waiting for a response. "When I bought the damn thing, I never thought I'd have to shoot it beyond my original shooting class. Now that I've used it three times since, well, I thought it was a good idea if I picked up some skills."

She smiled at me.

Pamela Coe was one of those beautiful natural blondes you'd instantly hate if you didn't already like her. I smiled back.

"Don't hold the gun too tightly," she said. "You're overcompensating for the coming kick and messing with your aim."

I looked down at the gun. "Thanks." I think.

She put the headphone back over her ear and shot at her target again, indicating our conversation was over, which didn't surprise me. Pamela never said much beyond what needed saying.

What I wanted to know was what she was doing at the range. But it looked like I wasn't going to get that right now. I'd ask at the agency sometime.

I put my own headphones back on, checked my clip, and then tried what she suggested. The first missed the target altogether. The second hit the navel area. And the third hit the head straight on.

Bingo.

THE GOOD THING ABOUT TAILING a ballplayer was that there were times when I knew exactly where he was because I could follow him via a live game. As I did with my car radio when I drove from the shooting range to Shea Stadium some miles away as the game ended. It was after dark and I was the only car going toward the stadium, with the waves moving away from it. I hadn't bothered tailing Reni earlier in the day because I figured Gisela had known exactly where he was. I decided I'd pick him up later after the game.

Car horns honked in celebration of the local boys' most recent success and I couldn't resist rolling down my window and doing a little arm waving and hooting of my own even as I pulled off Roosevelt onto Casey Stengel Drive and drew to a stop at the curb to wait for Reni to exit the player's lot. I kept an eye out for the guards in front of the stadium in case they decided to chase me off, the post 9/11 security measures making even fans' bags subject to searches before they entered the stadium.

Muffy reminded me why it was better to keep the windows up when he poked his bony back paws into my lap and barked viciously at a group walking past.

"You were so quiet I'd almost forgotten you were in here." I rolled the window back up, but not without it collecting a bit of saliva from where the Jack Russell terrier got in as many snarling barks as he could before I nearly closed his head in it altogether.

He circled back to the passenger's seat, did his round and round bit, and then sat down, panting as he looked out his closed window, as if wishing it were open.

It was at times like these that I almost felt sorry for the little dog. Almost. I mean, dogs deserved houses to live in with big backyards to play in. And his previous owner, the late Mrs. Kapoor, had had exactly that. Then her friend had pet-napped Muffy, I'd found him, and Mrs. K had proven that not even massive doses of curry could stop heart disease and died, leaving me as owner by default of the white and brown spotted terrier who'd grown up with a predilection for Sofie flesh. And he'd been forced to trade his house for my apartment, a nice grassy yard for my building's rooftop that he gained access to via the fire escape. And the only time he got out was when I took him with me. Not to the park like any good owner might do, but to follow cheating spouses.

And that's exactly what I hoped to find out Reni was now, tonight, so I could close this case as quickly as possible. No matter the stack of bills I'd have to give back to Gisela.

I was about a hundred feet up from where the players' cars and limos would leave the lot. The high, blacked-out gate opened and I immediately made out the shiny grill of the yellow Hummer that Gisela had been in earlier. Was she in there now? I didn't think she was, but I needed to get down Reni's routine, anyway. And if that included his wife meeting him after the games, so be it.

If he was meeting someone else . . . so be that, as well.

I blindly plucked my brother's borrowed, broken, and then replaced Olympus off the floor behind my seat and squeezed off a few shots and then I started my car as the limo drove toward the parking lot exit.

"Buckle your seat belt, Muffy, it's going to be a boring night."

Three

MUCH LATER I LET MYSELF into my apartment, yawning as I went. If only I'd known how boring the evening would be. I'd followed the Hummer straight to Venezuela's Astoria McMansion doorstep near Astoria Park off Ditmars—a five-bedroom, four-bath hacienda-type house that took up four lots where more modest houses had once stood—and then waited outside to see if he'd go anywhere else. At around midnight when all the house lights except those kept on for security reasons went off, I finally called it a day and went home.

If Reni Venezuela were having an affair, he hadn't met his lover tonight. Instead, his behavior spoke of a devoted husband and father, just as I'd once believed him to be. No post-game carousing with the other players. No stops to any seedy or up-scale hotels to rendezvous with groupies he'd sent ahead of him.

I banged my leg on the hall table inside my door and groaned. Probably I should have flipped the light switch. Instead I'd thought myself capable of making it to the kitchen and the light there after having lived in the place for the past six months. Muffy barked and I shushed him, nudging him out of the way with my foot where he circled my legs.

"Yes, yes, that means dinner. Yeesh, you'd think I was starving you or something."

But in a way, I was, wasn't I? After a considerable gas problem a month or so ago, the vet had suggested I put him on a strict diet of regular dry dog food, so I had. Of course, I'd had no idea that Mrs. Nebitz across the hall had been feeding him fried chicken liver from the fire escape. But after supplying her with a brand of dog biscuit that Muffy loved, the terrier and I had lived in gas-free harmony ever since.

Well, once he finally gave in and accepted that the dry food was it.

Unfortunately that also meant no midnight stops at the souvlaki stand on Broadway and Thirty-second on my way home. But I'd decided the sacrifice was more than worth it.

I switched on the kitchen light, poured his dog food, and refilled his water bowl. He went straight to work as I scoured the refrigerator for what I might eat.

An empty plate sat on the top shelf. One of Mrs. Nebitz's with a delicate rose design that had held a knish for all of fifteen minutes before I'd snatched it from the refrigerator and ate it. Namely because there was nothing else to eat.

"I really should go to the grocery store."

Scaring up half a package of crackers from the cupboard, I turned on the stove light for Muffy, switched off the overhead light, then cracked open the window over the fire escape before heading to my bedroom. I wasn't amused with the prospect of being single and eating crackers in bed.

"I wouldn't kick him out of bed for eating crackers."

I remembered the saying as I crunched on one of the saltines and then switched on the bedside lamp. Efi had surprised me by using the adage recently. Only she'd been talking about the actress Angelina Jolie and had earned an open-mouthed gape from me. Wasn't it bad enough that Grandpa Kosmos thought she was gay, or at the very least bisexual? Did she have to go around saying stuff like that?

Thankfully Grandpa Kosmos hadn't been around at the time. Nor had any other family members or I would have had to spend the next year trying to convince them that Efi really didn't mean it.

I put a cracker between my teeth and then stripped out of my clothes, draping them over an armchair before shrugging into my nightshirt. Then again, maybe she did mean it. Hell, at this point I would be hard pressed to be motivated to kick anyone out of my bed, much less someone as sexy as Angelina. Especially if she brought Brad with her.

As I lay back in bed, crunching on my crackers, I thought of Porter and wondered where he'd been lately. He seemed to have this uncanny way of showing up whenever I needed help. And I hadn't needed any help recently. Well, not of the nonsexual variety, anyway.

I glanced toward the wall of still wrapped wedding gifts I hadn't touched in at least a month. Periodically I liked to pop open a bottle of champagne meant for my reception and choose one or two of the gifts that looked like they weren't small kitchen appliances. But none of them had interested me since . . .

Since Porter had suggested that I wasn't over my relationship with Thomas because of the presence of the gifts.

I brushed crumbs off my shirt and grimaced when they slid down onto the sheets. Ugh. I could just imagine what kind of dreams I was going to have while I unconsciously rolled around. With my luck it would have something to do with fish and breading and being fried.

I heard Muffy's toenails on the polished wood floors and then he jumped up and sat next to me. I absently petted him and decided a cracker was bland enough for him to snack on. I gave him the second to last one, and then finished them off.

"What do you think, boy? Should we finally get rid of the presents?"

He was too busy sniffing around for stray cracker crumbs he could inhale.

"Maybe I should throw a party. You know, kind of like a reverse bachelorette party. Invite the female members of the family over and everyone can take turns opening a gift, taking home anything they like."

Muffy couldn't have been less interested as he did his round and round bit and then lay in the middle of the empty pillow next to mine, putting his furry butt directly in my face. I made a sound of disgust and turned the other way so that I was facing the gifts.

I'd tried calling Thomas-the-Toad earlier. You know, to politely ask him to drop the charges against my grandpa Kosmos. I'd gotten his voicemail and hung up without leaving a message. I knew that resolving the situation was going to take a lot more than a simple phone call, but I'd hoped otherwise.

As my eyes began drifting closed, I imagined my grandfather hauling off and socking my ex-fiancé right in the kisser. I smiled and snuggled down deeper into the bedding. Ah, yes. Just the right note I needed to drift off to sleep . . . before images of Jake Porter and his sexy Australian accent took over.

LIFESTYLES OF THE RICH AND FAMOUS. There was a time when I'd been more than a bit taken with the topic. You know, when I was twelve and my parents wouldn't let me go to a Madonna concert, or when I turned sixteen and a brand-spanking-new

BMW convertible wasn't in the offing, but rather a rustmobile with plates. And given the flood of shows like *MTV Cribs* and *The Fabulous Life of* insert-star-name-here, and countless other programs designed to make you feel part of an exclusive clique, seemingly putting it within your reach . . . well, I have to say that I used to be a sucker for finding out where Paris Hilton partied. Still, I always have a seat up front and center in front of the tube to watch the red carpet lead-up to an important awards ceremony. Even though I couldn't afford most of the designers mentioned when it came to clothing, I did have a deep-discount Louis Vuitton handbag and a couple of XOXO and Chanel knockoffs. A true product of American consumerism that kept people like J-Lo and P. Diddy and Paris Hilton in Bentleys while I drove around in a 'sixty-five bondo special Mustang even as I fantasized about MTV's *Pimp My Ride* restoring her to better than original glory.

But after spending the better part of the past day and a half following Reni Venezuela and his two-miles-to-a-gallon Hummer limo around Manhattan, from Hugo Boss where he'd been fit for a hand-tailored suit, to a late lunch—alone—at Elaine's, then to the stadium for practice followed by a trip to a day spa, I reasoned that their way of life would bore me to tears in no time flat. Okay, maybe after six months or so.

While I don't consider myself what my mother called a *tsiggouna* or cheapskate, I was picky about those things I chose to spend my money on, much less sit through. It was all I could do to get to my hairdresser Manos once a month for a cut and to have my highlights freshened. And I only did that because the color of my shoulder-length brown hair was plain and the strands curly, meaning going without regular visits left me looking like Medusa in dim light (of course, it didn't hurt that Manos told me that the golden highlights brought out the green in my eyes). Sitting in a chair for three hours straight having somebody fuss over me wasn't my idea of a good time. I'd rather catch a rerun of *House* or *Rescue Me*, preferably while eating a Greek delicacy or whatever Jewish goody Mrs. Nebitz had made that day. And if not for my mother commenting about how I needed to get my hair done nonstop around the time I was due for an appointment, I probably would.

Thankfully the Mets were due for a doubleheader today, which meant that I would have much of the afternoon and evening to myself.

Correction: which meant I could catch up with some loose ends around the agency and see if I couldn't catch the weekly call from my uncle Spyros.

I lucked out and found an empty spot right in front of the agency. I parked Lucille and then locked the old Mustang up before going inside the agency.

"Three of 'em. And the day ain't even over yet," Rosie complained without turning from her computer monitor. She waved three request sheets at me over her shoulder.

I ignored them and her, deciding I didn't want to know what she meant. I could do without thinking about cheating spouses or missing pets right now. As she had for the past month, Rosie had a portable radio tuned in to the first of the games. And her cell phone next to that, on call in case her sister Lupe went into labor with her first child.

"Any progress on collecting on the Pappas bill?" I asked.

She stared at me as if I was a *koulouraki* short of a full dozen.

Pappas was more definitely Apostolis Pappas, also known as Uncle Tolly, and he and his wife Aglaia owned a dry cleaners near Ditmars. Last month Tolly had gone missing and Aglaia had hired me to find him. Not so she could bury him, mind you, but so she could sell his new Mercedes. Only after figuring out that the two sets of books he'd kept were for his own skimming purposes and had nothing to do with the mob, and after I'd been given an unwanted view of the hungry waters of the East River from the Hell Gate Bridge, I'd figured out that Uncle Tolly hadn't been missing at all, but had decided he'd had it with life with Aglaia and moved to the Bahamas to open a tiki bar.

After all the trouble I'd gotten into looking for him, I'd decided I'd never call him "uncle" again.

I'd also decided to charge the couple my regular going rate instead of the reduced family rate that usually went hand-in-hand with anyone my mother arm-twisted me into helping.

Of course, they had yet to pay anything toward the reduced rate, much less the full one. And I was beginning to suspect they weren't going to.

"Oh, and this came in."

Rosie got up and slapped a request sheet down in front of me, followed quickly by the other three.

"Three more missing pets?"

"Uh-huh." She popped her gum. "That makes, what? Ten? I dunno about you, but I think something funny's going on."

"Maybe it's mating season."

She gave me an eye roll and then sat back down to wrestle with her computer. "That might make sense if all of 'em weren't cauterized, or de-balled, or whatever it is they call fixing them."

"Spaying or neutering."

"Whatever. None of the words sounds good." She paled slightly. "Maybe that vampire Romanoff ran out of human blood donors . . ."

"Stop right there. If you were a vampire, would you go for dog blood? No. I didn't think so."

Thankfully, I'd nipped that one in the bud before she could take out her perfume bottles filled with holy water.

I moved the three top sheets aside and scanned the fourth one even as Reni struck out the third batter in the top of the seventh.

"Venezuela's on fire today," the radio commentator Ed Coleman said. "After a rough six innings, he's pulled the team back into the running with a one-two-three turnover . . ."

I jerked up my head to look at Rosie and waved the request. "Is this for real?"

"As real as it gets."

I raised my brows as I reread the job description. "Investigate an ear found in split pea soup."

I sat back in my chair. Really, I should be going through the invoices, making notes on closed cases, and seeing what I could dig up on Venezuela when he was scheduled to travel out of town. At the very least, I should check out if his last name was really the same as his native country instead of waiting for Rosie to do it. Instead, my attention was glued to the request sheet.

The woman owned a small restaurant on Steinway a block or so up from the agency. Rosie and I frequently picked up meals on the run there because of the good cosmopolitan selection. In addition to offering up pretty good gyros, she had American staples like meatloaf and fried chicken.

And, obviously, a rotating soup of the day.

I caught myself rubbing my right ear and read what Rosie had written.

> Last Tuesday a couple came in for lunch. They'd been in maybe three or four times before, all within the past couple of weeks. In the middle of eating her soup, the customer jumped up and screamed, claiming that something was in her bowl in addition to the soup. Upon visual investigation, it was suspected to be a piece of a human ear.

"What, is Mike Tyson her cook?" I said aloud.

Rosie popped her gum. "That's what I said. Either that or Holyfield. You know, maybe the plastic surgery didn't take and the piece fell off or something. 'Cept the ear was white." She shook her head. "People. Always trying to get something for nothing."

I remember the finger in the chili scam somewhere out west a few years back. The couple responsible ultimately got prison time for their stupid little scheme.

But in that case the people targeted were part of a nationwide chain that could afford to buy the best private investigators in the world.

Phoebe Hall, the owner of this restaurant, couldn't. As she'd explained to me a couple of weeks ago, while I enjoyed a gyro that had served as my lunch and dinner. In her twenty-three years of running the restaurant, she'd come to understand that there was a certain cycle to business. And right now she was experiencing a slump that the monies made during peak times helped her through. I also knew this firsthand to an extent from having grown up in the business, what with my father owning his own semi-upscale steak restaurant and my grandpa Kosmos' Greek-themed café.

But in Phoebe's case she couldn't afford to upgrade her refrigerator much less try to defend herself against such a claim. Hell, I don't know if my father or grandfather could professionally survive such an accusation. Stories of human body parts being found in food tended to negatively affect business. While all restaurants were required to carry insurance, and the New York health department did its best to certify on a regular basis that restaurants met with code standards, all of that meant little in the end when you considered attorneys and investigators and court fees. I knew that something like this was a disaster in the making for any restaurateur.

I rubbed my forehead.

"Maybe she'll give us free lunch for life or somethin' if we take the case," Rosie said.

"Maybe she'll close down if this couple sues her."

"Come on. This is a scam if ever there was one."

Yes, but how did you prove that with limited monetary resources?

And what if the claim was true? What if somehow the ear had accidentally fallen into the soup or been part of the ingredients Phoebe had used to make it? What then?

"You gonna take it?"

"I don't know." I sat back and stared at the far wall that was in dire need of painting and the faded posters and maps covering it. "We have all our resources working the Venezuela case."

By "resources," I meant me.

Rosie gestured toward the radio. "Yeah, but you don't have to be doing nothing now."

"Sleep might be nice every now and again."

"In the middle of the day?"

She had a point.

I fingered the request, and then handed it over to her. "Find out what you can about the couple. See if they have rap sheets or if they've maybe tried to pull something like this before."

She smacked the side of her computer in a way that made me jump. "Sure thing, boss. Just as soon as this stupid thing stops freezing up."

Four

BETWEEN YOU AND ME, THERE was something else I also had
to do in my downtime that I hadn't shared with Rosie. While I
wasn't entirely sure why I hadn't told her, I reasoned that it was
probably because I liked that people were no longer linking
Thomas-the-Toad's name and what had gone down six months
ago with me. And I wanted to keep it that way.

Wasn't it bad enough that my rep was being seriously threatened by the fact that in a week my grandpa Kosmos would be
facing criminal assault charges for breaking Thomas' nose protecting my honor?

Forget that my grandfather might become a convict. I had
my reputation to think about.

So I swung by my place to pick up the Muffster and then
headed out to Bayside where Thomas' parents owned what had
once been a large house that they'd chopped into apartments
and added onto over the years. It was a pretty good bet that he
was still living in the apartment above his parents' because, let's
face it, there was no reason to go anywhere—beyond his

mother's harping on him to get married and move out. He had everything he needed right there at his fingertips.

Which, of course, I'd figured out a bit late that was where I fit nicely into the picture. He could move from his parents' place to the apartment building my parents had bought me as a wedding gift, without lifting a manicured finger and with nothing more major to worry about than where to put the leather Barcalounger I'd bought him as a wedding gift that now served as Muffy's regular snoozing spot.

I reminded myself that, thankfully, Thomas' place of residence was no longer my problem. Not anymore. No, that honor now went to my former best friend and groom-shtupper Kati Dimos.

My knuckles were white from where I gripped the steering wheel too tightly. I released my fingers one by one and shook them out, earning a bark from Muffy who was probably wondering what was going on. More likely, he was happy to be out of the apartment, even if it was just in my car, and was telling me to get over myself.

"Put a lid on it or no doggie treats for you."

His ever-present panting tongue disappeared and he snapped his mouth closed.

"That's more like it."

As I turned the corner onto the Chalikis' street, I felt strange somehow. Was it really only six months ago that I'd driven here as frequently and as comfortably as I did to my parents' house? It seemed like a lifetime ago. Then again, just yesterday.

Funny how the memory played those kind of tricks on you. Whenever I needed to travel anywhere in the area, I made a point of avoiding going anywhere near this street.

Now I was purposely driving straight to the Chalikis' house.

I found a spot halfway up the block and parked, ignoring the curtains that fluttered inside the house opposite me. Probably old Mr. Davis recognized me. Or maybe not. Maybe he was calling the NYPD now and Pimply Pino was on his way to torture me with his presence.

Than again, I think this was out of Pino's district.

I counted that as a good thing.

I approached the door to the house—now apartment building—and pressed the doorbell for Thomas' apartment.

"He's not there," Mrs. Warren from next door told me.

I squinted at her. "Do you know where he is?"

"Depends."

"On what?"

"On whether or not you tell me why you want him."

"I have some things I need to give to him," I lied, but only partially, because I did plan on giving him a big piece of my mind.

She made a face that indicated her disappointment. "Oh. Well, then, he's down at Mikey's place."

Probably she'd wanted to see some action. And if I'd said my purpose was to chew him out she wouldn't have told me where he was but rather would have waited until she had a ringside seat when he was home. Either that or she would have put on her fuzzy pink slippers and followed me to Mikey's.

"Thanks."

"Don't mention it."

She closed her window and disappeared from view.

Mikey's. A semi-Greek modern café. Semi because it held a refrigerated display case that held Greek sweets and, well, was owned by a third-generation Greek American. Modern because any Greek columns on the walls had been traded for red wallpaper and white-shell light fixtures.

God, had I really forgotten that's where Thomas had spent the majority of his downtime?

I got back into my car and drove the few blocks to Mikey's, the wave of earlier nostalgia returning tenfold. More often than not, I'd met Thomas here rather than back at his place. For the same reason he was probably here now: his mother.

I parked in a spot nearer the front of the nearly empty side lot and then walked inside. As usual, there were at least ten Greeks around the same age as Thomas in the place. And they all stopped talking when they spotted me. And I was sure a few of them were in danger of having their jaws hitting the black-and-white tiled floor.

"Mikey," I said by way of greeting. "Thomas, can I speak to you for a minute?"

"Sure. What's up?"

I shuddered as I recognized his reaction as one he would have made while we were still engaged. As if he hadn't screwed my maid of honor on the day of our wedding, threatened to sue me for half the building I now lived in, or given me a CZ engagement ring that had held a diamond when he'd gotten it from my grandpa Kosmos.

Of course, it didn't help matters that he was as hot as ever. The epitome of Greek tall, dark, and handsome. And in direct contrast to his friend Mikey who was at least six inches shorter, had inherited the telltale Greek hawk-like nose and weighed a buck ten at the most.

"Outside," I said.

He was parked in front of a television that was wheeled in during the day and was playing a video soccer game with Mikey. I'd never had a problem with him playing Xbox and PlayStation. My only request had been that he not do it during couple time. I likened the experience of watching him play while I waited for him to finish to the idea of watching him masturbate.

And right then I wasn't up to sharing what group game playing reminded me of. I'll just say that it gives "circle jerk" a whole new twist.

Thomas said, "Hold on, I just . . . need . . . to . . . goal!"

I gave an eye roll as he put down the control, threw his arms up in the air, and then smacked a grimacing Mikey hard on the back. "What's that make now? Fifty bucks that you owe me?"

"Forty."

Thomas. Overgrown child who still got into beating his friends out of their beer money. Attractive.

He came up to me, taking extra care to give me his usual long appraisal, apparently agreeing with the slim jeans and clingy white top I had on. I led the way out front.

"You look great, Sof," he said as the door closed.

I ignored him. "What's it going to take to get you to drop the charges against my grandfather?"

He slid his hands into the pockets of his cargo pants and then leaned back onto his heels. "I don't know. What you offering?"

"A clear conscience."

He chuckled. "I already have that."

I raised my brows.

"What else you got?"

I'd never been one for confrontations unless they involved my immediate family, and even then I tended to handle them with humor rather than anger. In fact, up until I'd caught Thomas wedged between Kati's thighs, we'd never had an argument, which should have been enough to set off alarm bells, but hadn't.

"Drop the charges, Thomas."

"Oooo. That sounds like a threat. Okay, I'll bite. Or else what?"

At least a dozen answers came to mind. First and foremost how easy it would be to jam my knee between his legs. But I'd already done that, hadn't I? And since Grandpa Kosmos had already broken his nose, that left out socking him. Hey, I strove for originality. You had to give me credit for at least that.

"Or else I'll make a point of letting every woman you date from here on in know about your inability to keep your penis to yourself."

His grin widened.

I turned to walk away from him before I did break his nose again.

His chuckle followed me. "Come back when you have something to offer."

I debated letting Muffy out to have at him as I got back into the car. If only I didn't suspect that Thomas would probably press charges against *me*.

ON MY WAY BACK TO the office, I'd listened on the car radio as the first Mets game had ended. The second game was scheduled to start later that night. I entered the office to find that Rosie still had the portable on and I stepped to turn it off before going to my desk.

"What's up?" she asked.

"What? Does something always have to be up?"

"Uh-oh. Looks like that would be your temper. What happened?"

"Nothing happened." I fumed.

I'd come back to the office precisely because I didn't want to talk about what had gone down at Mikey's. I didn't know what I'd been thinking when I went. That perhaps Thomas had grown a sense of right and wrong between now and the time he'd had Grandpa Kosmos arrested? The chances of a category five hurricane hitting Long Island were greater.

"Anything going on?"

Rosie shook her head. "Nope." She stopped chewing and

stared at where Muffy sat with his legs spread wide as he indulged in some loud licking.

"That's disgusting."

"Don't look."

"Spyros ain't going like his being in here."

"Yeah, well Spyros isn't here, is he?"

"No, but Nash just came in."

I stared at the closed door to Lenny Nash's office. Lenny was a silent partner of sorts to my uncle. The silent part may have come from his not saying much of anything, because the hefty entries into the income column of the agency's ledgers told me his actions, whatever they were, spoke loudly. He wasn't around much, and even when he was it was easy to forget he was there, but there was something about him that put me off my game when he was in the office.

I reached for the stack of newspapers on the corner of my desk. I was usually one for gossip and comic sections, but now I turned directly to sports. A confirmed Mets fan—as evidenced by my getting kicked out of the game a couple weeks ago—I'll be the first to admit that when it came to stats, outside how many games away from winning the pennant my team was, I didn't know squat.

The first paper didn't say anything more than I already knew. The second, a headline immediately caught my attention: VENEZUELA GOING LEFT?

The reporter was listed as George Fowler and he went on to say that for the past four games Reni Venezuela had pitched with his left hand exclusively, leaving his special mitt with two thumbs so he could switch off in the locker room. (In all honesty, the mitt creeped me out anyway. I understood it was especially made for him, but I would have liked to take scissors to it.)

So what? The guy was on a winning streak. Maybe he didn't

want to mess up a good thing. Hell, I didn't want him to mess it up, either. And Lord knew that sports players had tons of superstitious rituals. Who was the player who wore the same pair of socks for every game? I couldn't remember but I figured by the end of the season those socks could have run the bases themselves.

Rosie cursed at her computer and smacked it.

"That'll work," I said as I opened another paper, happy to be back to good news about the Mets in this one.

"I swear, I'm going to throw this thing out of the window one day."

"Then you'll have to pay for a computer and a window."

She glared at me.

Against my better judgment, I looked at the new papers littering the top of my desk. There were two completed reports on two cheating spouse cases, a copy of a spot tail statement that had been mailed to Con Ed, and a smeared printout of something I had trouble making out.

"What's this?" I asked, half-afraid Rosie would tell me it was another missing pet case.

"That's what I was able to print up before my computer and printer pooped at the same time."

I blinked, waiting for more.

She waved a hand at me. "That's the background check on Venezuela. Only his real name's not Venezuela. It's Bastardo."

"Bastardo?"

"Uh-huh. He changed it immediately upon immigrating here to play for the Islanders." Rosie looked disappointed. "Doesn't have the same ring to it, does it? Venezuela. Bastardo." She wrinkled her nose. "I can see why he changed it."

I leaned back in my chair, trying to make out the words on the half-eaten page. "Huh."

I was aware that a lot of Greeks changed or truncated their

names when they came to the States. Nicola Gatzoyiannis became the Nicholas Gage of *Eleni* fame. Jennifer Anastassakis became America's best friend by becoming Jennifer Aniston. And I'd gone to school with a girl whose father had changed Andricopoulos to Andricos.

Then there were the stars that changed their names for obvious reasons. Would Tom Cruise be the celebrity he was if he'd stayed Tom Mapother? Who would Caryn Johnson be without Whoopie Goldberg? And would Woody Allen be the New York icon he was if he'd remained Allen Konigsberg?

Of course, Reni's reasons for changing his name went well beyond anything merely cultural. If I was up on my Spanish, "bastardo" literally meant bastard.

Good for a gangster rapper. Possibly bad for a baseball player.

Then again, maybe not.

"Isn't there another player somewhere with the name Bastardo?" I asked.

"Yeah. A pitcher for the Dodgers."

I nodded. Maybe that was part of the reason Reni had changed his name.

"Anything on his family in Venezuela yet?"

She stared at me as if I'd grown a second head.

The telephone rang and Rosie immediately picked up. "Metropolis Agency."

She instantly relaxed at the sound of whoever was on the line. Then she said, "Spyros, I need a new computer."

My uncle and my employer. Even though I tended to forget about the second part beyond his name being on the window Rosie had just threatened to break.

Why did I have the feeling that she told him she needed a new computer every time he called? I put the paper down and waited to talk to him for the first time since he'd left for Greece months ago.

Five

"RULE NUMBER SEVENTEEN IN THE PI handbook is that you never draw your gun unless you intend to use it," Uncle Spyros said to me when I picked up.

Since he could have been referring to shooting my own client Bud Suleski in the knee, or giving Panayiotis Rokkos two ear jobs, I decided not to say that I'd fully intended to use the gun in all three cases.

"Is this book in print somewhere?" I asked. "Because if it is, I want to track down all copies and burn them."

His warm chuckle made me smile. "How you doin', Sof?"

"Me? I'm fine. It's you I'm worried about."

"Nothing to worry about. I just decided to make up for all the years I haven't been able to make it back to Greece."

"Weeks I can understand. But months?"

"Hey, from what I hear, you're making it easy for me to stay away."

I leaned back in my chair, trying not to feel too smug.

"You know, when you first hired on, I didn't expect you to make it past a week."

"I made two at Aunt Sotiria's." My aunt owned a funeral home. I'd been taken with the novelty of working around dead bodies. But when I found out that I'd be working with them more closely than I'd planned (Did you know a body's fingernails grew even after death? And that they needed to be cut prior to viewing? That's right, that job had been given to me), I'd sprinted straight for the door and never went back.

"That's not what I'm talking about and you know it. What I mean is that I'm surprised that six months in you're still there."

"What, you thought I'd rather wait tables at Dad's?" I pulled a pad in front of me. "Actually, that's something we need to discuss."

"Your father?"

"No. The fact that I have been here half a year and am more than pulling my own weight."

"And?"

"And, I want a raise. Commission rather than salary. Oh, and more autonomy around here."

"Define 'autonomy'?"

I watched Rosie feed an ancient floppy disk into her CPU. "I want to update some of the office equipment. Invest in some surveillance tools. Hire additional staff. Stuff like that."

I figured I'd sounded pretty good. Until I'd said "stuff like that." Probably it made me look like a kid who was putting in an order for high-end school supplies she didn't expect to get.

"Okay."

I snapped upright in my chair. "Okay?"

"Within reason. Let me talk to Nash. He'll tell you how much you have to work with. But judging by the numbers Rosie shared, well, it looks like you're going to have a wide margin."

"Cool."

I felt like that kid again, but forgave myself for the momentary lapse. If any situation called for a "cool" this was it.

"When are you planning on coming back?" I asked.

"I don't know."

"Is there direct number where I can reach you?"

"No."

"Any way I can get a message to you?"

"No."

Well, so much for feeling important.

"I call every week, Sof. Anything comes up, you go to Nash."

Essentially the same thing he'd told me the day I signed on.

We said our good-byes and then I transferred him to Nash.

"Were you guys just talking about what I think you were talking about?" Rosie asked, taking out one floppy then feeding the machine another.

"It sure does," I said, pushing the papers aside. "Grab your purse, Rosie, baby. We're going computer shopping . . ."

"I'M SENDING YOU TO MIAMI."

Eugene Waters stared at me like I was the one wearing gold teeth. He stuck his finger in his ear and joggled it. "What? I know I couldn't have heard you right. Did you just say you're sending me to Miami?"

I fought a smile. He'd been bugging me ever since coming to work for the agency for more responsibility and I'd ignored him.

"What, am I delivering papers?"

"Now that would be an expensive set of papers. No. The agency's sending you to tail Venezuela while they're down there playing the Marlins."

I'd considered going on the trip myself. For all of five minutes. But now that I had more power at the agency, I intended to get straight to work using it. Not to mention that I was getting pretty bored following a man who didn't seem to ever do anything out of the ordinary.

"Miami," Waters repeated.

"Uh-huh." I held up the tickets I'd had Rosie arrange through the Greek travel agency up the block. "Unless you're not interested."

He snatched the tickets out of my hand so fast I got a paper cut.

"Ow." I stuck my finger into my mouth.

"Why we tailing Venezuela?" he asked.

I noticed he moved from the "agency" to "us" in a smooth fashion. "I think this is where your 'don't ask, don't tell' policy takes effect."

He waggled a finger at me after sticking the tickets into the front of his shirt, as if putting them in his pocket wasn't safe enough. I remembered doing the same with the envelope full of bills Gisela had given me. It was those bills that were financing this trip.

Rosie's humming caught our attention. We turned to watch her clacking away on her new state-of-the-art laptop. A guy had come in to install a wireless networking system so that my uncle's office computer could access hers, along with broadband. She was in seventh heaven.

"I love this thing!" she said, completely oblivious to us. She caressed the sides of the screen and then continued clacking away.

"Doesn't take much for some people," Waters said, then looked back at me. "When do I leave?"

NOW THIS WAS DEFINITELY SOMETHING I could get used to.

Hooked up through Rosie's new computer, I sat at my uncle

Spyros' desk, scanning court decisions I'd gotten through a legal database search on restaurant scams. While the door was open and I could hear Rosie talking to someone on the phone, I could have been on another planet for all it affected me. I concentrated on the work in front of me instead.

No, I hadn't gone to visit Phoebe Hall yet. I wanted to do a little background work first to see if hers was a case I could take on with at least a little certainty of a successful outcome. I didn't want to jump in and promise something I couldn't deliver on. And since Phoebe didn't have much by way of resources, I couldn't afford to devote a huge chunk of time to her without some sort of payoff.

This from the girl for whom the greater percentage of her cases had been favors for her mother and missing pets not too long ago.

A brief knock at the door. "You wanted to see me?"

I finished a notation then looked up to find Debbie Matenopoulos considering me.

I stared back at her.

Debbie and I went way back. To St. Demetrios Greek School, to be exact, where she attended classes with my brother Kosmos. Inside the Greek community everyone knew that her real name was Despina. But that wasn't what I remembered every time I saw her in her sexy outfits. Rather, I saw her hanging from Jake Porter's arm, acting as his decoy.

It had taken a lot for me to get over the image of their having a connection outside the professional. But when Debbie had asked me for a job, I'd given her one as a process server. Partly because I'd wanted something from her at the time. Mostly because I was a sucker when it came to a good sob story.

"Yes," I said, getting up to move the files I'd placed on the visitor's chair. "Sit down."

She looked over her shoulder at where Rosie had squealed in delight.

"New computer," I said.

"Ah." She tried to appear like she understood but I knew she didn't. No matter. I wasn't going to be asking her to do computer work.

She sat down, her long legs growing even longer when her micromini hiked up. Yikes.

"Is this about upgrading me?" she asked. "I hope this is about upgrading me, because I could really use the money."

"Rosie tells me you've been doing a great job with the process serving."

"I guess. My sister says to me, 'It's because nobody expects you to be doing anything official,' but I'm not sure if that's a good thing or a bad."

"Good. Definitely good."

I'd expected to have mixed feelings during this meeting. After all, Jake Porter was the reason I had crossed paths with Debbie again after a number of years. Maybe it was because Porter wasn't a part of my life outside my fantasies right now, or because I'd managed to mature in some way not even I had recognized, but I felt nothing but professional courtesy toward the striking blonde.

A definite improvement over raging jealousy.

"I'd like to give you a cheating spouse case."

Debbie's squeal resembled Rosie's minutes earlier. "Really? I mean, I'm going to work on an actual, honest-to-God case?"

"Cheating spouse case. And one." To start. I wanted to see how she did before I committed to anything more.

"Great!" She got up too fast, flashing me . . . was she really not wearing underwear? Double yikes.

She was acting like she'd just won the lottery. Was that how I'd appeared when my uncle Spyros had offered me a job at the agency? God, I hoped not. Then again, I was no longer there, so what did I care?

"What is it? Can I see the file?"

I fingered through the items on the desk and held out a manila folder. She took it.

I was a little more reluctant with handing over the other item she would need. If only because of what it had taken to get it.

I held up the new, palm-size digital camera I'd bought along with Rosie's computer. I had planned to use it so I could finally return my brother's top-of-the-line Olympus, complete with fresh film and a zoom lens. (Actually, it wasn't my brother's. The camera I'd taken from him had met with a bad fate a few months ago while I'd been shooting pictures through a motel window only to find someone shooting back at me . . . with real bullets.)

But faced with handing over the new digital to Debbie, or the Olympus that she might lose or break or worse, or handling more cheating spouse cases myself, I gave her the camera.

"Now, you have to be very careful with this," I said.

She gripped it but I found I had a hard time releasing my own hold despite the fact that it was insured. Maybe I should have her pick up a disposable. Even though I knew a disposable wouldn't deliver the quality we often needed because such shots were sometimes taken from long distances and needed to be zoomed in on, not just with the camera, but after the shots were developed. And it was always a good idea that the client be able to recognize her or his no-good, cheating spouse in the picture.

Debbie pulled and I finally relented.

She stared down at it. "How do I use it?"

Okay, that was it. She was going to have to get a disposable—

The phone buzzed. "Sofie, I got a call for you on line two," Rosie's voice came over the intercom.

I looked around Debbie. "You could have just shouted it," I called out.

Rosie's gum-chewing grin put me in a worse temper. How long was this computer honeymoon going to last? I didn't think I could take much more of this good cheer.

"Who is it?" I called out.

"I dunno. Some guy. Says it's personal."

Guy. Personal.

Porter?

I looked at Debbie. "Here's the manual." I handed it to her. "You can reach me here or on my cell if you run into any problems."

"Thank you, Sofie. Thank you. I promise I won't screw this up. I'm going to get the best damn money shot you've ever seen."

I gave an eye roll. "Just get the shot and I'll be happy."

She tottered out of the office on her stilettos as I shook my head and picked up the telephone.

If my palm was a little damper than usual, and if my finger hovered above the connect button a little longer than it should have, I wasn't admitting it.

I cleared my throat, punched the button, and said, "Metro here."

A soft chuckle. Male. Nice.

Definitely not Porter's. Even his chuckle had an Australian accent.

"Sofie? Is that you?" someone asked in a thick accent, not Australian.

"This is she. With whom am I speaking?"

"Oh. Sorry. I didn't say, did I?" He cleared his throat. "This is Dino. You know, Constantinos Antonopoulos?"

I nearly fell straight off my chair.

Six

THE LAST PERSON I WOULD have expected to find on the line was Dino, the guy my mother had tried to fix up with my sister Efi. The man who had ended up staying for dinner after Efi left for a date with another guy.

The delicious Greek who owned a *zaharoplastio* or sweets shop.

"Dino! Yes, of course, I remember you," I said, hoping I didn't sound like I'd just nearly fallen out of my chair. "How are you?" I asked, trying to figure out why he would be calling me. "Do you need to hire a PI?"

He chuckled again. I decided that I liked the sound. "I'm fine. And, no, I don't need to hire a PI."

My mouth opened but nothing came out. I caught Rosie watching me from the other room and swiveled the chair to face the opposite direction. Still, I couldn't think of anything to say.

"How's the *pasta* business going?" came out and I cringed.

Greek *pasta* wasn't the same as Italian pasta. Think chocolate tortes designed to ruin your taste buds for any other sweet.

"Fine. Business is good." He paused. "Look, I don't want to keep you. I was just wondering if you could meet me for coffee or something sometime. Tomorrow, maybe?"

"Coffee?"

Of course. He wanted to talk to me about Efi.

Sometimes it was difficult for me to remember that once I'd kicked Thomas-the-Toad to the curb, that as a twenty-six-year-old Greek woman I was officially a *yerotokori*. An old maid.

"You want to talk about Efi?"

A pause, then, "Yes. We can talk about Efi."

Seeing as he'd been born in Greece, and had immigrated to the States only a year or so ago, his English was about as good as my grandpa Kosmos'.

"Fine. That will be okay. When and where do you want to meet?" I asked.

"Omonia? At eleven tomorrow?"

I made a face. Omonia was a Greek café and bakery on Broadway a short ways from my father's restaurant and my grandfather's café. While this might be about my sister, I didn't want anyone getting the idea that this was about us. So I suggested a place in Jackson Heights instead.

"All right. Eleven o'clock then," he said.

"Eleven," I agreed.

Silence.

"I look forward to it. Bye."

I quickly hung up the phone, curiously holding it down on the cradle with both hands.

Rosie was still staring at me.

"What?" I asked.

She *tsk*ed with a smile. "Conducting personal business on Spyros' dime."

"It's my dime. And besides, it wasn't personal. It was about my sister."

How, exactly, that made it not personal didn't make sense even to me. But I left things there and turned back to the computer, wondering how I was going to break the news to Dino that Efi was in love with another guy. . . .

ALL THINGS CONSIDERED, I SUPPOSE I was pretty happy with the way things were going. If I was bored with the Venezuela case (God, the guy didn't even look to be cheating on his wife, although during an earlier phone call she insisted that I keep working because she was even more convinced that something wasn't "right" with her husband), well, with Waters tailing him to Miami, that meant I only had to tuck the star pitcher into bed tonight, in a manner of speaking. I wouldn't have to worry about him for a few days outside conversations with Waters.

I sat parked in the mostly empty Lot B at Shea, waiting for the gates to the players' lot to open, and picked up the souvlaki I'd put on the passenger's seat. Since I'd taken Muffy home, I didn't have to feel guilty about not giving him any of the grilled pork bits. In fact, while I didn't own a scale, I think I'd dropped at least five pounds as a result of my forced home dieting. I could tell by the way I didn't have to exhale every time I sat down in my usually tight jeans.

That meant I could indulge myself a little. I tore into the warm pita.

I spotted an old Pontiac I'd seen the last time I was there. And the same fifytish-year-old guy got out, hiked up his striped polyester pants held up by a worn brown belt that was paired with a faded light green short-sleeved shirt bearing a black pocket protector. A reporter, I was pretty sure, because he'd also been in the press area when Waters had taken me to meet Venezuela, you know, before I'd hired on to get dirt on him I wasn't sure existed.

I squinted at the reporter. Didn't they have a special lot for the press? If they did, I was pretty sure it wasn't here in Lot B. To my right, most of the parking area was fenced off where the new Citi Field Stadium was being built.

I took another bite and then immediately put the souvlaki down when the first of the team members began exiting the players' parking lot through the blacked out gates. I wiped my hands against the front of my jeans and picked up the Olympus in case anything interesting should happen. A loud sound on the top of my car made me jump. I fumbled to put the camera down even as I turned in my seat. Not that I had to. One of Venezuela's goons moved so I had a real good view of him next to my open window, a breath away.

"What you following Venezuela for?" the steroid-inflated specimen who looked like he could double as a bar bouncer asked.

"What?" I said, nudging the camera farther aside even as I licked *tsatsiki* sauce from the corner of my mouth and tried to swallow.

"You've been spotted on the boss' tailpipe for at least the past two days. What, you one of those stalkers or something?"

I blinked at him, the thought that I might be mistaken for a stalker never having occurred to me. "No, I'm not a stalker." Truth was, I was insulted someone would think that. Although I questioned whether or not it was a good idea to identify myself as a PI instead. Probably should have let him think I was a stalker.

"Hey, do I know you?" he asked, leaning in closer to squint at me.

"Me? No. I'm sure you don't." I shoved my hand out of the window, forcing him to straighten and take a step back. "Hi, my name's . . . Pamela Coe and I'm a sports reporter for *The New York Gazette-Times*."

Okay, so the first name that came to mind was Pamela's, and I'd made a grab at a newspaper name. It was the best I could do considering the time I had to work with.

"You're a reporter?" The bouncer chuckled at that and I took great offense. What, the guy with the pocket-protector was more reporter material than I was? Why wasn't it reasonable to think I was one?

"Yeah, I'm a reporter," I said emphatically.

"Right." He slapped the top of my car again and I concealed—I think—my jump. "Look, I don't care who in the hell you are. Just stay the fuck away from my boss, ya hear? If I spot you on our tail again . . ."

The words, "or else what?" were on the tip of my tongue, but thankfully I was able to keep them there. I didn't need a diagram of what the walking ape would do to me.

"Oh, and I'm pretty sure I'll remember who you are. I never forget a pretty face," he said.

He walked away and I wondered what it was like to have one's knuckles drag on the ground when you moved.

Yikes.

So I'd been made. It would mark a first of sorts for me. But I suppose it shouldn't be all that surprising. After all, players like Venezuela probably had fans and baseball groupies following them all over the place. I'd even spotted a fair share of them myself.

I just hadn't factored in my being fingered as one of them.

I made a face, stared at where the camera lens was dripping with cucumber sauce, and then watched as the bodyguard got into a black Mercedes that was parked nearby in Lot B. Then the vehicle fell in behind the Hummer limo as it exited the players' lot. Both cars drove off.

Shit, shit, shit.

Now what did I do?

Of course, tonight would prove the night when Reni tipped his hand. When he met his married lover for a one-night rendezvous at the Ritz and ordered up chocolate-covered strawberries and champagne from room service. And I couldn't follow him without the risk of having the Incredible Hulk snapping a few of my bones in two.

"Hey, aren't you that PI?" pocket-protector guy asked from the other side of my car, apparently having seen me as he returned to his own car.

"Who wants to know?"

He lifted the press credentials I hadn't seen hanging around his neck earlier (probably he'd had them tucked into his puke-green shirt). "George Fowler, sports journalist for *The Gazette-Times*."

I found it mildly amusing that he was an actual reporter for the paper I'd cited.

"Who are you following?" he asked.

I eyed where Reni's entourage was exiting the parking lot, grabbed my camera, my purse, and as an afterthought my Glock, then got out of the car.

"Want to find out firsthand?" I asked.

"SO YOU'RE FOLLOWING VENEZUELA THEN," Fowler said, maneuvering his car at a safe distance behind the Mercedes that had fallen in behind the boss, the Hummer hard to miss in front of it.

"Maybe."

I didn't think it was a good idea to give him more info than I had to. Obviously he was hoping for some sort of scoop. And obviously I wasn't going to give him one. I'd had enough coverage for the time being, thank you very much.

I rolled down my window to combat the musty smell of the old car.

"That's not a good idea," he said, catching papers from where they flew from somewhere in the backseat. "This is kind of my traveling office."

I got the impression that it was his office, period.

Cripes. I thought my car was bad. This was a moving disaster that wasn't waiting to happen, but had already long since taken place. At my feet, countless disposable coffee cups, most rimmed with the sky-blue Greek key design, littered the floor. Under me something poked into my butt. I was pretty sure it was a pen, but it could have as easily been a spiral notebook. All over were newspapers folded back to the sports sections, outlining stats. There was at least an inch of dust on the dashboard. And neither the exterior nor the interior of the car had seen soap and water for at least a decade.

I eyed Fowler. He looked like he could use a good bath, as well. Maybe I could talk him into going through a car wash and leaving the windows open.

"You hot? Here, I'll turn on the vent fan."

A blast of hot, street-smelling air hit me full in the face and I started.

"Sorry," he said. "No air-conditioning. They say I've got to get a whole new system installed. Hell, the car isn't even worth as much as they want me to pay."

"A new car might be an option."

He grimaced. "On my salary?" He stuck his fingers into his pocket protector and then handed me a card. "No one does what I do for the money."

I took the card. "Then why do you do it?"

"For the love of the game, of course."

"Of course."

If it meant living in a car like this, no one could pay me enough to do what he did, much less *not* pay me.

"You got a card?" he asked.

"A business card?" No, I realized, I didn't have one. And I told him so.

"You need business cards. Helps people remember you."

"Yeah, well, I could do with people forgetting me more often."

"You're that Sofie Metropolis, right? You got booted from the game a couple weeks ago. You're a PI, right?"

"Maybe."

He took his eyes off the road, scrambled around in the backseat, then came up with a faded newspaper that looked almost as old as the car. "Wait . . ."

He rustled around, his lack of attention causing the Pontiac to drift into the opposite lane.

"Car," I said.

He looked up, righted the wheel, and then continued sorting through the papers.

"Yes, yes, here it is."

Correction: the paper was three months old. And an inside, tucked away piece included a small, grainy picture of me. The headline read: LOCAL PI SHOOTS CLIENT.

Well, now, that was good for business, wasn't it?

"You got one of those photographic memories?" I asked.

"Something like that. You've got to have one in this business. Know the stats. The players." He looked at me. "By the way, I'm interested in Venezuela myself."

"Of course you are. He's going to win us the World Series." I didn't want to talk about Venezuela. Mostly because I didn't want my face popping up in the paper again, this time in the sports section under Fowler's byline.

"You married?" I asked to change the subject.

I'd noticed the ring on his left hand and wondered what Mrs. Fowler looked like and whether or not she picked out his clothes for him.

"Nah. She left me six years ago."

"And you're still wearing the ring?"

He nudged the item in question around his finger with his thumb. "Yeah. Pathetic, isn't it?"

"Yes, pathetic would about cover it." I removed the notebook from under my behind and put it on the dusty dash. "Look, Fowler, I was just hoping for a favor. This . . . ride, and the possibilities of my need for it, are strictly off the record, okay?"

He considered me for a long moment, taking his eyes off the road again.

"Truck," I said at the same time a UPS van driver laid on his horn.

Fowler righted the wheel again.

"You mean I'm not going to get anything out of this?"

I plucked a five-dollar bill out of my purse. "I can give you gas money."

"Gee, thanks. That should get me around the block."

I gave him a twenty. "Are we clear?"

He nodded and pocketed the money.

And as we followed Venezuela, not to the Ritz like I wanted—or anyplace that would have made the trip in the Pontiac with Fowler worth it, for that matter—but home, I wished I would have driven straight home myself.

Instead, I asked George to let me out on the corner of Ditmars and Thirty-first, figuring I'd take the N or the W home and get a ride over to Shea in the morning to pick up Lucille.

"Oh, by the way," I said before closing the door, "why are you interested in Venezuela?"

He smiled at me, showing me light brown teeth that said while he didn't smoke now, he'd probably smoked for years. "You show me yours, I'll show you mine."

I gave him an eye roll and then closed the door. I didn't need any information that badly.

Seven

WHEN I ARRIVED AT THE Jackson Heights coffee shop the following day, I found Dino already sitting at a table in the back, adding sugar to a small cup of coffee. I ordered an extra-large (while it wasn't my usual frappé, when push came to shove, any ol' liquid caffeine would do), then walked to his table.

He immediately rose to his feet. The attempt at chivalry was both quaint and awkward. "I was afraid you wouldn't come."

I held my arms out. "I'm here." I put my cup down, and then sat, placing my handbag on the back of the chair. In my mind, I was going over exactly how I was going to tell him that Efi was not only not interested in him, but that she was actually dating someone else. A non-Greek to be exact. And the situation was driving my mother to distraction. Where I used to get countless calls a day that focused on me, now I got panicked messages that said, "You've got to talk to your sister! She's going to ruin her life."

What, exactly, she expected me to say to Efi was beyond me. Especially since I thought it was cool that she was in love, no matter the man she was in love with. And no matter that she was nowhere near admitting this was the case.

At any rate, I also had a lunch appointment with her later in the week, partly to get Thalia off my back, but mostly for her Name Day and so I could see my kid sis grin like the sea urchin I remember her being way back when. Before she developed an appetite for all things metal (body piercings) and ink-based (tattoos). While I saw her every Sunday at dinner, whenever the two of us tried to have a quiet conversation we found Thalia hovering nearby, sometimes with an empty glass in hand to press against the wall should we decide to take our conversation into another room.

"Like a little coffee with your sugar?" Dino asked.

I blinked, realizing that I'd added nearly half the sugar decanter into my cup and that it was about to boil over. I smiled, lifted the cup to my lips, and sipped, no matter that it burned my lips. "It's been a rough morning."

Had somebody warned me that getting Rosie a new computer would be akin to upsetting the peace around the agency, I would never have taken her shopping. From reading me baby horoscopes related to the impending birth of her niece, to her sharing the latest greatest database site she needed to subscribe to, every moment was filled with some sort of computer-related chatter.

"So . . . ," I said slowly. "How's everything?"

"Fine, fine. You?"

"Okay." I shifted. I'd expected this to be much easier than it was turning out to be.

Truth was, Constantinos Antonopoulos was a looker. He embodied every positive aspect of being Greek (the sexy, slightly hooked nose, olive skin, and ink-black hair) and none of the negatives (he didn't appear to have excess body hair or to be balding and his thick accent was charming rather than irritating). He had a single dimple that came out to tease whenever he smiled, revealing straight, even teeth. And, well, he was physically as yummy as the items in the display case back at his *zaharoplastio*. And I knew what he had in the display case because I'd gone to his shop once. It may have been an accident, but buying nearly every sweet in the place hadn't.

I caught myself staring and shifted again in the hard chair. "Look, Dino, I don't see any reason for drawing this out, do you?"

His brows rose. "No, no. Of course not."

"The truth is, my sister is interested in someone else."

"I'm not sure I understand . . ."

"Efi . . . well, she's dating someone." He continued staring at me. "A guy. His name is Jeremy and he's not Greek, which bothers my mother to no end. He's an ex-football player. And I'm not sure it's going to last but she looks really happy so what does it matter anyway, right?"

Dino blinked slowly at the winded explanation.

Okay, so it wasn't one of my most eloquent, but I was pretty sure I'd gotten my point across.

So why, then, was he looking at me as if I'd just explained to him the basic conventions of Greek Orthodoxy?

"I see," he said, continuing to stir his own coffee. He removed the wooden mini-Popsicle stick then took a long pull. I found myself overly interested in the action, thinking that he had a great mouth.

"Well, then, I suppose the thing to say is that I'm happy for her."

I smiled. "Yes. Thanks."

"But I don't understand how that affects me."

Okay, so the guy was dense. There always had to be a catch somewhere when it came to men as attractive as he was. In my ex's case, it was his allergic reaction to monogamy.

"It affects you because, well, she's not going to date you."

"Oh." He sat back as if I'd just told him he only had two weeks to live. Then he grinned. "Ah."

"I'm sorry to just blurt it out like that."

He shook his head. "No problem."

"Hey, you're a great guy. And I really liked the thought of having a baker in the family. And Lord knows you're being from the same area in Greece as my father's family is a definite plus, but . . . well, Efi does what Efi wants to do."

"That's nice."

I squinted at him.

"I think it's my turn to apologize," he said. "Because I . . . you and me . . . I believe we got our wires crossed somewhere."

"Wires?"

"Mmm. You think I invited you for coffee to discuss your sister."

"Uh-huh."

"When the truth is it's your company I was hoping to share."

I stared at him.

Had he just said what I think he had? That it wasn't Efi he was interested in? That it was me?

I remembered a few months ago when my mother had seemed to have potential grooms floating about the place nearly every day. I'd assumed they'd been for me, because I'd just gone through a wedding disaster and marrying me off would be a good way to save face. Only I quickly discovered that the hand-picked men hadn't been for me at all, but for Efi.

Dino had been one of them.

Had I just called *him* dense? It seemed there was nothing at all wrong with his mental capacities.

My own, on the other hand, appeared to be in need of a tune-up.

"Did you just say you're interesting in dating me?" I practically croaked.

I cleared my throat and quickly sipped my coffee, instantly regretting the careless move.

"Actually, I believe in some countries this would be considered our first date."

I was half-afraid my brows had just flown straight off my forehead.

"Look at the time." I stared pointedly at my watch. "I've got an appointment at . . . I'm already late."

Oh, that was lame. But in my experience, lame worked, so why fix what wasn't broken?

I stood so quickly my purse fell from the back of the chair. I bent to pick it up and spilled my coffee.

"Go, go," he said, rounding the table with a handful of napkins. "I'll get this."

I'd just insulted him and he was offering to wipe up my spill?

Mmm . . . what was that smell? I realized it was him. A mixture of vanilla and something clean and fresh. Not quite like soap or laundry detergent but similar with a lemony zing.

"Okay," I said quickly. "Oh, and thanks for the coffee."

I held up the cup I had bought myself and hurried toward the door, trying for the life of me to remember if my ass looked good in the jeans I had on.

Then mentally kicking myself for even going there.

"HEY, YO. EARTH TO SOFIE." Rosie waved one of her long-nailed hands in front of my face, her silver bangles clinking together. "Did you even hear a word I said?"

"Huh?" I blinked her into focus.

How long had I been out of it? For at least the half hour since I'd returned to the office after coffee with Dino.

"What did you say?"

She gave me a world famous eye roll and then *tsk*ed. "I was just outlining my plan to revolutionize this agency with this new computer."

"Oh that." She'd been going on about that for two solid days and I'd tuned out long before Dino had even called.

I sat back in my chair. Had he really asked me out?

Was that even the proper question?

I thought of my mother and winced. If Thalia caught a whiff of my meeting Dino for any purpose, she'd have the wedding invitations in the mail yesterday. Probably she'd even use the ones she had left over from my last wedding.

I could hear her now: "And the champagne you have at your apartment is still good. We could use that for the reception. And how about the dress? A few alterations and it'll be as good as new."

If there were a Greek hell, I was afraid I was glimpsing it.

Date Dino?

My mind froze.

"I'm continuing that search on that couple like you asked." Rosie's words cracked the sheet of ice.

"Which couple?"

"The couple trying to extort money from Phoebe."

"And?"

"And I still haven't found anything."

"Which means this might be an honest event."

"Or that they've been really good or lucky or both."

I nodded.

"Have you been over there yet?"

I shook my head.

"What's with you today, anyway? I swear, talking to you is like talking to a pole or somethin'."

"I don't know . . ." I stared at her. "I think I just got asked out."

I didn't think, I *knew* that I had. I just still wasn't clear on how it had happened. How I hadn't seen it coming. And I was waiting for it to sink in.

After would come how to avoid it.

"That's great!" Rosie exclaimed. "What's his name? I'll enter him in the computer and see what comes up."

"I am not giving you his name."

"Why? Is he a criminal or somethin'?"

"No, he's not a criminal."

"Married?"

My throat tightened on that one. "No."

"Then what's wrong with him?"

That was the question of the moment, wasn't it? What was wrong with him?

Absolutely nothing, which made this all the more puzzling.

"He's Greek," I said.

LATER THAT NIGHT I SAT in front of my television set and scanned the satellite and local sports channels covering the Mets game, settling on ESPN over channel eleven, a small pile of newspapers in front of me, both local and national. I realized I didn't have the channel programmed into my favorites list and spent the next half hour figuring out how to do that so I wouldn't have to spend another half hour trying to find the channel in the seemingly infinite number of other satellite channels.

Finally, I finished and watched as Venezuela struck out a Marlins player in the bottom of the seventh and the teams switched sides, the screen fading to commercial. Figured.

I'd stopped by my mother's on the way home and piled a plate high with *keftethes* (small meat patties with mint) and *spanakorizo* (spinach in a spicy red sauce with rice) and had it in front of me now. I eyed where Muffy was sitting at my feet facing me while his sniffing nose kept shifting toward the table though his eyes kept me in focus. Sneaky devil.

There was a light knock on the door. "Sofie? Sofie, dear, are you home?"

Mrs. Nebitz, my across-the-hall neighbor and rent-collector. When I'd first moved into the building, I'd found asking for money wasn't really my thing, especially considering the tenants, namely the still-unemployed Etta Munson and her evil incarnate daughter Lola in 2A, and the DeVry students in 2B. So Mrs. Nebitz had taken to collecting the rent for me. Probably it gave her something to do. And it more than made up for the fact that she'd been paying the same rent for the past thirty years.

"Hi, Mrs. Nebitz," I said. "How are you tonight?"

"Good, good. I got in a bit of shopping today and thought I might bring you a fresh knish from Knish Nosh."

I accepted the plate and smiled. At this point, I had more of Mrs. Nebitz's plates in my cupboards than my own. Something I'd probably remedy if I ever opened the wedding gifts stacked in my bedroom. In the beginning I gave the cleaned plates back to her empty. Recently I began thinking I should put something on them. But since I had yet to fix anything in my kitchen beyond frappés, I was coming to accept that that might never happen and I probably should just take her plates back over there.

"Mmm. Looks good."

"They make the best."

"Thank you, Mrs. Nebitz."

"Bah. No thanks necessary. A single girl such as yourself shouldn't be spending so much time by herself."

I smiled at that.

"Good night."

"Good night. Oh, and if you could bring back some of my

plates tomorrow, I'd appreciate it. I'm running out. Not that there's any hurry or anything. When you get around to it."

"I'll do it first thing," I promised.

"You're a good girl, Sof. Too bad you're not Jewish. I could fix you up with my grandson Seth. Although I think he's already dating somebody."

"That's nice."

"Not so nice, I think. Because none of us knows who she is."

I remembered my coffee with Dino earlier and swallowed. I got the distinct impression that Jewish families were much like the Greeks; namely that they were in your business, always. Dating? They wanted the name, rank, and Social Security number of the person. It was enough to make a body terrified of dating. "I'm sure he'll be fine."

She waved her hand. "Yes, yes, I'm sure he will. He always is." She waggled her finger. "It's me and his mother who should worry."

She shuffled back across the hall to her apartment and I quietly closed the door. Putting the plate next to the others on the coffee table, I sat back down, mildly impressed that Muffy had sat quietly throughout the exchange and hadn't touched a single *keftethaki*. I looked at them closely to make sure he hadn't licked them or anything.

Figuring the beef patties couldn't cause too much trouble (if I were lucky, any gas would smell of mint), I broke off a piece and fed it to him, feeding myself the rest even as I pulled the first of the newspapers closer to me with my other hand.

I'd never been one for current events beyond what led the news and was featured on the front page. Same old, same old, was what I usually discovered. Someone trying to slant one story one way, someone else the other, the truth on average falling somewhere in between. But so long as it didn't affect me here in Astoria, Queens, well, I figured I was okay.

I tugged out the sports section to find a full-length color picture of Reni Venezuela along with the headline: STAR PITCHER LOSES COOL.

Just underneath was the byline with the reporter's name. I was mildly surprised to find it was George Fowler.

Ha. Show him mine, indeed. Looked like his was plastered all over the paper for me to read.

I scanned the piece, looking for the reason he was overly interested in the new pitcher, you know, beyond his doing so incredibly well for the team. Nothing immediately jumped out at me beyond that it appeared Reni had begun copping an attitude with reporters where he'd been accommodating before. Having met Fowler myself, I wasn't surprised that the talented pitcher wasn't as friendly with him as he might have been previously.

I read the piece a second time, this time carefully. What I was looking for, I think, came during the second-to-last paragraph and seemed more of an aside than anything. Edited by his boss? I chanced a yes.

"Despite Venezuela's winning streak, this reporter finds it curious that his change in demeanor came about around the time I inquired why he's pitched only left-handed for the past eight games straight. . . ."

My phone chirped. Holding my place with a finger, I reached over and picked up my cell.

"Hello?"

"Metro?"

Waters. I looked up to see the game was back in full swing. "What's up? You're at the game, I take it?"

"I'm at the game."

"Has something happened?"

"Happened? No. Except that I'm having the best damn time of my life."

"That's why you called?"

"Do you know what temperature it is here in Florida?"

"I don't care."

"Eighty."

Eighty degrees at ten o'clock on a September night. Here in New York it was in the low sixties. Sweater weather.

"Shouldn't you be doing something?" I asked, aggravated. Probably I should have gone down there myself.

"I am. I'm talking to you." He shouted something at the ump who'd just called a strike. "And tell you I'm seriously thinking about not coming back."

I considered the cash I'd given him to cover expenses and wondered if it was enough for a month's rent on a studio apartment.

"Call when you have something useful," I said.

"And if I don't?"

"Then I'll have to hunt you down and kill you."

He laughed heartily at that. "Sure, Metro, sure."

I absently rang off then put the cell back down. Surprisingly I wasn't that concerned about Waters. He'd proven as good as gold over the past month he'd worked for the agency. And that he'd called tonight told me he was taking the assignment seriously. If there was something to be found in Miami, he'd find it.

I pushed the paper aside and chose another as I bit into more *keftethaki*. As for my finding something . . . well, that remained to be seen.

Eight

"AND YOU ARE?"

And I was Sofie Metropolis, PI.

But I couldn't tell Venezuela's sports agent's secretary that the next day as I stood facing her across her desk. Probably her sneer would grow darker. Probably she'd call security to escort me out of the swanky midtown Manhattan office with a knockout view of the Empire State Building.

So I engaged in a Mexican—or rather Greek—standoff with the twenty-something blonde who looked like she weighed all of a buck five. I figured that with the pitcher out of town, and Waters tailing him, I had time to do some poking around in other areas. I figured his agent Troy Aikman—no relation to the ex-pro–football player so far as I could tell—was as good a place as any to start. Especially since he was the first on the short list that I'd made that morning at the agency.

"Pamela Coe," I said, flashing the fake press credentials I'd had a skeptical Rosie make up for me that morning and that I had pinned to my purse. "Of *The New York Gazette-Times.*"

Troy's secretary eyed me much as Reni's goon had a couple

nights ago, as if questioning whether I could be a reporter. I tried to hold my ground without stiffening, even as the Queens girl in me wanted to ask, "What, you don't believe me?" and park my hand on my hip.

"Take a seat over there. I'll see if he has time to see you."

I turned.

"And next time make an appointment."

I didn't think sticking my tongue out at her would put me in good stead so I bit it and then took a chair like she asked.

A moment after she put her telephone back in its cradle, a door opened and a man looking remarkably like Tom Cruise from *Jerry Maguire* came into the waiting room. "Pamela," he said as if we were old friends and he hadn't seen me for years. The greeting was so intimate that I almost looked over my shoulder to see whom else he might be addressing. Not that he would have noticed. He was too busy pumping my hand and pulling me to my feet. "I'm Troy Aikman. No relation. Good to see you, good to see you."

"Thanks for agreeing to talk to me without an appointment," I said, wondering if I should fight the way he was leading me back to his office. Hey, I didn't know the guy, and he was being more touchy-feely than I was comfortable with.

"Come in, come in," he said.

Did he make a habit of saying everything twice? Perhaps it was because it took him that long to get to his next thought or maybe he was a few cleats shy of a full pair of baseball shoes.

He closed the door behind me.

"So," he said, sitting on the edge of his desk as if posing for a portrait, his capped teeth glinting in the bright light shining in from the floor-to-ceiling windows. The sports agenting business must be going very well indeed. "Tell me what I can do you for today."

I made a point of walking over to one of the visitor chairs and sitting down, taking a pad out of my purse where I'd written a few questions that sounded reporter-like.

"Your client Reni Venezuela is having a very good season so far, wouldn't you say?"

His smile slipped a bit. Apparently he'd thought I was there strictly to interview him. Probably he had the headline all worked out: STAR SPORTS AGENT TROY AIKMAN (NO RELATION) OUTSHINES HIS STAR CLIENTS.

Probably he was wrong about stuff like that all the time.

"Great, great," he went back to repeating himself as he rounded his desk and sat down. "We all fully expect him to take the Mets to the pennant and the World Series beyond." He rapped his knuckles on his desk. "Knock wood."

I didn't know why people always thought they had to announce what was already obvious. It's not as if the superstition were new; even the Greeks used it dating back to the Cretaceous period.

"How do you think, compared to your other successful clients, that Reni is adjusting to the whole fame game?"

"Adjusting? He was born to be a star!"

Of course. Weren't we all? "I understand that the two of you used to be in contact daily, but the norm nowadays is that you leave messages that aren't returned."

Rosie had scared up Reni's home phone billing records, along with those connected to his cell phone. And when added to Gisela's verification that the agent had voiced displeasure at his inability to get through to the closing pitcher, I thought that would be a good place to start.

Troy stared at me. "Are you implying he might be looking for another agent?"

"No. I'm asking you a simple question."

He stretched his neck and I had the feeling he would have

liked to pull at his collar. "Then I'd have to say that he's been very busy."

"Any plans on pressing the Mets to move him from closing pitcher to opening?"

"I couldn't possibly discuss anything of that nature."

"No problems on the home front?"

"Home front?"

"With his family?"

He didn't appear to know how to respond. Probably he didn't even know Reni was married without referring to his secretary or computer notes.

"His wife . . . his two young children. Are they adjusting well?"

The smile completely left his face. "Which paper did you say you were with?"

"*The New York Gazette-Times.*"

"How come I've never heard of you?"

"Because I'm new. Now, you've signed Reni to only a two-year contract before he goes free agent. Have you been talking to other teams yet . . ."

Troy was ignoring me. Instead he was pressing the intercom button for his secretary. "Nancy, get me *The Gazette-Times* on the horn."

"Right away, sir."

Shit.

It was then I realized that if Gisela had hired me, she'd probably made a few noises to Reni's people, his agent being one of them. Probably she was calling him all the time and asking him to find out why her husband was acting strangely.

And probably I was two words away from being arrested for impersonating a reporter.

"Actually, you can call my boss directly," I said, pushing a card across the desk.

The move could either be categorized as a stroke of genius when I realized I still had Fowler's business card with me, or an act of desperation. I suppose it all depended on the outcome.

I hadn't anticipated that Troy would actually try to verify my identity.

Apparently he noticed the name on the card. "Fowler."

"Yes."

"I see."

I tried not to show visible relief at his new interest. Especially when he picked up the telephone and began dialing George's number.

Double shit.

"George? Hi, this is Troy Aikman." A pause. "Troy Aikman, sports agent?" Another pause. "Reni Venezuela among others."

George finally appeared to recognize him.

"Sorry to bother you, but I was hoping you could verify the identity of one of your reporters."

I expected he received silence.

"Sure. I'll put her on."

"Metro," Fowler said into my ear.

"Hi, boss," I responded. "I'm here at Aikman's just like you asked. And, go figure, he didn't believe I worked for you."

"Shocker," Fowler said. "This is going to cost you, you know that?"

I ground my back teeth together. "How much?"

"More than you can imagine. Now put Aikman back on the phone."

"Sure thing, boss." I held out the receiver to Troy and he took it.

Moments later, he hung up and then sat back in his chair. "You check out."

"You know, that's not exactly the way to establish a good

working relationship with somebody. Do you do this to every reporter that walks through your door?"

"No, just the ones asking stupid questions."

Well, it looked like verifying my false ID hadn't warmed him any.

"I see." I put my pad away and got up from the chair. Hey, things could have been worse. I could have been escorted out by security to find the police waiting for my lying butt in the lobby. "I take it that this interview is over then."

"Smart girl."

Moron. "I'll just let myself out."

THAT HAD GONE WELL, HADN'T it? I scooted the restaurant chair closer to the table and considered the scant notes on my non-meeting with the shiny sports agent, and then sighed. Of course, I had no idea what I'd expected him to tell me. Namely because I didn't know what I was looking for. "My husband's acting strange," covered a wide variety of bases. He could be going through some sort of pre-midlife crisis. Suffering from a bout of fame shock. Or even ED, erectile dysfunction.

Hell, I didn't know.

Interestingly it never entered my mind to give Gisela her money back and tell her there was no case, however. Why was that? Could it be that instinctively I, too, felt something was off kilter?

"Would you like to hear our specials?" Phoebe Hall said. "Oh, hi, Sofie, it's you. I didn't recognize you sitting."

That's because I usually took my order to go and ate at the office. "Hi, Phoebe." I flicked the page on my notepad to a clean one. "I'd love to hear the specials."

I gave my full attention to the restaurant owner whose business future depended on the outcome of my investigation into the split pea soup with ear case.

"Lentil is our soup of the day." She made a face. "Without ear, of course. And meatloaf with garlic potatoes and green beans is the main."

"Dessert?"

"Rhubarb pie."

Mmm. There weren't many places I knew that offered rhubarb pie.

"I'll take the soup and a piece of pie."

She looked disappointed as she turned away.

"And bring yourself something, too," I said. "So we can talk."

Having worked in a restaurant for a good portion of my life, I knew the average turnaround. And Phoebe was quick. I'd no sooner written the date and time and the name of the restaurant (which was simply Astoria American Restaurant, and the only place you saw that was on the photocopied menus—the sign outside read RESTAURANT) across the top of the page, then she was seated across from me with a piece of pie of her own, my soup and dessert and silverware in front of me.

I tasted the soup. Good. I told her so.

"So," I said after eating a few spoonfuls. "Tell me how everything went down."

I already knew everything secondhand from Rosie, but it never hurt to have the client repeat the story in case they could add something that might help.

Unfortunately, Phoebe's version was as direct and detail-free as Rosie's. It was a New York thing, I think. Nothing but the facts, ma'am. Although Joe Friday was L.A.-based, no?

"Are you taking the case, then?" Phoebe asked. She had yet to touch her pie beyond pushing a few crumbs around on the plate with her fork. "I know Rosie said not to worry about having money to pay you, but I'd like to pay the going rate."

I smiled as I took a bite of my pie. "Well, seeing as this is the first time I've taken on a case of this nature, there really isn't a going rate."

She smiled in return, putting some color back into her round face.

"So why don't we just play this by ear?" I suggested and then grimaced. "No pun intended. I'll go talk to the couple, have Rosie do some more research, and see if we can't make this all go away with little or no effort."

Of course, what I was leaving out of that neat little scenario was that nothing was ever easy or neat when it came to my cases. But, hey, there was always a first time.

And I hoped for Phoebe's sake that this would be it.

"Have the tests come back from the police department yet?"

I shook my head. "They have a three-month backlog. All they could verify was that it did come from a human and that it was a piece of an ear. Do you have an attorney yet? Maybe he could arrange to have a sample taken for defense purposes."

I realized that what I was proposing would take more money and tried not to flinch.

When she didn't immediately answer, I said, "Okay, then. How about we just go with what we got right now and deal with the rest as it comes?"

Twenty minutes later, after three other customers had come in for lunch, and I'd finished my soup and pie, I told Phoebe I'd be in contact and then found myself standing on the street outside the door. I considered the businesses lining Steinway. The sound of cars filled my ears, a subway train passing under my feet rattled the grate nearby, and the smells of various restaurants teased my nose.

Although I'd worked at both my father's restaurant and my grandfather's café since I was old enough to tie on an apron, and had pretty much been on my own at the agency for the past few months, I'd never really given close consideration to what went into making a business work. Truth be told, my parents had done a good job of steering me clear of many of life's potholes. I'd never paid rent, ever. The only loan I'd gotten was for my Mustang, and that I had paid off in six months. I'd gotten an apartment building as a wedding gift, and aside from one biannual property tax bill (which had been enough to send me into shock for a week), and paying the utilities and insurance, I hadn't run into many problems.

I'd recently read in a national newspaper that an alarmingly large number of people were two paychecks away from being homeless, but mostly those had been just words to me. Something to which I couldn't really relate. I looked over my shoulder through the sparkling glass to find Phoebe wiping down the table we'd been sitting at and repositioning the single flower in a vase and reconsidered the quote. What happened if I couldn't get the couple to back down from their claim? Not file a lawsuit? What happened to the restaurant? What happened to Phoebe?

I began walking back toward the agency with a takeout bag Phoebe had put together for Rosie and pushed those thoughts aside, remembering Uncle Spyros' famous rules.

"Don't get emotionally attached to a client."

I remembered hearing the advice; I just couldn't recall what number it had been. Probably it should be number two. Right behind, "Don't take on cases you have no hope of solving."

Too late.

Nine

I WAS JOLTED AWAKE THE following morning by the ringing of my cell phone. I'd tried several times to call Waters in Miami before apparently dropping off to sleep, so the cell was under my cheek, causing a particularly rude awakening when it rang and vibrated.

"Hello?" I croaked, instantly sitting upright. I squinted at the clock. A little before 7:00 A.M. and the time my alarm was set for.

"Sofie?"

I scratched my shoulder even as Muffy lifted his head from where it had been tucked under one of his paws. "Eugene? For the love of God, what in the hell are you doing calling me this early on a Saturday morning?"

"Early? Oh, yeah. I guess it is early. For you. For me, it's still last night."

"You mean you haven't been to bed yet?"

"Nope."

I imagined that he'd been up partying to all hours. "Have you forgotten you have a job to do?"

I threw off the sheet covering me, accidentally burying Muffy in the process. He barked, making like a canine phantom until he could free himself.

"What in the hell do you think I've been doing all goddamn night, Metro?"

"You've got something on Venezuela?"

"Something? Try three somethings in tight little skirts and high heels that just toddled out of his hotel room across the hall from my room five minutes ago."

I rubbed at the creases on my cheek. "I'm still half asleep. Can you repeat that? With details, please?"

"Last night after the game I followed Venezuela back here to the hotel where the team is staying. He went to his room and after watching his door for a half hour through the peephole of my door, I thought that was going to be it. I decided to go down to the bar for a drink before calling it a night, but who should catch the elevator door to get in, freshly showered and ready for a night on the town?"

"Reni?"

"Bingo."

I'd followed the guy for four days straight and had gotten nothing but bored for my efforts. Waters goes to Miami and strikes gold.

If only I didn't suspect Gisela would see the information as so not what she was looking for.

"How did you get a room across from his? Doesn't the team reserve the whole floor for security purposes?"

"I'll have to invoke the 'don't ask, don't tell' thing again," he said.

I gave an eye roll that he couldn't see.

He continued. "So I follow him to the hotel bar, you know? He doesn't suspect me because, of course, I'm a longtime fan and all that and everybody knows me. Although he hasn't re-

ally said two words to me since we got down here. Other players say it's because he's getting too big for his britches, what
with his being credited for the team's turnaround. Anyway, the
bar's some fake-looking sports thing that serves watered down
drinks. And before you know it, he's hooking up with three
baseball groupies right there in a corner booth."

"He had sex with them in public?"

"No, idiot. He met them, gave them his room number, then
probably told them to follow him in five minutes. Because
right after he left, they were checking their watches, then they
left straight after. I followed them directly up to his room.
Where they went in and didn't come out until just now."

"Are you sure you had the right room, Waters? I swear, the
guy could be nominated for sainthood given the clean life he
leads here."

"Yeah, well, the devil must come out to play when he's on
the road, because this guy was definitely making up for lost
time judging by the noises coming from his room."

I imagined Eugene parked outside the room with a tape
recorder and made a face.

"Would steroids do that?" I asked, trying to work things out
in my muddled brain.

"Steroids shrink your balls and put a crimp in your game, if
you know what I mean," he said.

"More information than I was looking for."

"Just giving it to you straight."

"Yeah, well, be a little more vague next time." I sighed. "I
don't suppose you got any pictures?"

"What do you think?"

Seeing as this was the first time I'd put Waters on anything
else than process serving, I didn't know what to think.

"Of course I got pictures. You'll see them when I get back."

"Fine."

"Now if you don't mind, I need to go get some sleep. Their next game is in a little over nine hours and I need my beauty rest."

The reference made me remember the first time I'd laid eyes on Waters. He'd been wearing a hot pink robe—that bowed open a little too much for my liking—with feathers at the cuffs, the hem barely covering his ashy brown, stick-thin legs.

I blinked to banish the disturbing image.

"Okay, Waters. Call me when you get up."

I rang off, gripping the cell phone tightly in my hand as I considered what he'd just told me. So Reni liked to get his freak on when he went out on the road. While I was sure he wasn't the first athlete to do the same, I thought the information would be enough to convince Gisela that his road warrior ways were what was behind his strange behavior lately and close the case.

My alarm buzzed, scaring the living crap out of me. I slapped the top of it, thinking it interesting that it chose to go off at the same time that I was taking note of my own internal alarm.

Had Gisela managed to convince me that simple infidelity couldn't be all that was at the heart of Venezuela's changes?

Maybe I wouldn't tell Gisela until Waters got back with the pictures.

And maybe by then I might have something else to go on rather than my instincts.

AFTER SPENDING THE MORNING TRACKING down the driver of the yellow Hummer limo, the only thing I came away with that was mildly interesting was that the driver was new, hiring on immediately after Gisela had dropped by the agency and taken me for a ride (I only hoped it would remain in the literal

sense and not bleed into a metaphorical tale like at least one of
my previous cases had).

No, the driver told my alter ego, *Gazette-Times* reporter
Pamela Coe, he'd never taken Mrs. Venezuela anywhere. He'd
been instructed that the limo was for Mr. Venezuela's use
only.

As I sat in Lucille outside the Venezuela McMansion, I
checked my notes. I wanted to see if Gisela had the contact information for the previous driver (the current one didn't know
who he was), and Reni's security detail. While two guys had
gone out to Miami with him, another two had stayed behind;
that much I knew from firsthand observation and from Waters'
reports.

Thankfully the goon I'd had personal contact with had been
one of the two that had gone with him.

It was midday and a definite autumn chill had crept into the
air. I shivered in the light breeze as I climbed out of the car,
wishing I had thought to bring a jacket along.

A jacket. Was summer really over already? It seemed incredible. Especially in light of the baseball fever that had overtaken
the city given the Mets' growing success. Just last night as I'd
scanned through the sports channels, I'd been shocked to see a
pro football game being aired.

Yes, football and cooler weather were harbingers that summer was definitely reaching its conclusion. Which meant
sweaters and boots and heavy coats.

I tried to remember where my heavier clothes were and realized they must still be at my parents'. Gad. Did I really still
have stuff there? And why not? I still took most of my meals
there, "took" being the operative word, Sunday aside.

And here I'd called Fowler pathetic. I was twenty-six and still
had boxes of clothes at my parents'. What did that make me?

I spoke into the intercom to the person who had asked who I was.

"It's Pamela Coe here to see Mrs. Venezuela."

Silence. There was no buzzing of the gate. No sign that I'd been heard at all.

I sighed and pressed the intercom button again. "Hello?"

Finally the gate clicked open and I went inside, walking the short distance to the steps. I raised my hand to knock but the door swung inward before my knuckles met wood. Or, rather, thick steel.

"Omigawd, what in the hell are you doing here?" Gisela said, wrapping a silky white robe more tightly around her slender, va-va-voom body and tying the sash. "I told you never to come here."

She ushered me inside, looked both ways down the street, and then slammed the door shut.

"You never told me not to come here."

"Did to."

"I'm sure you didn't."

She *tsk*ed. "I'm having you follow my husband. And my husband's goons are following and watching me. What does that mean?"

That I'd just tipped her hand.

Then again, maybe not.

"If he or anyone else says anything, just tell them about some nosey reporter named Pamela Coe skulking around."

"Skulking?"

"Sneaking."

"Oh. That's why you used a name I didn't know. If I hadn't have seen your face in the security monitor, I wouldn't have buzzed you in." She considered me for a long moment, and then appeared to relax. "What do you want?"

I'd decided that I wasn't going to tell her about her husband's extracurricular activities in Miami just yet. News like that went down better with photographs. Without tangible proof, women like Gisela tended to not believe it.

I only hoped the photos were good. More than shots of the girls going into a room that could or could not have had Reni Venezuela inside.

"I was wondering if you could give me the contact info for Reni's old driver."

"Sure," she said, leading the way into what looked like a study. A study full of trophies and plaques and the decor of which appeared very masculine. Reni's, I had little doubt, which made me feel odd standing in it. "Can you believe he won't let me use the limo anymore? Banned me from it, he did. Just because I was late one time coming home and he couldn't use it to go to the park."

"The new driver told me."

She made a sound of disgust. "'New driver.' He's a frickin' thug."

I silently agreed. Getting information out of him had been like squeezing water from a stone. And I had little doubt that he'd compare notes with the goon who had spotted me in Shea Stadium's parking lot the other night. Their two brains might combine to make one and they might figure out who I really was.

"Here it is," she said, taking a card out of a Rolodex. I copied the info into my pad and handed it back to her. "What about the contact info for his security detail?"

She crossed her arms. "What's that got to do with anything?"

"Do you have it or don't you?"

I didn't ask what she, as a mother of two young children, was doing getting up at noon, even if it was a Saturday. I didn't appreciate her questioning how I did my job, especially since I didn't know where I was heading, either.

"Okay, okay. But I don't know what good it's going to do you. He changed all the guys when he changed the driver."

Interesting. I think. At the very least, it was unusual. Why would he feel the need to change his driver and security detail? A simple upgrade now that his celebrity was growing? Or something more unsavory?

"Hmm, that's funny. It's not in here," she said. She tipped the cards back to rest in the same direction. "Let me look again. I probably missed it."

While she searched through the box, I walked around the office. Above a gas fireplace was a series of pictures. Of Reni Venezuela when he'd played for the Islanders. Of his first day with the Mets.

My gaze caught on a faded old print from which most of the color had faded. I picked up the frame.

"Where was this taken?"

Gisela glanced at me then gestured with her hand. "In Venezuela, I think. That's his older brother Santos and younger sister Marietta."

Reni couldn't have been any older than ten in the shot. But it was hard to tell. All three children had the same big grins and dark good looks.

"Have you ever been to Venezuela?"

"Me? No. Reni goes down by himself at least twice a year."

"His family still down there?"

"Of course, they are. Where else would they be?"

"So his family has never been up here to visit?"

"Never. Reni says they're simple country folk and wouldn't feel comfortable in such a big city." She paused. "Well, except for his brother. He wanted to come up for a visit last year, I think, but they wouldn't give him a visa on account of he tied his wife to a chair for a week when she tried to leave him."

I raised my brows. One could only hope that Reni hadn't inherited the same genes his brother had, or else he might do the same to Gisela when he learned she'd hired a PI.

She took a card out. "Here it is. At least I think this is it. It's the name of the first guy he hired. It must have been misfiled."

I put the picture down and accepted the card.

"Thanks," I said. "I'll be in contact if I need anything else."

I started toward the door and then hesitated, turning to face her again. "Oh, I was wondering if there was anything new you might be able to tell me. Anything that might have happened between now and the last time we talked."

She stared at me blankly.

I gestured with my hand. "Like, how's your sex life?"

"What do you think is the biggest reason I hired you? Reni hasn't laid a hand on me ever since he got back from Pittsburgh."

"Before that?"

She fussed with the front of her robe. "Two, sometimes three times a day."

I was afraid my eyeballs might drop out of their sockets.

"At the very least, one." She shrugged. "And now . . ."

And now Reni was saving his energy for the road.

Go figure.

Ten

I'D BEEN JOKING WHEN I'D told the family at Sunday dinner that I was thinking about getting a tattoo. I'd wanted to shock my mother. Make my grandmother cross herself. Certainly I hadn't any intention of actually getting *one*.

Then what I was doing letting Efi drag me to her favorite tattoo artist Bruno?

One minute we'd been grabbing a quick lunch together to celebrate her Name Day, just the two of us. Me trying to keep from blurting out that Dino had asked me to coffee, her chattering on about her new boyfriend Jeremy. And then she was leading me to a place she visited frequently, but I'd never been to, determined to force me to make good on my word.

"Come on, Sofie, it's not like you're going in for a root canal or anything. You don't have to get a big one. Just a small one somewhere where no one can see it."

That piqued my interest.

If only I wasn't afraid that no one would ever see it, given the sad state of my sex life.

"I only wanted to shock Mom when I joked that I was

thinking about getting a tattoo," I complained, dragging my feet.

"Mom won't be shocked unless you actually get one."

She had a point there. Thalia Metropolis had come a long way in the twenty-six years since she'd first had me. Where getting my ears pierced when I was thirteen had been scandalous enough to be the topic of hotly whispered conversation for a week, Efi had to have a body wand moved over her every time she went through airport security. Beyond asking Efi to take her tongue ring out during dinner, everything was copasetic.

"Yes, but in order to shock Mom, I'd actually have to get one she could see."

"So show her your ass. It's not like she hasn't seen it before."

I raised my brows at her and skidded to a stop in the middle of the sidewalk on Thirty-first. Above us, the W train rattled the tracks. "I'd prefer to keep my ass to myself, thank you very much, Mom and especially Bruno the tattoo artist included."

She smiled. "You really are a prude, aren't you?"

"Yes, well, somebody had to inherit the priggish genes, because obviously you didn't." She released my arm. I sagged with relief. "Look, Ef, I really appreciate you trying to shove me into the twenty-first century and all, but there's this thing with me and needles."

"Do it for my Name Day."

In the old country, as my grandparents liked to point out, Greek Name Days were bigger than birthdays. Essentially a Name Day was the day on which the saint you were named after was celebrated. Pick any day of the year on a Greek calendar and you'd see a list of saints' names.

As far as I could tell, the holiday had been invented as a way for the Greek Orthodox Church to keep a presence in the family . . . and a finger in your pocketbook. Both Efi and I had stopped by St. D's on our way to lunch to light a couple of candles in honor of her patron saint Euphemia, who, it was said, had lived as a virgin until she was martyred in the fourth century AD. (Wishful thinking when my mother had named my sister after her.) And, of course, we stuffed the requisite monies into the collection box to more than cover the cost of the beeswax candles as well as gain special favor.

The holiday had also been invented as an additional excuse for the Greeks to celebrate, with dinner usually served by the host or hostess when guests stopped by to present them with boxes of sweets in their honor.

Today happened to be Efi's Name Day.

What worked in my favor was that tomorrow happened to be mine.

"And what could you possibly do to equal that for me?"

She grimaced. "I promise, you won't feel a thing."

Pain, I'd come to learn over the years, meant different things to different people. My threshold for pain might be much lower than Efi's. In fact, I knew it was, which gave her promise the power of a twenty-watt lightbulb.

She sighed heavily. "Okay, look. Bruno won't even give you a tattoo, anyway. Not until after you've tried a temporary one for a couple of days," she said.

I narrowed my eyes. "I didn't think you were capable of subterfuge. You're just trying to get me in there."

"Am not."

"Are too."

I recognized the juvenile quality of our exchange.

"Seriously," Efi raised her hands, "his rules are posted on his window. You don't even have to go inside to read them. And rule one is that he doesn't give anyone a tattoo until they follow a few simple steps first."

"Bruno has rules?"

She gave me an eye roll. "You talk like he's a monster."

I'd seen Bruno. With his neck-to-foot tattoos, he resembled something akin to a monster.

"Come on, Sof. What do you have to lose?"

"My sanity maybe?"

But I followed her anyway. And, like she promised, there were a list of five rules posted on the window of Bruno's shop, between a purple neon sign that read TATTOOS and a red neon sign that read PIERCINGS. I supposed I could count myself lucky that Efi wasn't trying to talk me into one of those.

At any rate, right there under rule one was that no amount of drunken begging would convince him to draw a permanent tattoo on an ink virgin who hadn't worn a temporary tattoo of the same design for at least forty-eight hours.

Seemed my uncle Spyros wasn't the only one fond of rules.

"See?" Efi said.

I grumbled a response and grudgingly went inside when she held open the door.

"Do you have to wear temporary tattoos before he does yours?"

"What? No. He made me with the first, but not since. I'm a tat pro now. I tell him what I want, he finds the stencil and does it."

A tat pro. Now there was a title of which to be proud.

In the corner a woman was stretched out face-down on a reclining chair that looked like it would have been right at home at a dentist's office. In fact, the whirring instrument that Bruno, himself, wielded sounded like a dentist's drill, making my back teeth suddenly hurt. He scribbled on the woman's lower back, dabbed at his work with a white cloth, and then scribbled again.

"Excess ink?" I whispered to Efi.

"Blood."

I gaped at her.

She smiled and steered me toward a wall filled with tattoo designs.

Okay, I'll admit, I've been secretly envious of Efi's open attitude when it came to body art. While I periodically labeled myself a rebel, she was the real deal, a Greek biker chick with attitude. I liked to think that if I were a little braver, I'd like to be her.

I looked over the tattoos.

Then again, no.

Winged hearts seemed to be very popular. Especially cartoonish hearts sprouting evil-looking wings. One of them almost looked like bat wings, and in another, the heart had teeth. Apropos, say, if you were a vampire. I thought of the man believed to be the neighborhood vampire, Vladimir Romanoff, and shuddered.

The sun and variations on the moon were also everywhere. Ladybugs came next. Who would put a bug on their skin? Didn't we spend time trying to keep them off? Then there were the roses and flowers. I don't know. I preferred my flowers to have a scent. I told Efi this and she said that I could apply perfume there. I stared at her.

"Who puts something like this on their skin? Yikes." I pointed to a particularly detailed gargoyle that looked more wolf than bird.

Efi pulled up the back of her T-shirt and right there on her right shoulder was a duplicate of the picture I'd referred to.

"Oh."

She straightened her shirt. "It wards off evil."

The Greeks wore evil eyes and spit on people to do that. I guess Efi was deeper into the Goth culture than I'd imagined.

"Did you have to temporarily wear that around for two days?"

She gave me an eye roll. "No."

Probably he should have made her wear it around for a month. God, had Mom seen that? I bet it gave her nightmares. No wonder she was always after me to talk to Efi. I could just see my sister at eighty, sitting in a sleeveless summer housecoat, her pale, wrinkled skin sporting a gargoyle that would scare her grandchildren.

I stabbed my thumb over my shoulder at the woman getting a back tattoo that would be visible just over the waist of her jeans. "Do you have one of those?"

"What, a tramp stamp?" she asked.

I nearly choked on my own saliva.

"Nah. I thought about it, though."

I opened my mouth to ask her why she'd opted not to, and then changed my mind. I didn't want to know.

I hit a section of the wall that was dedicated to Tinkerbell-like fairies. Now these were cute. I looked at my ankle, where I'd decided to get the tat and decided they were too cute. A section on the zodiac, butterflies that captured my attention for a minute, and a cute little bumblebee.

I could do that. A bumblebee. Float like a butterfly, sting like a bee. The old Ali motto floated through my mind. Maybe not. I went down farther, and then came back to the bee. It appeared to be the smallest tat featured outside a ladybug.

"Don't even think about it," Efi said.

"What?"

"Going for the smallest tattoo. I'll never let you live it down."

I made a face at her. Sometimes I hated my younger sister.

"I think I have something you'll like." Bruno had finished with his client, and come to stand behind us.

I looked around him at where the teenager stood in front of a full-length mirror to get a look at her tramp stamp. Hello, Grandma. Gave a whole knew meaning to granny panties.

"Hey, Bruno," I said, although it looked like greetings weren't the norm in his environment.

"I've been thinking about what would suit you ever since Efi told me she was bringing you in."

Usually I got a kick out of any man thinking about me for any reason. Especially lately. But the idea of Bruno concentrating on me for any specific length of time made me uncomfortable.

I stared at the tail of a dragon on his right forearm and swallowed thickly.

He'd moved to a series of drawers and opened the top one, shifting through several sheets of paper. "Here we go."

"A unicorn!" Efi said. "That would be perfect for you, Sofie."

I looked down at the drawing, admitting that it did hold a certain appeal. I'd always been partial to the mythical animal with a single horn. I had decorated my room with them when I was twelve.

But that was when I was twelve and now I was twenty-six.

I spotted a design lying partially covered in the drawer. I reached in and fished it out.

A simple outline of a small lizard.

It made me remember one of my first visits to Greece with my family. Well, at least it was the first that my young mind could recall, because according to my mother, we'd gone before then. At any rate, I'd been put to bed in a relative's bedroom when I spotted a small, pale lizard no longer than my index finger scurrying across the ceiling. I'd screamed and my father had come in to comfort me.

"It's just a *molitiri*, Sofia. They're good luck."

I'd watched as he caught the tiny lizard, and then brought it back to the bed, holding it so I could get a closer look.

"Why don't we take it outside?"

I'd nodded and we'd both gone down the hall in the opposite

direction of the voices in the living room. He'd opened the back door and we'd stood on the steps.

"Make a wish," he'd said.

I had, and then he'd bent over and put the lizard on the hot cement. It immediately ran for the garden nearby.

I'd seen plenty of *molitiria* since then during subsequent visits to Greece. And if they were in the house, I did what my father had and took them outside. Otherwise, I'd just watched them in fascination.

"Thanks, Bruno!" the satisfied customer called out as she left the shop.

He didn't acknowledge her.

"You're not thinking about getting that?" Efi asked.

"Why not?"

"It's so . . . odd."

This from the queen of odd.

I handed the drawing to Bruno. "Can you give me a temporary tattoo of this?"

"Yeah, I can do that. I'll feed the design into the computer and print it up on transfer paper. But you know it won't last long."

"It'll last long enough for me to decide if I want to go permanent."

His eyes smiled at me. I think he suspected I wouldn't want it permanent. I squared my shoulders. What, didn't I look like the tattoo type? I'd had my share of temporary tattoos over the years, you know, the kind you buy at Claire's.

I guessed that the temporary part was probably written all over me.

"Maybe you should go henna," Efi said.

"And risk henna poisoning? No. A transfer is fine." When I was fifteen, my friend Joyce Lionas had made me wait while she'd gotten a henna tattoo at Coney Island. She'd had a fever for three days and it had taken a good month before she was completely back to normal. I understood that the chances of poisoning were small, but having seen the effects firsthand, I wasn't going to chance it.

Bruno's mouth followed his eyes and he grinned at me.

What a sheltered life I must lead.

"Okay. Fine," Efi said with a sigh. She turned toward Bruno. "When you're done with her, I want my cross freshened up."

"I thought we were here for me." I objected to spending any more time there than I had to.

She lifted her pants leg to show me the gray Byzantine cross she sported on her right ankle. It had been her first tattoo, I remembered. I also recalled that it had been much darker then. Either that, or my imagination had exaggerated the memory. "It won't take long. I just want to make it look newer."

I scrunched my nose. "Okay. Fine."

FORTY-FIVE MINUTES LATER EFI AND I walked out of Bruno's, Efi with her right pants leg rolled up to keep her freshened tat clear of material, me with my left pants leg rolled up so I could stare at the green little lizard that appeared to be crawling up my ankle.

"Actually, that's cute," Efi said. "But I think the unicorn would have been better."

"I like this," I said.

I nearly walked into a pole as I fought to keep looking at the temporary tattoo and Efi laughed.

"Let's go see Mom," I said.

———

A COUPLE HOURS LATER I was back in the office, considering the pile of paperwork on my desk. Efi and I hadn't gone to see my mother. My sister had told me she wanted to save that for when my tat was permanent. Besides, I would be stopping by later to participate in the official family celebration of her Name Day.

Me? While I liked the lizard, I wasn't all that sure that I liked him enough to see him crawling up my leg forever. Probably I'd have dreams that he was scurrying up and disappearing into my underpants. Not a pleasant thought.

However, Rosie's reaction was almost as good as my mother's might have been. She gasped and slapped her hand over her heart.

"Now what have you gone and done? Just look at you. You've got a snake on your leg."

I looked down, realizing that the lizard's legs weren't clear unless you got closer. The thought of people thinking I'd tattooed a snake on my skin was unsettling.

Lizard, cute. Snake, not.

"It's a lizard," I told her.

"Uh-uh. It's a snake."

I grimaced and rolled my pants leg back down, her words taking all the fun out of it. "It's only temporary."

"Thank God. I can't imagine someone wanting a snake tattooed to their leg."

"It's a lizard."

She showed me her palm as she walked back to her desk. "Whatever. Here. These are your messages. Your grandfather called twice and even stopped by. Brought some of those yummy cream puff things with him."

I looked around for the Greek answer to éclairs, called *coke*. "Where are they?"

"I ate them. Of course."

"Of course."

Truth was, after my visit to Thomas' the other day, I'd completely forgotten about my grandfather's upcoming court date.

I got up again and took my purse from my desk drawer.

"I'll be back," I told Rosie.

"Where you going?"

"Jewelry shopping. Call on my cell if you need anything."

"Bachman's having a sale."

"I'll keep that in mind."

Eleven

I WASN'T JEWELRY SHOPPING, SO much as visiting those stores most likely to have reset my grandmother's ring for Thomas . . . with a CZ in place of the two-carat diamond it had come with.

I was on my third Queens jeweler, having struck out so far. No, they'd all said, they had no record of a Thomas Chalikis coming in during a month-long period the previous year, the time between my grandfather giving him the ring and the time he'd proposed to me during a date at a local club on Greek night.

I found a parking spot up the block from the fourth jeweler, Bachman's, and got out of my car to stare at the storefront. The shops I'd gone to first had been the more expensive-looking ones, with neat, designed windows and fancy lettering and well air-conditioned interiors. This one . . . well, this one had windows that looked like they hadn't been cleaned since old man Bachman had opened the place in 1949. And the lettering was missing pieces so that the name read "Paclman." A crude sign written on plain white paper with magic marker read FALL SALE: NEARLY EVERYTHING 25–75% OFF.

Nearly everything. Which probably meant everything but what you wanted would be on sale.

I pulled open the front door, listening as a rusty string of bells announced my arrival. Bachman himself was bent over a display case, a jeweler's glass affixed to his right eye, inspecting a ring. He blew on the gem and then brushed it against the front of his knit green wool vest before looking at it again.

Probably he hadn't heard the bell. Probably his hearing was about as good as his eyesight and I would have to wave my hand under the glass to get his attention.

"I know you're here, Miss Sofie," he said, startling me. "I'll be with you in a minute."

Yes, I knew Bachman. Everyone in the neighborhood did. Like Uncle Tolly at the Pappas Dry Cleaners, he was a fixture in the area, the place everyone went to get their jewelry repaired or cleaned.

Three display cases formed an "n" around me. Unlike the front window, the glass here had been cleaned to sparkling, and soft lighting focused on the myriad gems within. While the walls of the place were in dire need of painting (although it was hard to tell with all the fading certificates and framed photographs of Mr. Bachman with various of the city's historical figures—was that Ed Koch?), and the ceiling fan could do with a dusting, it stood to reason that the place did good business. Or else he wouldn't have been able to afford to stay open.

Finally, he wiped the ring with a clean cloth, slid it into a slot in a velvet box, and then placed the box out of sight under the counter. He looked up at me, the jeweler's glass still attached to his right eye.

"I thought I might be seeing you," he said.

I blinked at him. The guy had to be eighty if he was a day. But apparently Alzheimer's didn't run in his family because his memory was probably sharper than mine.

"Why's that?" I asked, stepping up to face him across the counter.

He moved his hand across his stomach and caught the eyeglass, replacing it with a thick pair of spectacles. "I have to say, it took you longer than I thought it would." He shook his head. "Kids nowadays. Too much to distract them." He waved his veined hand. "Television, computers, cell phones, jPods—"

"iPods," I absently corrected.

"Whatever. You think all those waves bouncing around everywhere are good for you? No, I say. One day they're going to figure that out, and then where will we be?"

"Mr. Bachman? Do you know anything about my grandmother's ring?"

He blinked at me. "It was your grandmother's?" He waggled a finger at me. "I knew it had to belong to someone like that. Told him that only a woman with taste would have a ring like that."

"Told who?"

"Your no-good rat *fershtinkiner* of an ex-fiancé of yours, that's who."

My heart skipped a beat.

At best, I had hoped I'd happen across someone who maybe had a receipt proving that Thomas had been there, a record that maybe he'd had the diamond changed out. I hadn't even dared imagine that I'd get someone who remembered everything as if it had happened the day before.

I opened my mouth to ask a question, but Bachman continued on his own steam even as he took the soft cloth back out of his vest pocket and wiped down the top of the counter in front of him.

"He comes in and asks if I can reset a ring for him. A ring, he says, he's going to use to propose to the woman he's going to marry." He pointed at me again, this time with the cloth in his hand. "I never trusted that boy. Not when he was knee-high to a grasshopper and his mother brought him in here while she shopped for a baptism gift. I swear, I'm still missing a tennis bracelet. It was fake, mind you, but it's still theft."

"The ring," I quietly reminded him.

"Ah, yes, the ring." He stared off into the distance as if remembering. "A delicate thing, really. Hard to believe it had held up as well as it had. The Greeks, their gold is softer than ours. More yellow. Makes for a pretty ring but isn't good for very sturdy pieces." He bent over, opened a sliding door, and then took a tray of necklaces out of the display case. "Like these. Wear them every day, shower in them, play whatever sports the kids are playing nowadays—what's that cricket stuff? Sounds like a bug to me—and they'll always look as good as the day you bought them. With the right care, of course."

I picked up a gold chain that had a circle pendant on it. "Of course."

"I tell him, 'It's good that you want to put the diamond into a sturdier ring. That way you guarantee that your bride will enjoy it for years to come. Even give it to her granddaughter,' like your grandmother did for you."

I nodded, not wanting to hurry him, but wondering if he was going to get to the point anytime soon. And I had little doubt that he had a point. He'd waited over a year for this visit. Had probably practiced what he'd say to me when I came in.

"Here," he said, holding out his hand for the necklace I held.

I gave it to him and he gestured for me to turn around. With movements more deft than I would have expected, he opened the clasp and fastened the chain around my neck.

"Only he had me make two rings."

I turned around quickly. "Two?"

"Uh-huh. Two." He pushed a mirror so that it sat in front of me, then adjusted the angle so I could see the necklace. "I ask him why he needs two rings, since he's marrying only one woman. He just gave me that smile. That same smile he wore when that bracelet came up missing when he was five. And he just told me to make them. A gonif, that's what his mother raised."

I admired the necklace in the mirror, and then remembered that I had the ring Thomas had given me in my purse. I put it down on the counter and rifled through it until I found the envelope.

"Do you recognize this as one of the rings?"

It seemed to take him eons to remove his spectacles and put the jeweler's piece back to his right eye. He opened the envelope, tipped the mangled platinum into his palm along with the diamond.

Or rather, the CZ stone.

He looked at me over his hand. "What happened to it?"

I averted my gaze. "Unfortunate incident with the garbage disposal."

He chuckled as he considered it. "Yes, that's one of the rings. And this," he held up the CZ between his right index finger and thumb, "is the CZ stone he had me put in it."

"And the diamond that came out of the original ring?"

"He had me make another. A gold one."

I felt as if a heating element had been turned on under my feet, bringing my blood to a low simmer.

"Hold on," he said.

Without bothering to take off the eyepiece again, he disappeared into the small office behind him. I heard some shuffling around as I put the mangled platinum back into the envelope with the CZ.

He finally came back out, looking like an old tortoise in the way he moved with his shoulders hunched over. "Here."

I held my hand out palm up and into it he dropped the setting of my grandmother's original ring.

My throat tightened.

"You kept my grandmother's ring?"

He waved his hand. "Without the diamond, of course. I suspect your old lover still has that. But I thought maybe one day you might like it back."

"Thank you," I said.

"No problem. Now, for the necklace. The price is $154.99. Minus fifty percent off and plus tax . . ."

"HE HAD TWO RINGS MADE?" Rosie asked incredulously when I returned to the office. "That nasty piece of work."

My sentiments exactly plus a few carefully chosen cuss words and imagery that involved goats.

Somehow I was still having a hard time wrapping my mind around the fact that Thomas had taken my grandmother's ring to a jeweler and had two rings made. And he hadn't given me the one with the original diamond in it, but rather the one with the CZ.

Had it been a mistake? Had he accidentally put the wrong ring in his pocket the night he proposed? And what had happened to the other, real, diamond ring? And if it had been a mistake, why hadn't he remedied it from the time he proposed until the day of our wedding?

"Nice necklace."

"Thanks," I said, turning to my desk.

"You gotta watch that old Mr. Bachman. You go in to have your jewelry cleaned and you come out with your credit card maxed out without realizing you'd bought anything."

I smiled.

Before leaving, I'd asked Mr. Bachman if he'd be willing to sign a sworn statement as to what he'd told me. He'd said he would. And that he'd even appear in court if the situation came to that.

"Oh, I almost forgot to tell you," Rosie said. "Waters called for you from Miami."

"Why didn't he call my cell?"

Rosie shrugged. "I dunno. And when I offered to transfer him to it, he quickly said that was okay, to tell you he'd called and that he'd call back again later. Then he hung up."

She said "hung" with a hard "g" like many New Yorkers did. Even I caught myself doing the same from time to time.

I was put through to his voicemail.

I hung up without leaving a message.

"Oh, and Pete's in his father's office."

I looked at where Rosie was busy at work on her new computer. While she didn't gush nearly as much as she had in the beginning she was obviously still very happy with the new purchase and the sense of power it gave her. Judging by the mountain of paperwork on my desk, that power was expanding.

Her cell phone rang and she picked it up and began talking to her sister who, I guessed, must be experiencing bladder problems.

I tuned out of the conversation and picked up a printout from my desk. It looked like a piece from a Spanish-language newspaper. A grainy photo of Reni was featured along with text that had been scaled down so it could fit on the page. I squinted at the words, but beyond making out the name "Bastardo" beneath the picture, and the fact that the piece was dated a year ago, my Spanish was spotty even with perfect copy.

Apparently Rosie had also been doing some additional background checking on Venezuela. Good.

I began to leaf through the rest of the items, and then sighed and instead went to my uncle Spyros' closed office door and rapped once before entering without being invited. My cousin Pete was bent over the safe Spyros had hidden in a cabinet in the corner. And was that a . . .

He had a power drill in his right hand and had just turned it on, which explained why he hadn't heard me.

I leaned against the doorjamb and crossed my arms over my chest, waiting for him to realize I was standing behind him, watching.

The drill bit shot off sparks as he pressed it against the safe. He cursed and fell back on his butt, pulling the plug from the outlet and cutting the power to the drill.

"You know, if you applied that energy to a real job, you'd probably being doing pretty well right now."

He dropped the drill and scurried to his feet, kicking evidence of his activities behind him as he closed the cabinet door. "Sofie. I didn't hear you come in."

I liked my cousin Pete, I really did. It couldn't be easy being him. His mother had divorced my uncle while he was young and she had struggled to raise the kid on her own. Of course, it hadn't helped that she'd had some misconceived idea that my uncle had enough money to completely support her and Pete for the rest of their lives. And when she'd realized that wasn't going to happen, she'd decided to get back at him. Namely through their son, Pete. Everything bad and challenging that had happened in his life, his father was to blame for it. Adolescent angst? Spyros should have prevented it. Teenage rebellion? Again, Spyros. His kleptomaniac ways? His father. (The reasoning behind this latest one was a bit roundabout. You see, as soon as Pete could tell the difference between a five-dollar bill and a twenty, his mother had directed him to lift the latter from his father's pockets and wherever else he might find them. But, still, Spyros was to blame, because how dare he hold on to an extra twenty when he could be giving it to her.)

Hell hath no fury like a woman scorned.

So essentially Pete had been programmed to hate his father, my uncle, and to believe his father owed him to infinity and beyond.

Forget that Pete was twenty-four now, still lived with his mother, and hadn't held down a job for longer than six months. Forget that my uncle Spyros kept hoping the kid (kid? he was way beyond that now) would wake up one day and indulged him until that happened by leaving stashes of cash in his office for him to take.

To maybe inspire some remorse? In hopes that Pete would grow a conscience by giving him incentives to steal?

Didn't make much sense to me. But so long as I wasn't involved, hey, all was fair in the father and son war.

The problem was recently it had begun to affect me. Because since Spyros had been away for nearly six months now, and the money stashes long since gone, money had begun disappearing from my purse when I wasn't looking. Approximately a hundred and twenty dollars worth over a two-week period. And, coincidentally, Pete had always been in the day the money had disappeared.

I'd asked Rosie if anything was missing from her purse and she gave me "the look," which told me that probably Pete had tried pulling stunts like that early on and that Rosie had done something to guarantee he would never go near her things again. Like suggesting that he stay well away from any dark alleys at night.

"What do you want?" Pete asked, regaining the ground he had lost when he discovered I was behind him. He almost managed to make it sound like I was the one in the wrong.

"I want to know what you're trying to do with that drill on the agency safe."

He looked down to find the drill's extension cord was wound around his left ankle. "None of your business."

I pushed myself from the doorjamb and stepped to pick up the drill. I unceremoniously yanked on the cord and began winding it around the body of the drill. "You know, Pete, I've looked the other way for the past few months whenever you've come in to steal money from your father's office. I've even managed to keep quiet when I started noticing money missing from my purse."

His face reddened but he still stared at me like I was the enemy.

"I won't pretend to understand what's going on between you and your dad. Because I don't. But break the law again and I'm going to call the police."

"Right," he said.

I gave him a long look that told him I wasn't joking.

"Get out of here. Now," I said.

He made for the door.

"Oh, and after you've had a chance to think things over, and decide that you might actually like to work for a living, come back and see me."

Twelve

SO THERE I WAS, DRIVING home after a very long day that had yielded a whole lot of results I hadn't been looking for (namely Thomas' misdeeds and Pete's criminal behavior and my own tat, however temporary) and leaving me empty-handed when it came to what I needed (namely I had yet to get Waters on the phone and, despite his report of the pitcher's extracurricular activities in Miami, had precious little on the case from that end).

I'd stopped by my parents' for the official celebration of Efi's Name Day only to find I was too late: There was no torte left and the woman of honor had gone out with friends for the night, nixing any hopes I had for dinner. Efi's leaving would have been a major violation should the house have belonged to her. But since it didn't, she was allowed to get away with such behavior. After all, as my grandmother had said, you're only young once.

I, on the other hand, would have to stay home all day tomorrow in order to accommodate any unannounced guests on my

Name Day. But my mother was bringing the torte so I wouldn't have to worry about that, at least.

At any rate, right now I was looking forward to nothing more than a long soak in a hot tub with a good book and quiet music.

Of course, I'd had to wait at my parents' before I could implement even those simple plans because the skies had opened up, unleashing a storm to rival all storms, including hail that had put a couple of small dents in the hood of my car and filled my back window well with water (I really needed to have that leak sealed).

Finally, I reached my building after doing a roundabout bit to accommodate the one-way streets (I only lived up the street from my parents'), already mentally seeing myself in the tub filled with bubbles up to my chin.

But it appeared I was going to be denied even that.

I first spotted the activity as I rolled by on my search for an empty parking spot. Apparently the business students in 2B had decided they also had reason to celebrate and my apartment building was party central. College students spilled out onto the sidewalk, the door was wide open revealing that there were even more of them sitting and lounging on the steps and in the hallway, hip-hop music filled the entire street, and Muffy was barking up a storm from the fire escape, his little furry body levitating with every effort. An effort that was lost because the music drowned out his barks.

It took me five minutes to finally locate a parking spot three blocks up and over, ironically past my parents' house. I sighed as I locked up the car, an accordion file with some paperwork from the agency pressed to my side.

"Sofie!" Don Myers called out as he saw me approaching. "How in the hell are you doing, baby?"

I tried to adopt my best strict apartment-owner stance, but had a hard time when faced with Don's big grin.

I gestured toward the people laughing and drinking nearby. Was that really a garbage can overflowing with the golf ball–size hail that had come down, beer cooling inside?

"Obviously I'm not doing as well as you are," I said to Don. "What's the occasion?"

"John's getting married."

John was one of the three DeVry students I'd let move into a two-bedroom apartment meant for families after they promised they'd be out at the end of the last semester. Instead, they'd stayed through the summer and now that a new academic season had already begun, I was afraid I was in it for the long run.

Don't get me wrong. Aside from loud music here and there, the guys weren't all that bad. And I'd sweetened on them when they gave Mrs. Nebitz their rent on time every month. (I'd had a hell of a time with them when I tried collecting it myself early on.)

But all things being equal, I'd prefer to have a nice quiet family in the unit. I spotted still unemployed Etta Munson staring out her closed window. Preferably a fiscally viable family.

John came up, beer in hand.

"Congratulations on taking the leap," I said.

"Thanks, Sof." He looked around. "You don't mind, do you? I mean, all my family's in Washington state and, well, the guys wanted to help me celebrate."

I shook my head and looked at my watch. It was only nine on a Saturday night. "So long as you guys try to bring things down to a low roar by eleven. And don't give the police a hard time if they get called in."

What was my responsibility in regard to the remainder of

my tenants and the neighborhood at large? Was I supposed to order them to take their partying elsewhere?

Don used his teeth to open a bottle of beer and then handed it to me. "Join us?"

I shook my head but accepted the beer. "No, but thanks." I lifted the file. "I have some work to do."

"You know what they say about all work and no play."

I grimaced. It wasn't long ago that I would have been doing exactly what they were on a Saturday night, but suddenly the group looked a generation away from me.

The problem with the dull girl thing was that no one was offering to spice things up a bit.

I remembered Dino and my throat tightened up all over again.

"Yeah, well," I offered up by way of an answer and then began to weave my way through the human bodies that lay between me and my apartment.

Then a thought occurred to me.

"Actually, Don, I think there's something I can contribute to the celebration . . ."

Five minutes later, Don and another guy had relieved me of two of the three remaining cases I had of six-month-old champagne that had been meant for my wedding reception. I kept one, you know, just in case I'd need it for something. Like late-night forays into the past when I opened one or two of the wedding gifts still stacked high in my bedroom.

"Thanks, Sof! The girls will love this," Don said.

I waved at him. "Don't mention it."

As soon as they had disappeared, Mrs. Nebitz's door cracked open.

"Sofie," she said by way of greeting.

"Oh, hi, Mrs. Nebitz." I looked down the stairwell. "I'm sorry about the noise. One of the guys just got engaged."

"Yes, I know. Nice girl."

She'd met John's fiancée?

"Everybody needs a reason to celebrate every now and again."

I was somewhat surprised to find I still held the beer Don had given me.

"I trust everything went well with your visit to Moshe today?" she asked.

I raised my brows at her. "Mr. Bachman?"

"Yes. We go to the same Jewish community center, Moshe and I. He mentioned you stopped in."

Sometimes I forgot how small the world could be. Especially when it came to the tight-knit neighborhood of Astoria. When Mrs. K was still alive, my mother had known my every move because Mrs. K hadn't had anything better to do than to watch my comings and goings.

So for all intents and purposes it appeared that the Astoria grapevine was still alive and well. I guess it was better that I knew that than not. Particularly since I was a PI and it really wasn't in my best interest for everyone to know about my goings-on.

"Yes, yes," I finally said in answer to her question. "My visit to Mr. Bachman went very well." I slid a finger under my new necklace. "I even got a really good deal on this."

Mrs. Nebitz waved her hand. "Deal, shmeal. Moshe could sell a Catholic priest a dreidel. A gold one."

I had little doubt that he could.

Catching on something, I looked at my neighbor a little closer. "How well do you know Mr. Bachman?"

Was it me, or had Mrs. Nebitz just blushed? Yes, that was very definitely a blush. From an eighty-something-year-old woman. "Noah and I knew Moshe for years. We attended, and I still attend, the same temple."

"Is he married?"

"Widowed. His wife passed on the year after my Noah." She said something in Hebrew or Yiddish then, but I couldn't be sure what it was.

"Have the two of you ever thought . . ."

Her eyes widened at me. "Sofie Metropolis! For shame."

I'm pretty sure I was the one who was now blushing, albeit for a completely different reason.

"Never mind," I said quickly. "Well, good night then, Mrs. Nebitz. You'll let me know if the party starts to bother you."

"I will. Good night. Oh, and thank you for bringing back my dishes."

"You're welcome."

I ducked inside my apartment for two reasons: first, to get away from Mrs. Nebitz as fast as I could; second to prevent Muffy from doing some damage to the party participants in case he'd found a way to get out of the bathroom I'd closed him in while Don got the champagne, as the smart mutt had been known to do on occasion.

He was still in the bathroom, so I let him out. He ducked and darted around my legs trying to lead me back to the door so he could have access to the hall. When he realized I wasn't falling for his cute display, he plopped his little fur butt on the floor in front of me and whined.

"No. No fresh human flesh for you."

As I walked to the kitchen and put the beer into the fridge in case I might want it later, I realized I wasn't being entirely fair to Muffy. While feasting on Sofie flesh had been one of his favorite pastimes while Mrs. K was alive, he hadn't bit a single person since he'd become my new roommate.

I remembered Tony DiPiazza and frowned.

Well, okay, not a single person I hadn't wanted him to bite.

And since car license plates belonging to Mafia goons also didn't count, I figured the Muffster had displayed amazing restraint in the past few months.

I opened the cupboard and took out a bag of doggie treats he liked, probably because they tasted like bacon.

"Who's been a good boy?" I asked. "Have you been a good boy?"

Muffy's tail stopped wagging at me and he cocked his head if to say, "You're not really serious, are you?"

"Never mind," I said, dropping a treat into his mouth, then following with another before putting the bag away and filling his bowl with dog food.

I leaned against the counter. I could feel the bass from 2B's sound system pulse beneath my feet and laughter drifted in from the open window. I figured a bath was out. Unless Mrs. Nebitz had a spare pair of earplugs she could loan me. So I grabbed the beer from the fridge and my portable chair from the front closet and headed up to the roof. Muffy followed, his toenails *click click*ing against the damp asphalt of the roof.

"Great minds."

I glanced over to where my neighbor Sloane was lying back in his lounger, staring up at the stars that were peeking through the wispy clouds that had remained after the storm. You could still hear the music from downstairs, but it wasn't as intrusive up here somehow.

I opened my chair and moved it to the short stoop that separated my building from the next. Since Sloane used the same stoop as a table of sorts, he was within arm's length.

"Hope you don't mind company," I said as I sat down and put my feet up on the stoop.

"Actually, I welcome it. It's been quiet lately. Almost too quiet."

Muffy ran the length of the roof a couple of times, barked at the party people, and then came to sit next to me, his tongue lolling out of the side of his mouth.

"I find that hard to believe."

Sloane chuckled and the mild smell of marijuana reached my nose. He lifted his right arm where he had it hanging over the side of his chair. "Does the smell bother you?"

I shook my head. "Compared to the city's other smells two days before trash collection? Nah."

He took a long draw off the handmade cigarette, held the smoke in, and then slowly released it. "Nowadays it's the only way I seem to be able to stimulate any appetite."

I didn't know Sloane well, but I liked him. When I'd escaped from the fiasco that was my wedding last March, and ended up on this very roof still wearing my wedding dress and smearing my mascara all over my face, he'd been where he was now. He'd asked if I was okay. I'd lied and told him that I was. Then we'd both sat there without saying anything while I watched my worried family members come and go, never knowing where I was.

I figured he was probably about thirty to thirty-five. And had come to understand since that fateful winter day that his family owned the building next to mine and that he lived rent-free in exchange for acting as the super. He was a comic book illustrator, and wasn't a bad-looking guy.

Well, actually, that depended on the day. Right now he appeared a little on the thin side and he must have gone through another round of chemo because his blond hair was patchy, the little bit of it I could see beneath the red bandanna he wore.

"You look a little wound up," he said. "You want a pass?"

I'd never been a big fan of illicit drugs. Oh, I'd smoked pot a couple/few times, but had never bought it myself.

"Sure," I said, accepting the joint from him and taking a hit.

The sweet smelling smoke filled my lungs and seemed to lick through the rest of my body, uncoiling my tight muscles, calming my stomach and relaxing my shoulders.

I took another brief hit, then handed him the joint, settling more comfortably into my chair.

"Better than a bubble bath," I said softly.

"What?"

I shook my head and smiled at the slight buzz I had. "Nothing."

We both sat for long moments staring up at the sky, taking turns finishing the joint, and listening to the party down below. Muffy had moved to perch at the edge of the roof and lay down, his head hanging over the side so he could at least salivate over the human flesh even if he was forbidden to taste it.

"Do you ever wonder about how strange life can be?" I found myself saying to Sloane.

I felt his gaze on my profile and I realized how stupid my question was in his case. "All the time."

"I mean, just when everything's going great, it's like some sort of unseen hand grabs you by the shoulders and shows you a view you hadn't noticed before."

"Like making you look at the clouds instead of the stars."

"Exactly." I took a sip of my warming beer and then set it down on the stoop. "I mean, right now I should be married, possibly pregnant with my first child, planning for a future I'd always dreamed about growing up, you know? Then everything changed and I became a PI."

"Not necessary a bad thing, considering."

I shrugged. "Not a bad thing at all. Most times."

Another long pause. I listened as a neighbor up the block shouted for the DeVry students to pipe down.

"My ex is pressing charges against my grandfather for breaking his nose."

Sloane shifted.

"This, after he switched the diamond out of my grandmother's ring and gave me a CZ."

Muffy must have spotted something interesting because he was instantly back on his feet again, barking his head off.

"Then there's my cousin Pete, who would probably steal the CZ and try to pawn it off as a diamond if he got the chance." I shook my head. "Every time I turn around, he's looking for money to pocket from the agency."

"Have you told your uncle?"

I shook my head. "Nah. I figure I can handle it." I turned to look at Sloane. "I offered him a job today."

"Who, your cousin?"

"Yeah."

"You trust him to work for you?"

"I don't know. But how much damage can he do, say painting the office and repairing the bathroom mirror? You know, something Rosie can watch him doing. Only he doesn't know yet that's what I'm going to be offering."

Sloane chuckled.

"I got asked out."

I didn't say anything more and Sloane didn't ask.

"Did you hear me?" I said after a long moment.

"I was afraid I was imagining things."

I reached over and lightly hit him on the arm.

"Who is it? That sexy Australian?"

An image of Porter entered my mind and I shivered all over. "No. I haven't seen him in nearly a month."

"Who then?"

I tucked my chin into my chest, suddenly overly interested in the way my jeans fit against my thighs. They didn't look all that bad, really. Being a New Yorker meant you did a lot of walking. Combine that with a forced diet because of a gassy roommate and you had slimmer thighs.

Not a bad trade-off.

"Sofie?"

"Hmm? Oh. Sorry." I laughed. "This guy named Dino."

I stopped there, biting lightly on my bottom lip to stop from offering more.

"Are you going to go out with him?"

I stared at him as if he'd suggested we go into the pot-selling business together. "Are you crazy?"

Sloane grinned. "Why?"

"Because . . ." I trailed off.

And just like that, all the reasons why I might have convinced myself that dating Dino would be a bad idea fled from my foggy brain.

"Because he's Greek," I latched onto.

"Ah. That makes sense."

I chewed that one over. "Does it? Because suddenly it doesn't seem to make much sense to me."

And it didn't. Not really.

"Are you attracted to him?"

I tilted my head as I considered my answer. What wasn't there to be attracted to? He was tall, dark, and handsome, with a great one-dimple grin and a funny nature. The problem lay in that straight off the bat I'd shelved him because I'd thought he wanted to date my sister.

Now that I knew he wanted to date me, instead, where did that leave me?

Flattered, for sure. And more than a little intrigued by the prospect of what it might feel like to kiss him. Preferably at his sweets shop behind the displays, sampling cream off his skin and having him do the same to me.

"So what's the problem then?"

I twisted my lips.

"Listen, Sofie, you know I'm the last one to pass judgment on anyone. Not given the current state of my own life."

I looked at him, granting him my full attention as I imagined what life was like in his shoes.

"But the way I figure it we only have one shot at this thing called life, you know? And if something catches your fancy, then you should go for it. Full out."

"But what if I don't want it in the morning?"

"Then you don't want it. Ask it to leave." He looked at me. "But just think of the fun you'll get to have while you move from point A to point B."

"He asked me out on a date, not to have sex," I said.

"There's a difference?"

I grinned.

"Hire someone to break Thomas' kneecaps, report your cousin Pete to the NYPD, and have great sex with Dino." He shrugged. "What's the harm in any of that?"

What was the harm, indeed?

Thirteen

IT'S ALL FUN AND GAMES until the police get called and you have to face them stoned.

When I woke up early Sunday morning, I groaned, the reason why I didn't regularly smoke weed hitting me squarely on the head.

Of course, I'd known someone would eventually call the boys in blue. Someone always did. There were probably scores of people who sat cross-armed in front of the clock waiting for the exact time they thought the party should end. In this case, it was ten o'clock on the button.

And I'd had to face none other than my best friend Pimply Pino Karras. He was no longer pimply nor my friend, but there you had it. The instant Sloane and I spotted the flashing red-and-white lights on the street below, I'd known I was the one he would be looking for. I figured it had been a good month since he'd had reason to harass me and probably he'd latched on to this excuse with both hands.

I'd thought about pretending I wasn't there for all of two

seconds. Until I realized he'd probably wait outside my apartment door until I materialized.

So even though Sloane assured me I looked fine, that Pino wouldn't be able to tell I'd indulged in illegal drugs by merely looking at me, I'd gone down to my apartment to splash cold water on my face, squeeze drops into my eyes, gargle with the strongest mouthwash I had, and then spritzed myself like crazy with my favorite perfume.

"Pino," I'd said, running into him on the stairs on his way up.

He stood with one foot on the step above him, his hand resting on his billy club. "Sofie." He sniffed.

I swear I thought he could smell the weed no matter my attempts to mask whatever scent clung to me. Probably the department could use him instead of drug-sniffing dogs.

Probably I was just a paranoid smoker.

"Can you come outside for minute?" he'd asked.

I silently agreed as I followed him downstairs and onto the sidewalk. At the first appearance of the police, most of the guests had magically dispersed, the sound of cars starting up and driving away was clear. Seeing as Don and his roommates were college students, well, it stood to reason that a lot of their friends might not be twenty-one yet.

Land of the brave. Home of the free. Or something like that. At eighteen you could vote and die for your country. But you weren't credited with the good sense God gave to a gnat to know whether you could handle a beer or two.

I'd caught the drug-induced internal dialogue and cleared my throat. "Sorry about the noise. I'll ask the guys to keep it down. One of them just got engaged and they're celebrating."

"By having sex in parked cars where the neighbors have a front-row seat?"

I made a face. "I'm sure that has nothing to do with the party," I said.

"It was the groom. And it wasn't his fiancée he was, um, doing it with."

Figured.

Well, I guessed the party was pretty much over then, in more ways than I cared to count.

"Are you sure? I mean they just got engaged."

He turned and I followed his gaze to where John was standing talking to police while his new, now probably ex-fiancée was being restrained by two other officers, a third girl sitting on a curb, her face buried in her hands as she cried.

Neither of the girls looked older than eighteen or nineteen. And both of them looked like they'd indulged in one too many.

Maybe there was good reason for the minimum drinking age after all.

Then again, I'd seen people much older than them do far worse things. And alcohol hadn't played any role.

I'd squinted at Pino. "So all of this affects me . . . how, exactly?"

He leaned closer to me and sniffed. I automatically stepped back. "You been drinking with them?"

"Of course not," I said, remembering the beer. "And what if I was?"

"I could run you in for willfully contributing to the delinquency of a minor."

"Eighteen does not qualify a person for minor status." I looked around, praying there weren't any people under eighteen there.

Yeesh. A person couldn't allow their tenants to have a party anymore without worrying about getting thrown in the clink. What was this world coming to?

Thankfully one of Pino's colleagues had distracted him and I was allowed to return to my apartment with just a warning.

Bless his twisted little heart.

I lay in bed for a long moment, staring at the ceiling, remembering the incident with amazing clarity considering my condition at the time. Muffy was still asleep at my feet. It was too early to go into the office on a weekday, much less a Sunday. And Venezuela wasn't due back in town until later that morning.

Speaking of which . . .

I reached for my cell phone on the nightstand and pressed the button to call Waters.

I got his voicemail and called again. And again. Finally, on the fourth round, Eugene picked up.

"What in the hell do you want, Metro? I was sleeping."

"I figured you were due a little payback."

"Funny. What's up?"

"I thought I asked you to call in with daily reports?"

"I did call. You weren't there."

"The agency. But when Rosie offered to put you through to my cell, you refused. Said you'd call back. You didn't. And you didn't respond to my calls or messages, either."

"Yeah, well . . ."

"Uh-uh. That ain't going to cut it, Waters. Out with it. What's up?"

Muffy was obviously awakened by the stern tone of my voice. He stared at me, and then nipped one of my toes through the sheet.

"Ow! You little mongrel." I edged him off the bed and the sound of his toenails clicked against the wood as he went to see about his business on the roof.

"I lost him," Waters finally said.

I sat up like a jackknife. "Define 'him'?"

"You know who him. Him him."

"Venezuela?"

"Yeah."

"For how long?"

He mumbled something.

"What was that?"

"Seven hours."

"What?"

"See. That's why I didn't want to tell you. I knew you'd just get upset."

"Of course I'm upset. You're down there specifically to watch him."

"Hey, look, I didn't know the guy was like Superman or something. I thought after those women left he'd go to sleep, you know, like any other normal man. But I found out through housekeeping that he must have left soon after. And the hotel driver told me he took him to the airport. Then picked him up again there at around two and took him straight to the ballpark."

"Did you find out where he'd gone?"

"No. I didn't even have a line on which airline he'd used. Anyway, it probably wouldn't have made any difference. Have you tried to bribe an airline employee since 9/11? I was nearly arrested."

"Maybe you should have been."

I ran my fingers through my tangled hair then scratched my scalp. "Would steroids do that?"

"Do what?"

"Give the guy the energy to have sex all night with three women, spend the day going who knows where, then return to play one of the best games of his life?"

"Not steroids. Maybe drugs, like coke or something, though. I was up for three days straight once."

More info than I wanted.

Cocaine. A multiheaded hydra I'd always taken great care to avoid. It was always around. At parties, being offered up as casually as beer. It seemed to be more widely available now, what with so much competition from crystal methamphetamine—also known as meth or ice—and the resurgence of heroin.

Oh, yeah, I was up on everything. While I preferred to avoid the drugs myself, I knew what the deal was. I'd never been one to stick my head in the sand and pretend something didn't exist. I had even been concerned about Efi every now and again, but she hadn't seemed to go beyond normal experimentation.

If there was such a thing as "normal experimentation" anymore.

"Have you found evidence that he's using?" I asked Waters.

"Not yet. But I'm looking."

"Actually, you're coming back here in," I looked at my clock, "three hours."

"Oh, yeah. Right. I forgot."

Sure he had.

"I want you in the office five minutes after your plane touches down."

"That's mathematically impossible."

"You know what I mean. Call me when you're back in town."

I rang off shortly thereafter and then sat in bed trying to put all the pieces together. I'd thought maybe steroids might be to blame for Reni's "strange" behavior. But it now appeared there could be a whole host of other reasons for him not sleeping with his wife.

And not out of the question was that he no longer found her appealing.

I thought about the party last night being thrown for a newly-engaged couple that was neither engaged nor a couple by the end of the night. For that matter, my own disaster of a wedding day made a command performance.

What was it about the human race that we were constantly compelled to seek out chaos where there was none?

There was a knock on my apartment door. Muffy started barking as if he'd just caught the scent of a cat, apparently having finished his business on the roof. It couldn't be anyone he knew, because he wouldn't bark so furiously otherwise. Mrs. Nebitz got a fast tail-wagging and a few licks of the chops because she was known to feed him goodies. My mother earned a dubious stare before he disappeared under the kitchen table, well out of reach of her and with a couple of viable escape routes. Pino got a low growl.

Who needed peepholes? I had Muffy.

I threw off the top sheet, oblivious that I wore only my old Mets T-shirt and hot pink panties, and then put Muffy into the bathroom where he couldn't take a chunk out of someone and put me next in line for a lawsuit.

I pulled the door open without looking through the peephole.

Probably I should have looked first.

Air locked in my lungs as I stared at the hot guy in the hall.

"Dino," I squeaked more than said.

Fourteen

I COULDN'T HAVE BEEN MORE surprised had Thomas decided to make nice and shown up holding a bouquet of flowers and my grandmother's real diamond and begged me for forgiveness on his hands and knees.

Coming a close second would be Jake Porter wearing his weathered leather cowboy hat and asking me if I'd like to go for a ride in my Sheila (that would be my Mustang Lucille), so that we could finally have that hot sex our flirting had promised but had yet to deliver on.

What in the hell was Dino doing at my apartment on a Sunday morning . . . *early* on a Sunday morning?

"*Chronia Polla*, Sofia," he said with a sexy grin.

I wasn't sure how to react. Not standing there, my hair a tangled mess, and my hot pink panties peeking out from under the hem of my T-shirt.

I slammed the door in his face.

Oh, but that was bright.

I closed my eyes and dug the heel of my right hand into my eye socket, hoping that the stars I saw would reveal that I was still in bed and had dreamed that Dino was standing outside in the hall.

And that I just shut the door on him.

A brief knock.

I opened my eyes. Nope. This wasn't a dream. This was startling reality.

"What are you doing here, Dino?" I asked through the door, lifting my hand to touch the wood, then pulling it back and fisting it at my side.

"It's your Name Day. I brought you a torte."

He'd . . . brought . . . me . . . a . . . torte.

I couldn't use the excuse that I'd forgotten my Name Day because of the simple fact that my sister's had been the day before. But I had to wake up enough to realize that.

I chewed on my bottom lip as I ordered my brain to produce a suitable action to my inaction.

"Good morning," I heard Dino say to someone.

I looked out the peephole to find Mrs. Nebitz in her open doorway.

Great. Now Mrs. Nebitz knew that Dino was coming over to my house early on a Sunday morning. She'd probably tell Mr. Bachman. And Mr. Bachman would tell whichever neighbor who happened into his jewelry shop. And just like that Thalia would be calling me in two hours flat asking for the wedding date.

I opened the door without revealing myself, and grabbed a handful of Dino's T-shirt in my hand, tugging him inside with little ceremony.

"Good morning, Mrs. Nebitz," I peeked my head around and said, then slammed the door again before she could respond and perhaps ask for an introduction to this latest nice young man who was visiting me.

"What are you doing here?" I whispered, although it was unnecessary. Mrs. Nebitz sometimes couldn't hear me when I was right in front of her, much less pick up what I was saying through an inch and a half of solid wood.

Then again, you never knew.

Dino stood holding a large white box from his bakery. I noticed he wasn't looking at my face, but rather the hem of my T-shirt and the silk-covered delicate areas that lay beyond.

I made a strangled sound. "Wait here."

As I gripped the bathroom door handle, I considered for a brief millisecond allowing the barking Muffy to have his way with the new visitor. But at the last minute I put my foot between me and the mutt and edged my way inside. It wasn't until I was seated on the commode that I considered the fact that I had a hot man in my apartment. And not only wasn't I happy about it, I was wishing like hell he would just go away.

"What?" I asked Muffy where he sat at my feet openly watching me. Probably because I was looking after business he usually didn't get to see.

He made an inquisitive sound and then cocked his head to the side.

I gave him an eye roll then finished, flushing the toilet when I was done. I moved to the sink, then remembered to close the toilet lid, nearly clipping Muffy's nose off where he was perched with his paws on the seat trying to get a fresh drink of water.

I stared into the mirror, aghast at my appearance.

What did it matter? Better I should turn Dino off now. Before I was tempted to take that torte out of his hands and devour it in front of him.

Worse, before I took the torte out of his hands and devoured *him*.

I decided to forgo the sink and dove straight for the shower instead. After I'd blown my hair dry and made an attempt with makeup (hey, the guy had brought me a cake, he at least deserved a civilized thank-you from someone who resembled a human being), I wrapped myself in a towel and made a mad dash for my bedroom.

"I'll be out in a minute," I called.

I slammed the door, only then realizing that I'd inadvertently let Muffy out of the bathroom with me.

I listened intently, reasoning that it wasn't my fault, really. I couldn't be held accountable if Muffy decided to sink his teeth into Dino's leg and then chase him from the apartment.

I heard growling.

Crap.

I hurriedly dressed in jeans and a white clingy long-sleeved top. But when I emerged a minute later, I found that Dino wasn't warding off Muffy with a fire poker. Rather he sat on the couch and was scratching Muffy behind the ears.

"Oh," I said. Here I'd gotten worked up for nothing.

Dino immediately got up. "You didn't have to get dressed on my account."

Was that a devilish glint I saw in his eyes as he considered my appearance? Yes, I reasoned, it was. And that one-dimple grin of his had a bit of a naughty quality that I hadn't witnessed before.

I decided that I liked it.

Perhaps a little too much.

Which compelled me to consider just when he'd gone from very attractive potential groom material for Efi, to poster man for those I might want to see make an appearance in my bedroom.

I found my gaze slanting in that direction and stopped myself.

I'd learned a long time ago that a woman's heart was a complicated thing. While there were four physical chambers, I could map out a maze without end to signify the times in my life when I'd taken a wrong turn.

Chalk it up to fear of failure. Or the fact that me and Greek men just plain didn't seem to get along. Thomas might be the worst of them, but he was by no means the first. Alex Nyktas held that distinctive honor. And Thalia still whispered that he was the one that had gotten away.

More specifically, he'd gone off to Boston to medical school and . . . well, he'd never come back.

But none of that helped me in the here and now as I stood staring at Dino like I was at risk of being bitten. Or, worse, that I was at risk of biting him.

I tried hard to focus on everything but him, reminding myself that we weren't in a club on Greek night, and that it was early on a Sunday morning. In fact, I'd promised my mother that I'd meet her at church, what with it being my Name Day and all, and it would mean weeks of emotional abuse if I stood her up.

"You brought me a torte," I said, zooming in on the box on the coffee table.

His reaction indicated that his mind, like mine, was elsewhere. "Oh. Yes." He picked up the box and held it out to me. "Chocolate. I hope you like it."

What wasn't there to like about chocolate? Or his delicious accent when he said the word?

I opened the top even as I moved toward the kitchen and more neutral territory.

Coffee. That was it. I hadn't had my morning frappé yet. How was a girl supposed to think without a little caffeine running through her veins?

The torte was to-die-for gorgeous. And my mouth watered with the desire to cut into it.

"Frappé?" I asked Dino.

I cringed when I realized I should have just thanked him and ushered him toward the door. I couldn't be blamed; hospitality was fused with Greek DNA. A visitor? Then you gave them at the very least something to drink. And most of the time something to eat.

Muffy had followed, his little nose wiggling as he sniffed in the general direction of the torte. I put the box down on the table.

"Do you have Greek coffee?"

"What kind of Greek girl would I be if I didn't have Greek coffee?"

Truth be told, I hadn't had Greek coffee until a few weeks ago when I'd opened one of the wedding gifts in the other room. The gift had been from one of Thomas' two grandmothers (nice old ladies to whom I really should have returned the gifts). Inside was a delicate porcelain Greek coffee set bearing decals of the Acropolis in twenty-four-carat gold. (If you've never seen a traditional Greek coffee cup, envision a little girl's tea set. You know, the fake kind where tea was never really poured or drank. I'd borrowed my mother's Greek set when I was five to have my own tea party with a neighbor girl and our dolls. I'd broken a saucer and still heard her complain about it today, you know, whenever I went to the house after she'd dusted.)

At any rate, I now had a tourist set of souvenir Greek coffee cups—albeit expensive ones—that I'd kept out of guilt, a small handmade copper *briki* (pan), and, of course, the coffee that had come with it.

I tried not to think about the irony of my using the items not to fix coffee for my new husband Thomas, but rather for another Greek man who had made me a chocolate torte for my Name Day.

"How do you like it?"

"*Metrio.*"

"*Metrio*" meant with a little sugar. Not too bitter, not too sweet. Much like the man himself.

For reasons I couldn't begin to fathom, I decided to fix coffee for both of us. Since moving into my own place, I usually fixed my favorite of frappé—iced Nescafé coffee. Now I craved something different.

I slanted a gaze toward Dino, wondering if that craving also extended to him.

He was watching my ass.

I raised my brows and turned back toward the coffee.

And why wouldn't he be? Watching my ass, that is? He was a man, after all. Not to mention a Greek man (I won't go there). And I'd purposely put on my nice-ass jeans. You know the pair. The ones that didn't droop too much at the base of the cheeks, the waist of which weren't too high to make it look like your rear end went on forever, or too low so that you had butt cleavage, and that fit just so that they were snug, but not too tight so that you could make out panty lines.

Not that I had any of those, because I'd also put on a thong.

Hot. It was suddenly hot in here.

I fanned myself. It was the open burner, that was all. Making Greek coffee was hot work. First you had to measure two cups of water from the cups you would be using. Then measure in two heaping spoonfuls of the coffee powder. And a teaspoon and a half of sugar. Then you stirred and continued stirring until your efforts and the heat nicely mixed everything, stopping only at the end so that the foam could rise to the top of the *briki*.

This was the part I usually screwed up. There was an art to cutting off the flame at the exact right moment. Too soon, and the coffee wasn't smooth. Too late, and you were scrubbing the dark liquid from your stovetop afterward.

Marking a rare occasion, I got it just right.

I poured the coffee into the cups and then moved them to the kitchen table.

"Let me cut you a piece of the torte," I said.

Then I realized that I should refuse his generous offering. Where would I say it came from? My mother had already told me not to worry about buying anything sweet, that she'd get a torte and I could pick it up from her house after church.

"That's okay." Dino held up his hands, still standing. "It's a gift. For you and your guests."

It was Greek tradition that if someone brought you a sweet, it was your duty to serve him or her a piece of it. And while I wasn't very good at pushing my will or Greek traditions on other people (Thalia had that market cornered), I found I wanted to do so now.

"Don't be ridiculous," I said, taking the torte out of the box and placing it on the table. I put the box on the counter and then took a knife out of a drawer and a couple of plates from the cupboard. Within moments I had placed two good size pieces in front of two chairs, even though neither of us had yet to sit.

Muffy barked, startling me where I stood staring at Dino.

I looked down at him. "Roof or bathroom?" I asked, distantly understanding that to him the roof was the bathroom.

He ran to the window and I heard him go up the fire escape to the roof.

"Cute dog."

"Mmm," I said, suddenly beyond words.

Because in that one moment, as I wondered at the deep brown of Dino's eyes that rivaled the chocolate of the torte he'd brought me, and took in the shape of his generous mouth that even now smiled at me suggestively, knowingly, I grew suddenly hungry. And it wasn't for the torte.

And just like that, I was kissing Dino for all I was worth.

And he was kissing me back . . .

Fifteen

THREE HOURS LATER I LAY across my bed naked, chocolate smears all over me and the bedding, the scent of spilled coffee filling my nose.

Dino wedged firmly between my thighs.

He shifted to move off me and I tightened my calves behind his back, forbidding him to move even as I stared at the ceiling and wondered what, exactly, I had done.

One minute I'd been the perfect hostess, offering him coffee and torte. The next I was a two-bit ho offering myself up right there on the kitchen table.

Which explained the coffee in my hair, and the chocolate on my shoulder.

Because once I'd begun kissing him, I couldn't seem to stop. His mouth had felt so damn good pressed against mine, the taste of him calling out to something fundamental within me, and his no-holds-barred response to my attentions made it virtually impossible for me to slam on the brakes. There were few turn-ons more potent than knowing someone wanted you as much as you wanted them.

So I found myself being hoisted up onto the table, for the second time in my life being responsible—however indirectly—for breaking good china, and ruining a perfectly good chocolate torte when Dino arched me back and I found my elbow hitting the center of the cake with little fanfare.

Not that that had stopped anything. In fact, when I lifted my arm to take a look, Dino had taken advantage of the opportunity to lean in and begin eating the sweet frosting from my skin.

There are few things more erotic than watching a great-looking man lick food from your skin. Especially when other areas of your neglected body immediately clamored for that same attention.

Somewhere in the back of my mind as I thrust my fingers through Dino's thick, dark hair, and welcomed him between my clothed thighs, I'd known that if one or the other of us hesitated for a millisecond, everything would come to a grinding halt.

But the only thing I'd been interested in grinding was my pelvis against his.

And, oh boy, had it ever been a great idea. I'd been rewarded four times for my recklessness. First right there on the table. Then we'd moved to my bedroom where I finally got a chance to see how my king-size bed provided exactly the sexual playground I'd hoped it would. No position required shifting as we moved this way and then the next in an urgent concert of sweaty flesh and burning needs.

It had been a long time since I'd been with a man. And now my body let me know about it in ways both big and small. My delicate parts throbbed. My breasts were ultra-sensitive from the attention of his mouth. My lips were swollen from his kisses. And my legs felt like I'd just gone a marathon round with the Thighmaster.

My conversation with Sloane the night before came back to haunt me.

". . . the way I figure it we only have one shot at this thing called life, you know? And if something catches your fancy, then you should go for it. Full out."

"But what if I don't want it in the morning?" I'd asked.

"Then you don't want it. Ask it to leave."

Seemed like simple advice then. But what happened when the incident had taken place in the morning? Did I just get up and say, "Well, gee, thank you, Dino. That was nice. Let yourself out, won't you? I'll see you around."

Pile on top of that the fact that I'd missed church and he'd missed his deliveries and that Mrs. Nebitz had seen him coming into my apartment and was probably watching for him to leave and . . .

I groaned.

"Esai kala?" Dino asked if I was all right in Greek.

Problem was that I wasn't okay in either English or Greek. Because an even darker thought had emerged in my head: I had just given Dino Jake's sex. . . .

"SOFIE, ARE YOU OKAY?"

Rosie asked the question the following morning at the agency. A simple inquiry to be sure, but one I'd heard at least a hundred times since yesterday morning, from every member of my family who had stopped by my apartment to wish me a happy Name Day, and even by Mrs. Nebitz who had caught me standing outside my apartment door, key hovering, for a full five minutes after I'd gone to my parents' house to get the replacement torte from my mother, who, thankfully, had still been at church when I stopped by.

Truth was, I was getting tired of everyone asking if I was all right. I'd had sex, not come down with the flu.

Although I wondered if the symptoms I was displaying were all that dissimilar. Shiny eyes. High color. Glazed-over expression.

You'd think I'd have been smiling. After all, I hadn't just gotten sex, I'd gotten great sex.

The problem lay in that I hadn't gotten it from the man I had expected to get it from.

Shortly after my revelation while Dino was still in my bed, he'd made a quiet departure, promising to call me later. When he had called, I hadn't picked up. Partly because my mother had been sitting next to me when it had come in. Mostly because I didn't have a clue what to say to him.

I mean, what did it mean that I'd slept with him, beyond that I'd been desperate?

Oh, that so wasn't nice.

But the fact remained that I'd used Dino in a way he hadn't deserved. Not that he hadn't enjoyed our morning. But I'm sure he now expected that things would progress from there. Perhaps he was looking forward to repeating the sex. He was a man, after all. More, he was a Greek man from Greece, where, from what I understood, most didn't indulge in casual sex. Well, at least not men from the small town he was from (lack of opportunity probably played a huge role in that regard). Those who frequented the high tourist areas were a different story. There were even popular songs written about wild sex with visitors.

But somehow I didn't think Dino fit that mold.

In fact, I was pretty sure that there were some places in Greece where having sex essentially meant you were married.

Okay, that was stupid. But probably not all that far from the truth.

And should my family find out . . .

I groaned aloud.

"You keep making those noises, I'm going to ask you to leave," Rosie said.

I made a face at her and fought to concentrate on the matters at hand. Venezuela was back in town, and I was still waiting for Waters to check in. And then there was the ear soup incident I'd promised to check into for Phoebe and the long list of missing pets owners wanted me to find. I stared at the stack of the latter request sheets, thinking that it couldn't be possible that so many pets were roaming the streets, lost.

At any rate, I had better things to do than to risk being bit. Or sit there waiting for a train to hit me.

The bell over the door rang and I automatically looked to see who had come in. To my surprise, my cousin Pete stood just inside, dressed nicely, his chin tucked into his chest.

"If that offer of a job still stands, Sofie," he said, "I'd like to take you up on it."

"You can't be serious?" Rosie mouthed to me from where he couldn't see.

I got up. "Of course it still stands," I told him and smiled first at Rosie then at my younger cousin. "Come on in . . ."

I FIGURED BETWEEN THE TIME Venezuela's goon had approached me at Shea until now that I'd been forgotten about, but I quickly discovered I'd been wrong. After waiting an hour up the street from the McMansion for Reni to leave, the yellow Hummer limo finally drove in to pick him up.

And I had to back off because the same goon had gotten out of the back and was walking in my direction.

Crap.

I put Lucille in reverse, backed into the nearest side street, and then hightailed it out of there.

"I need your car," I told Rosie ten minutes later, back at the agency.

"No way. I'm on baby alert."

"You can use my car."

"Your car is in worse condition than mine is."

"That's a physical impossibility." I waggled my fingers palm up. "Give me the keys."

Reluctantly she opened her desk drawer and took her keys from her purse. There was a ceramic charm of a garlic bulb on the key ring.

She made a sound of disapproval. I thought it was for me, but when I looked at her she was watching my cousin Pete working . . . at painting the office.

I didn't know what Rosie had expected. For me to give him a cheating spouse case, maybe? Or perhaps I should have sent him out on one of the countless missing pet cases that we were turning up left and right. But the truth was—call me stupid— I didn't trust the kid. It might have something to do with the hundred and twenty missing from my own purse.

At any rate, I told him I'd pay him fifteen bucks an hour to paint the office and see to some other small tasks. He'd *tsk*ed loudly at me, apparently expecting the same thing Rosie had.

"You do a good job, and I'll give you something else," I told him, still leaving a wide margin for definition.

Then he'd grinned, probably thinking he could milk the job for all it was worth. Only he forgot that Rosie would be supervising. And Rosie had her own ax to grind with my uncle's no-good-but-hopefully-with-potential son. Which meant that he was working his ass off.

"Wait!" Rosie said. "You didn't give me your keys."

"Oh." I handed them to her.

"And no dogs."

"Then you'll have to babysit him here."

"Better he should be here than my car."

I went out, let Muffy out of my car and led him inside the agency and he immediately ran, barking, toward Pete, where he was on a ladder cutting the corners with a brush. Muffy grabbed a hold of the hem of his white jumpsuit.

"Jesus Christ, get this effin' mutt off me!"

Okay, so I got a little bit of enjoyment out of the display. It was said that an animal could sense the true nature of a man with merely a sniff. And in Pete's case, Muffy was peg on.

Of course, I was leaving out that Muffy used to chase and bite me on a regular basis. But since we were getting along so well now, part of me wondered if the late Mrs. K hadn't trained him to bite me.

I put a growling, body-shuddering Muffy into Uncle Spyros' office and closed the door, listening as he jumped against it several times, his claws running down the wood. Well, it looked like no one would be going in there anytime soon. Especially not Pete. Hmm . . . I wondered why I hadn't considered doing something like that sooner.

"How long you gonna be gone?" Rosie asked.

"I dunno. If anything comes up, give me a call."

I only hoped that Venezuela hadn't gotten too big of a jump on me. . . .

Sixteen

I'D LOST VENEZUELA. BY THE time I drove Rosie's beat-up old Trans Am to the McMansion, the Hummer was long gone and so was he.

If it were true that when things went bad, they turned really bad, then maybe I should brace myself for the worst to come.

I returned to the office, exchanged cars and rescued Muffy from Spyros' office, and then left again, the paint fumes and Rosie's complaining about them too much to bear. She'd propped open the front door and had a fan blowing. I'd have told her to go home, but she needed to stay to watch Pete. And since I wasn't going to do that . . .

Instead I sat in my car with Muffy and referred to my notes, considering the list of other leads I wanted to follow up on. From dropping in on Reni's hairdresser to see if he would spill some sort of case-solving revelation while pumping up my highlights, to seeing if his expensive tailor might be willing to answer a question or two, my gaze was repeatedly drawn to the number Gisela had given me for the former head of Reni's security detail. Out of the three options, it emerged the path of least resistance if only because disgruntled ex-employees tended to be a little more cooperative than those whose loose lips might sink the Reni money ship.

So I called the number and instantly got an address for a guy named Jesus Gonzales. A short time later I found him on the street in front of an apartment complex in Woodhaven, his head stuck under the hood of an old Camaro. The site of snug jeans on a great male behind reminded me a little too much of Jake Porter for comfort, especially since I'd yet to return Dino's calls.

But as Jesus stood upright, wiping his hands down the front of his T-shirt, any resemblance vanished, along with my thoughts on the two men in my life. Or, rather, the one man who had effortlessly snuck into my life and the other that I had wanted in my life for so long I couldn't remember what it felt like not to want him there.

I was careful to keep Muffy inside as I climbed from the car and closed the door.

"Jesus Gonzales?" I asked, approaching him from across the street.

"Who wants to know?"

"Pamela Coe." At this point it was better to maintain my fake persona than deviate from it. Besides, how was I to know Reni wouldn't change his mind tomorrow and rehire Jesus? I didn't need him sharing our coming conversation with the very man I didn't want to know my real identity.

Of course, that meant that I'd have to come up with a good story to accompany the name. And I didn't think introducing myself as a reporter was going to do it in this case.

I stuck my hip out and struck a pose familiar to ballsy women everywhere. "I heard you used to work for Reni Venezuela."

He grinned as he looked me over. "Yeah, I used to work for

him." He made a teeth-sucking sound that made me shudder. "What's it to you?"

Probably Jesus had liked his old job. Probably he had gotten laid more than he regularly did.

Probably I needed to come up with a really good reason for him to stop looking at me like he was measuring me for the backseat of the car he was working on.

"Yeah, well, my old man just got your old job."

Jesus' expression changed. "Yeah?"

"Yeah. And I was wondering, what did you do that got you fired?"

He squared his shoulders. "I didn't get fired. I quit."

"That ain't the way I heard it. I heard you and all the guys that used to work for him got fired."

"Yeah, well, you heard wrong."

"Why would you quit such a cherry job?" I made a point of looking around. "I mean, it don't look like you got a better job or nothing."

"What's it to you?"

Now that seemed to be the question of the hour. I shrugged and smiled as if I had my own personal agenda. An agenda that might be interesting but that I wasn't about to share with him. "That's for me to know and for you to wonder about."

He chuckled at that.

"So . . . what went down? He find out that you were doing his old lady?"

He blinked at me. "Gisela? Oh, hell no. None of us could get within two feet of her." He shook his head. "No. It wasn't nothing like that." He shrugged. "I don't know what happened, really. I was out on the road with him—"

"Pittsburgh?"

His eyes narrowed. "Yeah, Pittsburgh. Who did you say you were again?"

"What happened in Pittsburgh? He ask you to do something freaky?"

"No, man. He didn't ask nothing. He just disappeared without saying nothing, and then popped up again from out of nowhere acting like a real asshole. I mean, he could be temperamental sometimes, but that day he was an out-and-out bastard. And then he fired us. Right there on the spot. Didn't even wait until we got home."

"Just like that?"

"Just like that."

"You didn't do nothing? Didn't say nothing? He just up and fired you?"

"Yeah. Really sucks because the job paid real good, you know? Probably I ain't going to find nothing that pays me half of what I was making working for him." He looked me over again. "Your old man know you're sneaking around asking people questions?"

"My old man's never home since he started working for Venezuela."

His grin made a comeback. "That means you're probably feeling like you might need a little attention then, right?" He sauntered toward me in that urban, hip-hop way that was a half-walk, half-dance step. "You looking for a little something to make you feel good about yourself? A little Latin love to make you feel like a lady again?"

I managed a smile instead of a grimace and backed up toward my car. I figured if things got too sticky, I could just let Muffy out to have his way with the amorous Jesus. "What, you crazy? If my old man even finds out I was talking to you, we'd both be dead meat."

"Yeah, well, what he don't know, won't hurt him."

"Thanks," I said. "But no thanks."

I got into my Mustang, started her up, then rolled the window far enough down for me to say something, but not far enough for Muffy to jump out.

"Hey, man, good luck finding a new job."

And then I pulled from the curb, watching in the rearview mirror as he stood in the middle of the street staring after my car.

Better I should have gone back to the agency to watch the paint dry.

SINCE RETURNING TO THE OFFICE while Pete was still painting wasn't an option, I decided my grandpa Kosmos' Cosmopolitan Café on Broadway would be just the place to have a nice, cold frappé and give me some space to go over my notes. On my way there from Woodhaven, Waters called to say he wanted to see me. I told him to meet me there.

"No dogs," my grandfather said as soon as Muffy and I entered the café.

I kissed him on both cheeks. "He's my seeing-eye dog."

I'd put Muffy's leash on and he was too busy biting it to think about biting anyone else.

"You don't need no seeing-eye dog," Grandpa Kosmos told me.

"Depends on what you're looking for." I called out for Ingrid to get me a frappé then walked to the far end of the counter, by-passing the tables in favor of one of the tall stools. I tied Muffy's leash off on the bottom then climbed up, watching as a couple sitting three stools up moved farther down. I smiled my apology.

The usual cast of characters was in the place. The same people I served coffee to myself not too long ago. Three tables in the back were essentially reserved for them, even though I don't think they ever vacated them long enough for anyone else to even think about sitting there. Most of the men were my grandfather's age, with graying or full out white hair, and pouches of varying sizes around their middles. They called out a hello and I waved, trading barbs with some of them.

"How's the new case going?" my grandfather asked, coming to stand next to me.

"It's going," I said with a frown.

I'd taken my notes out and spread them on the counter in front of me. Not that it made much difference. I didn't expect anything to jump out at me. Aside from a couple of absences and staff changes, and the indiscretion tripled in Miami, there wasn't anything there to jump out at me. Jesus hadn't even told me anything I didn't already know.

"Hey, Pappou," I said. "What do you know about game-fixing?"

I'd jotted down the thought while waiting for Venezuela outside the stadium one night last week. While he hadn't lost any games, who was to say he wasn't setting up an opportunity to throw a major game down the road? Say, for the pennant?

"What do you want to know about it?"

"That means you know something?"

He chuckled at me, then called out to his friends in the back. "Sofie's asking if we know anything about game-fixing."

Much guffawing ensued.

I took a moment to look at the bunch more closely.

It wasn't long ago that the Mafia to me was nothing more than a bunch of names in the newspaper and something to be featured in movies, usually B movies that relied on clichés and offered little by way of originality. Aside from *The Sopranos*. I liked *The Sopranos*.

At any rate, last month I'd gotten a firsthand view of the reasons why there were so many Mafia clichés. Namely because a lot of them were painfully true.

I remember asking Rokkos, a Greek-American, why he aspired to be a part of the Italian Cosa Nostra, you know, before I shot him. He hadn't answered me.

Now it was in this new light that I viewed my grandfather and his friends.

I don't know. Perhaps it had something to do with the fact that my grandfather had always seemed old to me. Gray, jovial, full of piss and vinegar and grandfatherly advice that included "learn how to laugh at the rain." And as his devoted granddaughter—I'd always thought myself more like him than anyone else in my family—I'd never looked beyond that. You know, to maybe see him as a person. As a man who had once been my age and had maybe done a few things that might not have been on the up and up.

And his friends . . .

It never occurred to me that Takis, Frixos, Andreas, and Christos were anything other than Grandpa Kosmos' retired friends.

And right now, with everything else going on in my life, I could have done without the reminder.

I held up my hand to ward off further discussion. "Never mind. I don't want to know."

The door opened and the place fell silent. I looked up from my notes to find it was because Eugene Waters had just walked in looking like a pimp in training.

I suppressed a chuckle.

"Hey," I said as he took the stool next to me after letting Muffy smell the back of his hand. While the two of them hadn't gotten along in the beginning, they'd long since settled into a "don't try anything with me, I won't try anything with you," type of relationship that didn't include biting.

"Hey, yourself." He folded his hands on top of the counter

and leaned closer to me. "What's with the silence? They expecting me to rob them or something?"

"Something. It doesn't help that you look like you just got done slapping one of your hos."

He grabbed his lapels and straightened his custard-colored leather jacket. In the month since I'd hired him, his hair had grown out a bit and he sported a neat two-inch Afro. "You like it? I picked it up in Miami."

"I hope you don't expect those receipts to be a part of your travel expenses."

"Hey, a guy's gotta do what a guy's gotta do."

"Then it'll come out of your paycheck."

He grimaced and then stuck his hand inside his jacket to slide out a large envelope. "How come you're not tailing Venezuela?" he asked.

"Never mind," I said for the second time in as many minutes.

I didn't want to admit that I was forced to abandon my tail because I'd been spotted . . . again.

At any rate, he had an appearance in a couple of hours at the Queens Center mall. I figured I'd catch up with him again there.

"These the pics?"

"Uh-huh." He grinned.

I pinched the metal fasteners and then opened the flap, sliding the eight-by-ten shots out onto the counter. The first few shots weren't anything special. Reni in the hotel bar talking to the women. Could easily be explained away as autograph hunters. The next was of Reni going back to his room—alone—and then the women going into the same room. There was no time stamp on any of them.

"These don't do me any good at all," I said, sighing. "Did I send you down there for nothing?"

Waters motioned for me to continue looking.

I slid the useless shots under the others and had to think quickly in order to keep my eyeballs from rolling out of my sockets and bouncing off the counter to where Muffy might bat them around a bit. There in living color was Reni in all his naked glory, somehow managing to service three women at once.

I rapidly sifted through the remainder of the shots, all showing one very married celebrity pitcher engaging in sex acts of all types. I made it through all of the shots once, then went through them again, slower this time, turning one to the side to verify that I was seeing what I thought I was.

I must have made a strangled sound, because even Muffy had stopped fighting his leash long enough to cock his head at me.

"Good, huh?" Waters waggled his brows at me.

I cleared my throat and stuffed the shots back into the envelope, folding my hands on top of it. "I don't even want to know how you got these."

"One of the maids let me into Venezuela's room right after he left for batting practice the first night and I planted cameras all over. In the lamp, a picture frame, the fire alarm."

"Where did you get that kind of equipment?"

"Rosie put me onto it." He shrugged, looking pleased with himself. As well he should, because he'd just delivered jackpot material. "And then I went to some friends who said they could get me like items at a discounted price. If you know what I mean."

I had an inkling (Was he telling me he'd had someone steal the equipment for him? Enjoyed a five-finger discount?), but decided it prudent not to pursue it.

"So did I deliver or did I deliver, man?"

"Oh, you most definitely delivered." The problem was, who

was going to deliver the pictures to Gisela? Even though I'd been the one to accept the case, I wasn't too keen on the idea of showing her such condemning evidence.

"Good job, Waters," I said. "You're permanently upgraded to full agent."

He grinned so wide his gold teeth flashed at me. "Cool."

"By the way, you wouldn't happen to still have that equipment . . . ?"

"HOLY SHIT. CAN YOU DO that?" Rosie asked back at the office when I showed her the pictures. She held one to the side as I'd done at my grandpa Kosmos' café. "Limber guy, I'll give him that."

I took the photos from her, a little disappointed. I don't know, since she was such a big fan of the successful closing pitcher, I'd expected a more outraged reaction. Instead, she didn't look any more put out than if she'd just thumbed through a girly mag and seen exactly what she'd anticipated.

"Boy, am I glad I'm not the one who has to show Gisela these," she said.

"That's all? You're not going to say anything else?"

She popped her gum. "Like what?"

"I don't know. Like what a no-good lying cheating pig he is?"

"He's a man. Goes with the territory." She shrugged and then turned back to her computer. "By the way, something popped up on that couple in the restaurant case."

I stepped to look over her shoulder. "What?"

"Nothing much. Just that they've moved a lot over the past year. See this," she pointed to a spot on the flat monitor with a long black-painted fingernail, "they're originally from Omaha. Then they moved to Kansas City. And here, a gas bill came up on them from Memphis. The last city was Philadelphia, where I guess they left for here."

"How can you tell?"

"Because the cell phone bill was issued to them from there a month and a half ago."

"Oh." I stood up. "Sounds like a grifter's life for them," I said aloud.

"My thoughts exactly. I mean, you don't move around like that unless you're up to no good."

"Or unless you're a vacuum cleaner salesman."

Rosie gave me an eye roll. "They don't do that no more."

"Says you. One came by my place last week. And I think Mrs. Nebitz invited him in for rugelach."

"If these guys were selling vacuum cleaners, something would have come up on MAFUC."

"MAFUC? Is that a resource database?"

"No, it's my name for this." She caressed the side of the monitor. "My awesome fucking computer."

I threw back my head and laughed.

"I told you I could do great things with a great computer. And I'm just scratching the surface. I used this one program to enter in all the missing pet owners' addresses earlier today. And look at this."

"I don't want to see it." I walked back to my desk. "Is that what you're wasting your time doing? What about the digging I asked you to do on Venezuela when he was in Venezuela?"

"It only took me something like five minutes. And at this point I figured that even you've got to be wondering why we've been getting so many requests to find missing pets lately."

"I thought word was out on what a good job I was doing finding them."

Rosie stared at Muffy. "Uh-huh." She popped her gum again and he growled at her.

"Anyway, I thought it was interesting that all the reports spiral outward for a ten-block area."

"You can really do that?" Despite my better judgment, I found myself walking back to her computer where she pointed again. "Yep. And the best I can figure it is that this is ground zero."

Seventeen

QUEENS CENTER. THE MALL SEEMED to be a rite of passage for most teens. Many of my friends' first jobs had been at a clothing store in the mall at the Gap or Banana Republic. But not mine. By fourteen I was working a few hours a week at my father's restaurant, and over the course of the next ten years I'd worked either there or at my grandfather's café, the exceptions being the brief stint at my aunt Sotiria's funeral home, and odd jobs I'd done for my uncle Spyros that were temporary in nature and had been literally odd at times.

Speaking of temporary, I hiked my pants leg up to get a look at my tattoo. It had begun to fade, but was still there. Dino hadn't even appeared to notice it during our impromptu sack session. Then again, I don't think either one of us had noticed a whole lot about each other that didn't have to do with hot, urgent sex.

I straightened my pants leg.

At any rate, while Queens Center hadn't been my regular hangout, I knew enough about it to find my way around. And right now I stood in the Time Warner Cable Living Room on level two in the JC Penney's wing where there was a Mets player meet 'n' greet. The longest line belonged to, who else, but Reni Venezuela, whose first Mets Topps card was being launched. It looked like everyone and their brother's kid had shown up for the event to get their new cards signed, and I had the cramp in my leg to prove it. I'd been standing in line for over an hour to "meet 'n' greet" the handsome new pitcher that looked like he was thoroughly enjoying the attention.

Me? I was having a hard time banishing the memory of the Miami pictures. Hey, that type of full-color, documented activity tended to have that effect on a girl.

Finally, I was four people away from Reni.

A kid of about ten tried to elbow in front of me in line.

"Hey, the line is back there," I said.

The boy glowered at me and I ignored the stab of guilt at my response. After all, he was just a kid. How could he know I had a leg cramp?

"What?" I asked, unable to help myself. "You think because you're a kid, you get a break? Think again."

"Come on, lady, Reni's my all-time favorite pitcher."

"Sure he is," I said, feeling uncomfortably similar to the way I had when I'd gotten booted out of Shea Stadium after flinging profanity at the ump. I eyed the stack of cards he held. "Probably you're just going to sell the stuff on eBay anyway."

"Look, my son's lived and breathed the Mets since the day he was born." His mother stood behind him and I gathered by the way she was holding his shoulders that she had probably been the one who'd tried to edge him in front of me. Probably she had a leg cramp, too.

"Yes, well, maybe you'd have been better off teaching him some manners instead. And not to think that just because he's a kid that he's entitled to special treatment."

The spot opened up in front of me, putting nothing but air

between me and Reni. I stepped forward only to have the ten-year-old jockey for and win the spot. I glared at the back of his head, whispering that somewhere down the line he was going to remember this moment and regret that he hadn't been polite.

"Reni! I'm your number-one fan. Sign my card for me?"

I watched as the ambidextrous closing pitcher signed. When the ten-year-old tried to hand him another card from his stack, a guy who had been standing off to the side stepped forward. "Sorry, kid, only one item per fan. There's a line behind you that stretches a mile."

"Pig," the kid said.

He stalked away from the table. I shook my head.

"Yeah, right. Big fan," I said.

Finally I stood in front of the table. I held up the Gridworks New York Mets Cooperstown bat I'd bought from the official team souvenir shop a couple of days ago. It had set me back more than I thought it would, but I figured it was worth it. In my case, it served double-duty: as a memento of my favorite team's winning season and of working a case that went beyond cheating spouses and missing pets.

I held up the bat. "Sign this for my sick nephew, please? He's a huge fan."

"What's your nephew's name?" he asked me as he accepted the bat.

He hadn't recognized me. Good. That meant that his security team probably hadn't told him about me yet. Either that or with my ball cap hiding my hair, big sunglasses despite the fact that it was dim in the mall and that they practically made me blind as a bat, and a swipe of bright red lipstick, maybe he didn't know me.

"Sofie," I said.

He chuckled and signed the bat with a flourish. I surreptitiously watched the action, tipping my sunglasses up so I could get a good look at the scorpion tattoo on his right arm.

"Here," he said, handing the bat back.

"Thanks, Reni. Keep up the great work."

I was instantly moved out of the way of the next person—who, I found, was the mother of the kid who'd cut in front of me. Probably she had taken his cards to get them signed for him. I continued on for fear that I might attract the attention of his security detail that hung out on the edges of the event.

"Nice disguise," I heard from behind me as I walked toward the mall stairs.

I spun around, half-expecting to find one or more of Reni's goons on my tail.

Instead, my fear exited on a loud sigh. "Fowler."

He grinned at me. "Miss me?"

"Bunches."

"I bet."

I continued walking and he drew even with me. "So did you get anything interesting out of the agent?"

"I don't know," I said. "Did anything interesting happen down in Miami?"

"Hey, Metro, you owe me. I saved your bacon with Aikman."

"Yeah, thanks for that."

"So give it up."

"Give what up?"

"What do you got?"

"Aside from photos of Reni screwing three groupies . . . nothing."

He made a sound of disgust. "That's it? Shit, I could have told you that."

I stared at him. "What happened to holding these guys up as hometown heroes? Role models for the children?"

"Hey, it's understood that what the people don't know, won't hurt them. Besides, everyone with half a brain knows that kind of crap's been going on since the advent of the Olympics, for God's sake. Did you know that they still bus in prostitutes from other countries for the modern games?"

I stopped myself from putting my hands to my ears and humming so I wouldn't have to hear him, but just barely.

"What else you got?" he asked.

I shrugged as I reached a crossroads and slapped the bat into my opposite hand. "That's it. How about you?"

His grimace told me he had the same. "But I know something's going on here. I can sense it."

"Is that part of being a reporter? Working on hunches?"

His gaze met mine. "Yeah. Isn't it part of a PI's job, too?"

Yes, I supposed it was.

He walked back toward the event. "Give me a call if you come up with anything."

I gave his back an eye roll. "Yeah. And you do the same."

"AND VENEZUELA HAS STRUCK OUT another batter! East Division National League Championship play-offs, here we come. . . ."

It was the top of the seventh inning—now the bottom—and the Mets were leading 2–0. Part of me was excited that my team was winning. Another part kept remembering the photos I had tucked into my purse.

I switched off the radio in my father's car, and then glanced at Muffy in the passenger's seat, where he looked out the window toward the McMansion then back at me.

"Too bad you can't take these in to her," I said.

I figured that the best time to approach Gisela was while Reni was playing. But since she'd flipped out the last time I'd gone to the house, I'd contacted her cell, instead, asking her to meet me. I watched now as she left the house and got into a silver Caddy. That was good. What wasn't good was the black Mercedes that tailed her.

Nuts.

The best I could hope for was that the goon would think her out on the emergency cosmetics run we'd come up with.

I started my father's fifteen-year-old navy blue Caprice and turned off the street the block before the house, heading for the Eckerd on Broadway at Thirty-sixth. Somehow I got there before Gisela did, searched for and found a place to park, and ducked inside, the same disguise I'd used at the Queens Center of Mets ball cap and sunglasses as I hung out in the cosmetics section. I picked up a box of those nose strips and pretended to read the back. Moments later, Gisela sidled up next to me.

"What's up?" she asked, not even giving me a second look as she fingered through mascara.

I took the envelope out of my purse and slid it to her.

The request for a public meeting place served two purposes: First, it would help us stay under the radar of Reni's security team; second, when Gisela saw the pictures, hopefully she wouldn't completely flip out and take her anger out on me.

I realized the idiotic nature of my reasoning. Not a day went by when I didn't see some sort of public verbal confrontation on the streets of New York. The kiosk guy had shortchanged a businessman. A car had bumped into another while parking.

A man had gotten caught two-timing his girlfriend/wife/fiancée.

I cringed and waited for Gisela's outburst.

Instead I felt the envelope prick my side. I took it back, looking into her face. While some of the color was drained from it, she didn't appear about to burst any blood vessels or anything, much less erupt into scorned woman revisited in the middle of Eckerd.

"Is this what you've been wasting your time on?" she asked between clenched teeth.

I blinked at her.

"I told you I didn't want you to see if he was cheating."

"Because you told me he wasn't."

"I told you he wasn't having an affair. What's in that envelope is not an affair. It's fucking. There's a difference."

I wasn't sure how to take her words.

"Look, you don't know what it's like to be the wife of a celebrity. Rap star, movie star, sports star, it don't matter. There are groupies everywhere. A girl's gotta accept that there's going to be some messing around." While her words said one thing, her deep swallow told me that it still hadn't been easy to actually see it. "So long as he keeps coming home to me and the kids, that's all that matters."

"Are you serious?"

"He only does it on the road. And not all the time. I already know about it. I don't like it, but I accept it's part of the game. Ego, celebrity, sex. It all goes hand in hand."

"Sounds like bad advice from a male psychologist."

She glared at me. "Do what I paid you for."

She swiveled on her heels without making a purchase and steamed through the doors, leaving me staring after her.

Okay, so this was a new one to me. I moved to the checkout counter with the box I held. I understood that in about half the cheating spouse cases I worked on, the couple worked things out. Meaning that the victimized spouse found a way to forgive if not forget so that they could move on as a couple or a family.

Fine.

But when so much money was involved in the Venezuela's case, Gisela could take him for oodles and live quite comfortably without the skirt-chasing husband.

So why, then, put up with a guy who screwed three strange

women on the road, then came home and said, "Hi, honey, I'm home"?

The cashier named an amount that made me look twice. "Pardon me?"

She repeated the amount.

"Are you kidding me? You want that much for that stuff? Keep it."

Then I followed Gisela's lead and left the store empty-handed. And as I did so, I realized that no two women were alike. While I had kneed my groom in the gonads on the day of our wedding because he'd been shtupping my maid of honor, someone like Gisela might coldly tell him to zip up his pants and wipe the lipstick off his mouth, and advise the woman to get lost, then go ahead and marry the slime anyway.

So where did that leave us? Was I right? Or just hardheaded? Or was Gisela right and allowing her husband some liberties was the only way she knew how to make her marriage and family work?

Over the course of the past six months I'd come to realize that there were just some mysteries—mostly of the human variety—that were too complicated to solve. And this was proving one of them.

TWO MORE CALLS FROM DINO. I sat outside the McMansion in my father's Caprice later that night after having followed Reni home from Shea, and scrolled through the missed calls on my cell. I clicked to retrieve voicemail messages against my better judgment. My thumb hesitated over the call button.

Okay, so I was a coward. I wasn't sure I wanted to hear what Dino had to say. What had happened between us the other morning was a momentary blip on the radar, an aberration of time and space, something better ignored.

But even as I recognized this with my head, my gut was telling me I at least owed the guy an explanation.

I pressed the button then closed my eyes as I listened to the messages.

"Hi, Sofie, it's Dino," his sexy, heavily accented voice tickled my ear. "I just wanted to tell you that I . . . really enjoyed this morning. Call me."

I could sense his smile as he'd said "really enjoyed" and I couldn't resist an answering smile of my own.

The next message came this morning. "Hi, Sofie. Okay, so right now you're probably wondering what happened yesterday. So am I. Despite evidence to the contrary, I don't make a habit out of ravishing women in their apartments first thing on a Sunday morning. And your silence tells me that you're not used to being ravished. What I'm trying to say is . . . Oh, hell. I don't know what I'm trying to say. Call me."

It was a surprise to hear that he was going through exactly what I had over the past day and a half. I'm not sure what I expected, if, indeed, I had expected anything. I'd been too wrapped up in my own thoughts and fears to give his feelings any real consideration.

His third message, left about three hours ago, summed up everything. "Okay, I've decided that maybe what happened wasn't the best idea. Not that it wasn't good . . . it, it was great. But I realize that we skipped a couple of important steps. So my proposal is this: don't call me. At least not until a week or so has passed. Then I'll call you and ask you out on a date. A real date. No sneaking around to meet at remote coffee shops. And your place and my place are out of the question because . . . Well, I think we should keep things public for the time being. So expect to hear from me sometime next week."

For long moments I sat there considering what he'd said. Don't call him? Did he really just order me not to call him? I glanced at the dash clock. After eleven. I pressed the button to call him.

"*Nai?*" a groggy male voice answered in Greek.

"Dino?"

Some rustling I guessed were his sheets as he sat up. "Sofie? Sofie, is that you?"

"Yeah, it's me."

More rustling. "Do you know what time it is?"

Why did people always ask that question? Of course I knew what time it was. "I just got your messages."

Silence.

"Look, Dino, the other day was . . . nice and all." Major understatement. "But I don't think I'm ready for this . . . ready for you right now."

"That's why I suggested we wait until next week to talk."

"Now, next week, what does it matter? The truth is that I came this close to getting married six months ago. And the 'm' word is so not on my wish list and I'm not sure I want it to be."

"Sofie, we had sex. I didn't propose."

I felt my face flush. "Yes, well, for a lot of Greeks that can mean the same thing."

"Who are these Greeks? I'd like to meet them, because I certainly don't know any."

I smiled and then tucked my chin into my chest.

"Call me next week, Sofie," he said quietly. "Now if you don't mind, I really need to get back to sleep. I've got to get up in four hours."

Four hours? Did he really get up at 3:00 A.M.? I shuddered. Few were the nights when I actually got to bed by then.

Just another example of why we were a bad match. Well, a bad match outside the bedroom.

Inside the bedroom was another matter altogether.

"Say good night, Sofie."

"Good night, Sofie," I murmured, doing a bad Gracie Allen impression.

I heard him ring off and then sat for long moments staring outside the car. I realized that the cell phone had illuminated me while I talked to Dino and had caught the attention of one of Venezuela's goons.

Great.

I shut the cell then started my father's car and backed up to the closest cross street, roaring away in the opposite direction.

If only the desire to point the car in Dino's direction wasn't looming large in my mind. He was, after all, only a few blocks away. . . .

Eighteen

I DROVE TO THE AGENCY the next day expecting the same old, same old. What I got instead was completely new.

I opened the door and walked into not the smell of old, musty office, but of fresh paint and cleaning products. I blinked, taking in the muted beige walls and white ceiling, the tile beneath my feet gleaming dark green and beige.

"Where did you get the tile? And when the hell did you lay it?" I asked Rosie.

She turned from her computer with coffee cup in hand, sticking her gum on the rim before taking a long sip. "I didn't get it anywhere. It was already there. I just had Pete clean it."

"Pete did this?"

"Uh-huh. Looks like a whole 'nother place, doesn't it?"

"I'll say."

The brighter colors made the office look at least 25 percent larger. And brought into stark relief the wall of dented gray filing cabinets that lined the one wall, and the old metal desks that both Rosie and I had.

"I'm thinking about bringing in a couple of plants from home," Rosie said. "Ferns, maybe."

"You have plants?" I couldn't keep even a cactus to save my life. My grandpa Kosmos said I didn't have a black thumb but was the kiss of death, period, when it came to vegetation of any sort.

"Of course, I have plants. It's a hobby with me."

"You really need to get a life." I sat down heavily in my chair.

"I got a life. I have a boyfriend, go out, and then there's that thing with my sister."

That thing with her sister. I found it interesting that it wasn't all that long ago when the topic dominated any conversation we had. But now that Lupe was due any minute, Rosie had gone silent. Well, okay, I didn't think it was possible for Rosie to actually go silent on any subject, but she didn't rattle on about it anymore.

Probably she and her sister had already done all the shopping and planning and talking to last for three babies.

Or maybe she was worried.

"You have a boyfriend?" I asked. "You never said."

"You don't have to know everything."

Yeah, but I at least found it funny that I'd never heard her mention him before. Rosie mentioned everything.

"What's his name? Do I know him?"

"I'm not going to tell you his name. And I don't know that you know him. At least not know him, know him."

I scratched my head, deciding that I hadn't had enough caffeine yet to interpret Rosie speak. I moved to the small refrigerator off to the side of the cabinets and went about making my usual frappé, the second of the morning.

"How do you mean I don't know him, know him? Like in I know who he is but I haven't really spoken to him?"

Rosie popped her gum back into her mouth then made a zipping motion across her lips. "I'm not saying nothin'. You know, on account of it might jinx me or something." She took in my glower. "Hey, it happens. You know, the minute you think it's safe to share the news of your dating, everything falls apart and then you're left answering questions like, 'how's that guy?' and you have to explain how you're not a couple anymore, and that's more irritating than the fact that you broke up because you opened the relationship before it was ready."

I spooned in a double heaping of Nescafé at this punctuation challenged monologue.

Definitely too early for this conversation.

"Fine. Keep it to yourself, then." I took my coffee back to my desk, trying not to draw parallels between what was happening between Rosie and her love interest and me and Dino.

What? There were no parallels. Dino and I had indulged in a one-morning stand. Nothing more. Nothing less.

Obviously Rosie had been seeing this guy for longer than that.

I stared at her.

I hoped.

"You know, I'm going to have to ask Spyros for a raise next time he calls," she said, typing away.

"I thought you asked him the last time he called."

"I did and he told me no because I got one six months ago." She motioned toward the computer like a game show model. "But with this new computer I'm doing at least twice the stuff I used to before. I deserve at least double my pay, is how I see it."

"Double? Good luck."

I pulled the Phoebe Hall file in front of me and sat back with my feet on my crowded desk. Actually, considering my expanded role at the agency, maybe I should ask for a raise, as well. Well, maybe not so much a raise, because Spyros had granted my request to work on commission. But maybe a piece of the action wasn't such a bad idea. Why should the agency reap all the rewards? I could use the extra money to get Lucille fixed up before winter descended. At least make sure she was in good running order so I wouldn't have to worry about her stalling out on me. And that her heater worked so I wouldn't freeze. Oh, and it would probably be a good idea for me to have that leak looked at.

Where was Jake Porter when you needed him?

I choked on my frappé at the unbidden thought.

And, there you had it. The true reason why I was avoiding Dino, last night's phone call aside. The true reason I was avoiding any sort of honest assessment of what had happened between us.

Could it possibly be that all the pent-up emotion I had for the mysterious bounty hunter had been projected onto Dino?

I put my travel cup down on my desk. "By the way, has anything come up yet on that bounty hunter guy?"

Rosie didn't say anything for a long moment, almost like she hadn't heard me, but I knew she had. First, because she heard everything. Second, because her gum chewing had slowed.

"That bounty hunter guy?" she asked with a raised brow. "Like that's all he is to you. Some guy who happens to be— maybe or maybe not—a bounty hunter."

"Just answer the question, Rosie."

"No."

"See, was that so difficult?"

"Not for me. But I'm thinking it is for you."

"Shut up."

"I didn't say nothin'."

The office went silent as I put aside the Hall file and then pulled a fresh pad in front of me and started making a list. Surveillance equipment topped the list, along with travel allowances. I swear, with the high price of gas, and the amount Lucille was chugging down, my entire paycheck would go for that. Well, okay, maybe not the entire check, but a good chunk of it. I should look into expensing the cost to the agency.

I made out a note to Nash, the silent silent partner, and then walked it into his office and put it in the middle of his empty desk. I didn't know when he'd be in again since he didn't keep any kind of regular schedule, but I wanted him to see my note first thing when he did make it in.

"What are you doing now?" Rosie asked without looking away from what she was doing.

"Asking for your raise."

Her fingers paused. "Did not."

"Okay, no, I didn't. That you'll have to bring up to Uncle Spyros."

"So what did you ask for?"

"Tell me the name of the guy you're dating."

"I don't want to know that bad. I figure I'll find out what you're up to soon enough anyway."

Yeah, probably when she went to read my note when I wasn't looking.

I sorted through the piles on my desk. The highest by far was the one holding the missing pet request forms. I picked them up and dropped them into the garbage can.

"Hey, you can't do that."

"You have duplicates."

"That's beside the point."

"I have no intention of working on them."

"Then put Pete on them."

I stared at her.

"What? You told him once he finished fixing up the place, you'd give him something else."

"Yeah, like errand-running."

"He even fixed the bathroom mirror."

I stepped into the closet between Nash and Spyros' offices and flicked on the light. Sure enough, the mirror had been fixed. Not only that, but he'd calked the bottom of the commode and the back of the sink and had cleaned the place up.

Who knew Pete was such a neatnik? Certainly not me.

Or perhaps he had a better work ethic than I'd given him credit for. Not only had he surpassed my idea of a good job, nothing had come up missing in the office or my purse. And he hadn't gone into his father's office once.

I sighed as I switched the bathroom light off. I was going to have to throw something his way for all this. Of course, I suspected that if Rosie hadn't been hovering over him, keeping him honest, he probably would have dragged his jobs out for at least a week.

But since he hadn't . . .

The door opened to let someone in.

Speak of the devil.

"Hey, Pete," Rosie said without looking up.

"Hi, Rosie." He tilted his head in my direction, looking a little wary. "Sofie."

"Morning," I said as I retook my seat at my desk. "Good job with the office."

"Thanks."

He was standing before my desk now, his hands folded behind his back. I expected him to ask me for a check for his time. Instead, he asked what else I wanted him to do.

I looked down at the missing pet cases I had dumped into the garbage can. But despite everything he had done over the past six months, I couldn't bring myself to give him those. Besides, the earnest expression on his face told me that he might be genuinely interested in working.

So I handed him the three cheating spouse cases that had come in over the past couple of days. "Here. What you need to do is arrange for a meeting with the clients, preferably at a time when their spouse or significant other isn't around, and get the information you need to start tailing the individual."

"And then?"

"And then . . ." I gestured with my hand. "You follow them. Do you have a camera? No? Then buy one of those disposables. I saw that some of them have zoom lenses now, but only thirty-five percent." I'd looked into that after having handed over the new digital to Debbie. I planned to ask for it back and send her for a disposable. Hopefully she hadn't already broken the digital. "So that means you'll have to get up close enough to get the money shot."

I went on to explain what the money shot was.

"And then?"

"And then you bring everything back here, Rosie or I will take care of the rest, and you're done. Case closed. You go on to the next one."

"That's it?"

I smiled. "That's it."

He had opened the first file and was nodding as he headed toward the door. "Cool."

I was getting a lot of "cools" lately. And I decided I liked it. There were so many things in life that you couldn't control, stop, or otherwise avoid. Difficult items, unexpected turns, and potholes that popped out of nowhere. It was nice when you were able to make the person navigating over and through and around their own problems look a little easier.

Besides, Pete reminded me of myself when I'd walked into the agency half a year ago. I'd asked my uncle Spyros if he needed help and he'd essentially done the same thing to me that I had just done to Pete. The difference lay in that I had ust come off having my own almost-spouse cheat on me and hadn't been looking forward to watching others' spouses cheat.

And then a couple of weeks into the job my uncle had seemed to disappear altogether—going to Greece was close to qualifying as dropping off the face of the earth, or at least off the western hemisphere—leaving me in charge.

Well, okay, Nash was probably in charge, but you know what I mean.

"I hope he doesn't get turned on by watching others do it."

Rosie's words snapped my head in her direction. "Oh, you so did not just say that."

"Oh, yes, I did. Spyros had a guy like that right before you hired on. Swear to God he got run in for public indecency. He *really* enjoyed watching others do it, if you know what I mean."

"Eeew."

"You can say that again." She gave an exaggerated shudder. "The guy gave me the creeps and I swear he hung around outside the agency for a couple weeks after Spyros fired him."

"What happened then?"

She shrugged. "I dunno. I think maybe he found somewhere else to do his pervert stuff."

I couldn't imagine getting off on watching other people have sex. Forget about it being extramarital (I think I've already established my thoughts on that issue). There was something . . . mechanical about the act, somehow, when you were an outsider watching it. I actually found myself trying to give the offending spouse a quiet pep talk.

"Don't do it, buddy . . . it's not too late to turn back. Just turn around and leave . . . that's it. Oh, no. You just had to do it, didn't you? Oh, gross . . ."

Then there were those people like serial cheater Lisa Laturno, who had some sort of sexual addiction and got a rush out of messing around on her husband, who always took her back.

I didn't get it. The reason why people needed to complicate their already complicated lives. But then again, that was me. And right now I didn't consider myself a good authority on much of anything having to do with sex.

My current Dino dilemma exhibit A.

I shook my head, determined to tackle my paperwork.

Nineteen

THERE ARE JUST SOME THINGS I'd prefer never to have to do. Like giving myself a pedicure. Or picking up Muffy's business from the roof. Or taking my paternal grandmother to buy new underwear.

What I was facing now ranked right up there with the worst.

This had to do with my ex-fiancé and his determination to press charges against my elderly grandfather for popping him in the nose—completely justified, if you wanted my opinion. But seeing as the court date was tomorrow, my opinion meant little.

At any rate, there I was again, parked on the street in front of Thomas' parents' apartment building watching the neighbor's curtains flutter. I hadn't run into his parents the last time, but I had the feeling I wasn't going to be so lucky this time out because it was dinnertime. And my suspicions were confirmed when I got out of my car to find Mrs. Chalikis stepping outside the front door, an apron around her expensive suit, her arms crossed over her chest.

I mustered every last wit I possessed and then went to stand in front of her.

"What do you want?" she asked.

Certainly nothing that had anything to do with her. You see, Mrs. Chalikis had thought that since I was the one who called off the wedding, that her son should be entitled to half the value of the wedding gifts. Up to and including the apartment building my parents had given me.

"Excuse me, but I'm here to see Thomas."

"What is it you want to see him about?"

"What, are you his secretary?"

The woman had bothered me to no end from the get-go but I'd always been polite to her, which made my response that much more surprising.

When Thomas had taken me home to dinner for the first time, Athanasia Chalikis sat across the table staring at me as if I didn't have enough dollar signs pinned to the front of my blouse for her taste.

Still, I'd always been taught that two wrongs didn't make a right. Just because she was a monster in an apron didn't mean I was entitled to be.

"Sorry," I mumbled for my slip, then held her gaze. "I have an important matter to discuss with him."

Actually, I had several, but this one would do for now.

"He's not home."

"Oh? Then why is he standing in the front window, waving?"

Thomas-the-Toad wasn't exactly waving at me, but he did appear to be getting a kick out of my standoff with his mother.

Athanasia looked over her shoulder, offered up a curse in Greek that had something to do with a goat doing something to Thomas, and then threw up her hands and walked back inside her apartment. Moments later, Thomas came out looking like he wanted to be anywhere than there. Probably he regret-

ed letting himself be seen. Probably his mother had told him
that since he was stupid enough to let himself be seen, then he
could take care of me.

"Sofie," he said.

"Thomas."

"I guess I don't have to wonder why you're here."

"I guess you don't."

He planted his hands loosely on his slender hips. My gaze
followed the movement, reminding me of how attractive he
was and what had drawn me to him in the first place.

Which just went to show you really couldn't judge a Greek
by his looks.

"I'm not going to drop the charges, Sof. I don't care how old
the guy is, he broke my nose."

"Is that really the reason why you're seeing this through? Or
is it because of the embarrassment of having my grandfather
break your nose in front of so many people?"

"The people I can handle," he said, but I was unconvinced.

He sighed, looked over his shoulder, and then rubbed his
chin. "Look, Sofie, I'm not really interested in going head-to-
head with your grandfather in the courtroom. Truth is, I liked
the old man."

"Hell of a way to show it."

He shook his head. "Probably. But if I don't go through with
this, my parents say they'll cut me off."

I looked to find that Athanasia had traded places with
Thomas and was now watching us through the window. I had
little doubt that she could hear us because I'd watched her open
the sliding window to the right.

I stared at the apron she wore and considered the strings
Thomas was still fully attached to. Strings that she really didn't
want to sever.

I turned my attention back to Thomas. "You know, it might

actually do you some good to get out from under your parents' thumbs."

He looked dubious.

And I couldn't blame him. Hey, I'd lived with my parents until the day of our almost-wedding. Had never even thought about moving out before then.

But considering all the changes my life had undergone since . . . well, in some strange way I wondered if I didn't owe the man in front of me a thank-you.

Maybe that was taking it too far.

Thomas didn't budge.

I cleared my throat. "Okay, then. I think it's only fair to warn you that if you push ahead, then I'll have no choice but to pursue legal action of my own."

He stared at me for a long moment, apparently weighing my words. Then he chuckled.

I took out a folded sheet of paper from my purse. "Remember the engagement ring you gave me? The one my grandpa Kosmos gave to you to give to me? The same one you had reset at Bachman's?"

He stopped laughing.

Good, I had his attention.

"This here's an affidavit from the old man himself stating that you'd had two rings made that day. And that the one you gave to me held a CZ."

He snatched the paper from my hand then looked over his shoulder at his mother. "The old fart doesn't know what he's talking about."

I crossed my arms. "That's your defense? Call me stupid, but I don't think the judge is going to buy it. Not given Bachman's impeccable memory and standing in the community."

"He runs a dive."

"He says that since the diamond you kept was marquise cut and of unusually high quality, you owe me at least twenty grand."

Thomas squinted at me and his mother made a strangled sound in the window. "You wouldn't dare."

"Try me."

He stared at the paper.

"I also think that this evidence goes a long way toward proving my grandfather's motivations."

Athanasia Chalikis had disappeared from the window. Probably she was calling the family attorney now. Probably she wanted to know if I could do what I was threatening.

"I can't drop the charges," Thomas said.

If ever a guy deserved to be popped in the nose . . . "If you're really that much of a coward, then don't show up for the trial tomorrow. Tell your parents you got caught in traffic or something."

The Chalikises would believe that. The running joke was that Thomas would probably be late for his own funeral.

Unfortunately he'd been on time for our wedding.

I snatched the affidavit back. "Have a nice day."

"And if I don't show tomorrow? You won't pursue the, um, ring matter?"

"How about we play this by ear?" I said. "You don't show up tomorrow and we'll talk."

More Greek curse words, this time from Thomas. I smiled as I walked back to my car.

I COULDN'T BE SURE IF my visit to Thomas had done the trick. He might be cocky enough—and his mother vindictive enough—to go ahead with the prosecution and deal with the rest when it happened. After all, they might be waiting for just such an opportunity to get the ball rolling on legally claiming part of my apartment building.

But I was pretty confident I'd gotten my point across.

A few hours later I sat in Shea Stadium Parking Lot B in my brother Kosmos' silver VW Rabbit convertible. I noticed Fowler's beat-up Pontiac a couple of rows over as the last of the fans rolled out, happy with another win. I eyed the blacked-out gate to the players' lot. I craned my neck to get a look past the fans pressing in around the exiting players' cars for autographs, then I got out of the Rabbit altogether. There. There was Reni now. He wasn't in his yellow Hummer limo, but rather was driving the black Mercedes that usually followed him. I got back into the VW, watching as Reni sped by . . . without anyone behind him.

No tail. No security. No goons.

That was odd.

I shifted into first and let up on the clutch, still not used to driving the VW stick shift as I *putt-putt*ed after the Mercedes. Seeing as no one else was with him, I'd have to be extra careful he didn't spot me. I searched for the windshield wiper button and ended up flashing my bright lights and squirting washer fluid before finally locating it. The wipers worked a million miles a minute, squeaking against the windshield until I could figure out how to slow them.

I followed the taillights of the Mercedes into the soggy night, squashing the urge to speed up as it turned right onto Casey Stengel Drive and then merged onto Roosevelt where he took a quick left, probably testing to see if there were any cars tailing him. Cute. I thought ahead and when he turned right at the next stop sign, I kept going straight, moving up to turn at the next street. Sure enough, at the next stop sign I found the Mercedes turning left, ending up passing in front of me.

We continued on with the zigzag game of tag toward Corona for a few more minutes before I lost him.

Great.

There was nothing more dangerous than thinking you had the jump on someone.

I backtracked and found that I hadn't lost him. Rather, Reni had parked. The Mercedes' headlights were still burning as I picked a spot up the block and on the opposite side of the street. Using a jacket as a guard against the rain, Reni got out and dashed toward the sidewalk and then a couple of buildings up, a bag clutched to his chest.

Now that was interesting.

I looked around me. I wasn't overly familiar with this area of Corona. While the whole of Queens had been undergoing an improvement of sorts, there were entire sections that had so far been left out. And this was one of them. Faux brick apartment buildings with peeling tiles and cracked windows were the order of the day and were mostly inhabited by multiple families. The vicinity was populated by the latest wave of immigrants from South America, I'd recently read. And not all of them were legal. As the piece had cited, there were over two thousand miles of unprotected border between the States and Mexico. And that wasn't mentioning the other thousands of miles of borders.

It was a neighborhood that creeped me out this late at night. The overhead lamps didn't seem as bright here for some reason. And the emptiness of the streets made me feel safe not at all. Forget that I was following a man who obviously didn't want to be followed, but just because his goons weren't on his tail didn't mean they weren't somewhere behind him. They could even have their laser sights set on me now.

I looked around, fighting a shiver.

I'd been a PI long enough to know to expect the unexpected, but not long enough to feel confident that I was prepared for those unexpecteds.

The rain began to let up. I started to get out of the car to go have a look around the building Reni had gone into. Was he meeting a mistress? If so, surely he had enough money to put her up somewhere nicer. Was he picking up drugs?

I had the door half-open, switching on the ceiling light, when I spotted Reni coming back out.

Damn.

I yanked the door closed, hoping that he hadn't seen me. He looked around, got back into the Mercedes, then took off.

I calmed my heartbeat and then started to climb out of the car to see if I could get any further details from the building and try to figure out what had brought him there when my cell phone chirped, making me hit my head on the roof.

Christ, but scare the crap out of a body already.

I picked the phone up from the passenger's seat and looked at the display. Pino.

What in the hell did Pino want? Were the DeVry students having another party? Maybe the broken-up engaged couple had reconciled, definite cause for celebration for that crowd.

I began to toss the phone back to the seat, then decided to answer instead.

"Metro, you might want to get over to Uncle Tolly's."

"Hello to you, too, Pino."

I hadn't been to Uncle Tolly's since I'd worked his missing person's case over a month ago. Forget that my dry cleaning was piling up and I'd soon have to decide whether to forgive him or find another cleaners. The reason was partly because he and his wife Aglaia had yet to make good on their promise to pay me for my trouble, a mild description of what I had gone through, mostly because I had to get over that trouble.

I realized that Pino had offered no smart-ass reply. "What's going on?" I asked.

"This is not something I can tell you, but something you have to see."

I rang off, closed the car door again, and headed in the direction of Astoria.

Twenty

I HADN'T BEEN TO THIS part of the neighborhood much lately. To some extent because I'd spent so much time there while looking for Tolly. But even if I had been there yesterday, I don't think I would have recognized the block on which Pappas Dry Cleaners was located. Not with four fire trucks parked at different angles in the street, accompanied by fire chief Jeeps and NYPD cruisers, flashing lights turning night into day. Not that the fire needed help. The dry cleaners was a ball of orange flames licking upward, thick dark smoke choking the sky.

I spotted Pino where he stood placing a blanket around Aglaia Pappas' shoulders. The butcher Plato Kourkoulis was next to her, staring at where the flames claimed his shop, located next to the cleaners. Firefighters were focusing more on preventing the fire from spreading even farther up the line of shops to the right. Luckily a parking lot to the left provided a natural barrier.

"What happened?" I asked, approaching the threesome.

Pino patted Aglaia's shoulders then nodded to his left, indicating he wanted to talk to me alone.

People from the neighborhood crowded the street, their faces painted a fluorescent yellow by the bright flame.

"Explosion," Pino said simply.

I squinted at him even as the acrid smoke coated my nose. "What?" I whispered more than said.

When Apostolis Pappas had initially gone missing, everyone had pointed to his possible involvement with the mob being to blame. More specifically, it was believed that Tolly was doing more than just laundering Tony DiPiazza's clothes, that he was in fact helping launder dirty money. But my investigation had proven that he hadn't been.

"Any idea what caused it?" I asked, turning to face the fire.

"You can guess what the rumor mill is saying."

Undoubtedly what I was thinking: that perhaps there had been a connection between Tolly and the mob. A connection that I had missed. A connection that had resulted in this.

"Uncle Tolly was inside when it happened."

I stared at Pino as if he'd told me that Astoria Park had just fallen into the East River. "What?"

He nodded and scrubbed the back of his neck with his hand, showing a human side I hadn't much glimpsed before. Usually Pino prided himself on making my life a living hell by harassing me, using his badge as a way of getting back at me for every stupid prank I'd ever pulled on him at St. D's.

That he had called me down, and was sharing the info with me now, told me that things were, indeed, serious.

"I don't get it," I said. "When I was working the case, you did everything short of arresting me to keep me away from the cleaners. Why call me now?"

"I'm thinking the detectives are going to want to talk to you," he said.

"Me? Why?" Then it dawned on me why he had called. I could finally be of some constructive use to him.

While Pino was a pain in the butt, he was a man who was serious about his job. I could imagine what would happen should anyone try to bribe him. He was about as up-and-up as they came. And right now, he wanted to try to piece together as many resources as he could to solve what could possibly be a crime.

"Because you have more information than any five of us put together, probably."

"What about Aglaia?"

We both stared at the woman who appeared twenty years older than her age, which made her looked way past dead.

"She was in the upstairs apartment at the time of the explosion. Managed to get down the back fire escape. Just barely. She said Tolly was still downstairs locking up. The paramedics are going to be taking her to the hospital just as soon as they can talk her into moving. She suffered a few burns to the back of her legs and hands where the fire engulfed the fire escape."

I swallowed hard, imaging the dire scene. "That's not what I meant. Surely Aglaia can fill the detectives in on everything that happened a month ago."

Pino looked at me. "There's a world of difference between the word of a grieving widow and a professional private investigator."

I felt a small pang of wonder that he was referring to me as a pro. But it was quickly buried by other more pressing emotions. "Sure, sure. I'll talk to whoever wants to talk to me."

"Good."

Plato motioned toward Pino.

"I'd better get back. I'll pass on your contact info."

I nodded and then wrapped my arms around my body to ward off more than the chill of the autumn night. I felt paralyzed standing there, watching the wrath of nature devour what had been such a fixture in my life. How many times, growing up, had I gone with my mother or grandmother to pick up dry cleaning, and then by myself as an adult? Or to the butcher's next door? Countless times. The shops had been as familiar to me as the back of my hand. The people who ran them more a part of the family than neighbors.

And they believed Uncle Tolly had been inside at the time of the explosion.

I shivered, realizing that in that one instant I'd forgiven him his trespasses and had gone back to calling him "uncle." Death had a way of doing that to a person.

"Hello, luv."

My entire body was instantly aware of the man behind me, the man who had uttered two simple words that touched something I'd forgotten about in the past few weeks.

I looked over my shoulder to find Aussie Jake Porter, the mysterious bounty hunter who had some interesting "friends," standing in the shadows. Oddly, not even the illuminating flames or flashing lights seemed to brighten his strong features. He was a shadowy outline, made identifiable by his tall, six foot four height and leather cowboy hat more than anything else.

"Jake," I said on a long exhale.

He didn't say anything for a long moment. Merely looked at me. And I suspected that what he saw went well below the surface of my jeans and shirt.

I wondered what he made of me, what he was contemplating. Was he thinking about the last time we kissed? About how close we'd come to delivering on the promise created by the hot chemistry between us? Or was he considering the way my ankles had healed, my left one still bearing the fading remainder of my temporary tattoo of a lizard?

Or, even more mind-boggling yet, was it possible that he understood that I had changed significantly since the last time our paths crossed? That I had given his sex to another man?

It appeared to take some effort for him to pull his gaze from mine as he looked toward the dry cleaners and tilted his cowboy-hat-covered head in that direction. "Interesting development, wouldn't you say?"

I didn't take my eyes from him. "I'd definitely say." That was, if I were capable of saying much of anything at all.

"The old man was inside?"

"That's the consensus. Aglaia barely made it out of the upstairs apartment." I swallowed hard. "At any rate, I think we'll all find out soon enough."

As soon as the flames were finally doused and Uncle Tolly's body was recovered in the fresh light of day.

Porter nodded slowly. "That, we will."

A thousand questions ran through my mind. Questions that had nothing to do with the dry cleaners or my previous case, but rather centered on the man who was within touching distance but whom I didn't dare touch. Did he think of me? Was he aware of how conflicted I felt in that moment? If I suggested we go for coffee, would he come? Or would he not answer me and leave me with another of his suggestively loaded grins? Enough to fuel a lifetime's worth of fantasies and secret longings, but never assuage the want I'd felt for him the moment I first laid eyes on him.

"Sofie?"

I turned my head in the other direction to find Pino descending with what looked like a fire investigator.

"I want you to meet Detective Hernandez," Pino said. "This is Sofie Metropolis, the PI I told you about."

I raised a finger. "Can you hold on just a minute?" I asked.

I turned to ask Porter out for that coffee.

Only he was nowhere to be found.

As I scanned the crowd, looking futilely for any sign of him or his cowboy hat, I thought that was the story of my life. . . .

MUCH LATER THAT NIGHT I sat at my kitchen table, every light in the apartment switched on, along with the television and the radio, Muffy sitting at my feet so he could catch the odd pieces of souvlaki I dropped his way. I took a bite of the pita stuffed with grilled pork, barely tasting it. I didn't even know why I'd stopped to get it on my way home. I'd been operating on autopilot, the backs of my eyelids flashing scenes from the fire every time I blinked. I suppose I needed something familiar to help me edge back into life as I knew it. But it wasn't working. If anything, every bite I took seemed to remind me that not only had things changed, they would never be quite the same again.

While the fire had been contained, it was still a long way from being cool enough to check for Uncle Tolly's body. But the fact that he hadn't shown up on the street was enough for everybody—enough for me—to understand that the odds were high that he had been in the shop when it exploded. To even consider that he might try for another escape to the Bahamas was so outrageous as to be ridiculous.

My cell phone vibrated on the table in front of me, next to my Glock. I wiped my hand on my sleep T-shirt and looked at the display. My mother. I didn't answer.

I'd talked to her earlier, after she'd heard the news via the church grapevine. It had been at her suggestion that I originally agreed to take on the Pappas case. And while she didn't have a clue what had gone down on top of the Hell Gate Bridge, she did know about the rumors of Uncle Tolly's connection to the mob. When he'd resurfaced, looking healthier than I'd ever seen him look after his stay in the Bahamas, everyone had gone back to life as usual.

But now that the cleaners had exploded . . . well, we were all essentially boomeranged back to that point in time.

I knew Thalia was worried about me. Hell, I was worried about me. Even though I knew Mafia-kingpin-in-training Tony DiPiazza was in Sicily, and would be for the next year, that didn't tell me where his second-in-command, Panayiotis Rokkos, was.

Was the Greek thug collecting on outstanding debts? If so, where did that put me on the list?

I stopped pretending to eat, fed Muffy a couple more pieces of pork, his diet on hold, then wrapped up the souvlaki and threw it away.

I called my mother back. She picked up immediately.

"Why didn't you answer?" she asked.

"I was in the bathroom," I lied.

"Are you sleeping?"

Was she kidding? I was afraid I wouldn't be able to sleep again. "No."

"Me, either."

At some point I'd come to understand that not sleeping was part of a mother's job. How many times had she been waiting up when I'd come home way past curfew? How often had I gotten up to go to the bathroom in the middle of the night to find the light on downstairs indicating she was down there, probably worrying about a sick relative in Greece, or a balloon loan payment coming due, or about my sister or brother?

And here she was losing yet another night's sleep because of me.

When I'd first hired on at Uncle Spyros' agency, yes, I'll admit, a part of me had done it because it was the absolute last thing everyone would expect of me. I made a point of avoiding thinking about what they had expected because I was pretty sure it had to do with taking Thomas-the-Toad back and opening the gifts still stacked in my bedroom with him.

And after the first time I'd used my gun, I'd gotten a thrill out of everyone knowing that I could take care of myself, not just in connection to my disaster of a wedding day, but against a man intent on killing me.

What I hadn't considered was how many sleepless nights I would cause my mother. This and she didn't know the half of it.

"Are you okay?" I asked.

"Me? I'm fine."

I didn't believe her. "What's up?"

A long sigh, then, "I don't know. I tried calling your grandfather earlier and couldn't get him on the phone."

Which meant she'd probably called him nonstop since and still hadn't gotten him.

"Would you like me to check in on him?"

Silence, then another sigh. "No. I'm sure he's fine. He's probably just avoiding my calls. Probably he heard about Tolly and is with his friends or something."

"Probably," I agreed. "But if you want me to take a drive by his place, I will."

"No, no. You're probably tired. Anyway, you're going to court with him tomorrow, right? So you'll see him then."

In light of all that had happened, I'd almost forgotten about tomorrow. Almost.

Had Grandpa Kosmos skipped town? I wondered. In fear for his freedom, had he decided to take a trip back to the homeland to lay low for a while?

The thought was so dumb I laughed out loud.

Thalia bid me good night for the third time that evening, and I rang off and then put the cell phone back down on the table next to my gun.

No, Grandpa Kosmos probably hadn't hopped on the next Olympic Airlines flight out to Greece, but he might have gone looking for the man responsible for his being due in court tomorrow. The man who had not only screwed me, but had made off with his late wife's, my maternal grandmother's, wedding ring.

Oh, crap . . .

Twenty-one

WHEN ALL WAS SAID AND done, I'd probably gotten as much sleep last night as Thalia had. Then again, for all I knew she'd slept like a baby after our last phone call, having removed the burden of worrying about Grandpa Kosmos from her shoulders and shifting it solidly onto mine.

Of course, that worry had to compete with the other things weighing me down. Like listening for strange sounds (even though I had Muffy for that, I worried that he would bark at the flower delivery man, but leave a burglar alone), and thinking I smelled gasoline.

It was more than the worry for my own well-being, although that was first and foremost in my mind. So shoot me. Then again, don't. At any rate, I now had more than just myself to think about. Aside from Mrs. Nebitz across the hall, who was nowhere as nimble as Aglaia and would never be able to get down the fire escape, there were the other tenants in the building. If my apartment were to be targeted, then theirs would go up as well.

Then there was always the chance that to get to me they might start somewhere else. . . .

I wasn't sure who the "they" were in the equation, but I was pretty sure it was Rokko. Who probably had never gotten over the fact that his boss had caught heat because of me.

Or that I had shot the tops off both his ears. Accidentally. Sort of.

Then there was the subject Rosie and I discussed about disgruntled cheating spouses targeting the agency and my uncle Spyros for revenge when their well-documented activities—compliments of the agency—resulted in the end of their marriages and the ruin of their savings accounts.

I'd heard of NYPD officers who had never fired their weapons in thirty years on the job. And while the private investigators I'd seen in TV shows and in movies certainly got roughed up from time to time, I'd somehow thought that was for entertainment's sake and that very little of that happened in real life.

Surely nothing had happened to my uncle Spyros.

At least not that I was aware of.

But I had never lived with him and didn't know what went on in his life on a day-to-day basis.

Was my job too dangerous? Was I putting too much on the line for a simple paycheck?

"Hey, Sof."

I blinked where I stood outside the courtrooms at the Queens Criminal Courthouse in Kew Gardens. I'd arrived a half hour early, long before everyone else. And now I stood staring at my cousin Nia, short for Antonia.

"What are you doing here?" I asked her.

Is that where Grandpa Kosmos had gone last night? To my cousin Nia's house? Is that why my mother and I hadn't been able to get a hold of him? Forget cell phones. My grandfather still didn't have an electronic cash register at his café.

"Actually, I was going to ask the same of you," Nia said. She snapped her fingers. "And then I remembered it's because of you that Pappou even has to appear in court."

"Not because of me. Because of my ex-fiancé."

"An ex-fiancé who is in Pappou's life because of you."

I gave her an eye roll.

I remembered that when we were kids the family used to joke that Nia could argue the mouse out of cat's mouth. And that probably she would make a good attorney as a result.

She'd taken it seriously and had gone on to college, then law school . . .

It finally occurred to me what she was doing there.

"You're not repping Grandpa Kosmos?" I said, incredulous.

Her Donna Karan–clad body snapped upright. "And why wouldn't I be?"

"Because he'll go to jail for sure."

Oh, God.

I paced down the hall and then back again.

What was Nia? Like all of twenty-five?

I realized that was only a year younger than me.

But still . . .

"*Kalimera sas,* Sofia and Antonia," my grandfather said as he approached where I stood staring down my cousin.

"*Yiasou,* Pappou," I said, kissing both his cheeks.

Nia did the same and I scowled.

Don't get me wrong. Nia and I had always gotten along. So long as she remembered her place. And this definitely wasn't her place. Only I was allowed to help Grandpa Kosmos. I was his favorite.

Ugh. Had I really just thought that? Yes, I realized, I had.

"So," he said, straightening the jacket of a suit that was probably as old as I was but thankfully didn't smell that way. Probably because he'd gotten it cleaned at Uncle Tolly's.

I cleared my throat. "Are we ready to go in and face the judge?"

My mother had assumed that Grandpa Kosmos had heard about what had gone down at the dry cleaners last night and had been tying one on with friends. Given his focus on the case, I reasoned that he might not know at all. That probably he had been avoiding all calls as he readied himself for today, likely wording speeches that he could make to the court.

The thought that he didn't know made me feel sick to my stomach somehow. And introduced a new somberness to the coming proceedings.

"Shame what happened to Uncle Tolly," Nia said as we entered the courtroom.

I tried to catch her attention on the other side of our grandfather to make the universal finger across the neck to indicate she should stow it.

Too late. Grandpa Kosmos had stopped walking and looked at Nia.

"What about Tolly?"

"You know. His place blowing up like that. His being inside."

I watched my grandfather turn ten shades of pale and I made sure I had a tight grip on his other arm. While he was no lightweight, he wasn't all that young anymore, either, and didn't need to hear such news right before he was to go in to face a judge.

"What?" he said.

"We'll talk about it later." I gave Nia a warning glance. "Right now we have a court date to keep. . . ."

A HALF HOUR LATER, AFTER the case was called before the judge, and she gave the prosecution ten extra minutes to deliver their witness, and after determining that he probably wouldn't show (thank you, God and Thomas), the case was dismissed and the assistant prosecutor was given a reprimand for bringing such frivolous charges against a pillar of the Astoria community.

My grandfather's puffed-out chest told of his satisfaction. "Probably he was afraid I'd pop him again," he said as Nia and I escorted him from court.

I smiled, willing to sit on the news that I may have had a hand in Thomas' not showing today. Let Grandpa Kosmos think what he would.

My cousin, however, wasn't pleased. "My first real court case and it was dismissed."

"Isn't that a good thing?" I asked. "One case toward a no losses track record."

She seemed to brighten up. "Yes. Actually, you're right."

All told, not a bad morning.

Until Nia left and Grandpa Kosmos turned to me, wanting to know the details on Uncle Tolly. . . .

Twenty-two

ALL THINGS BEING EQUAL, I was coming to hate weekends. I knew that my lack of a dating life had something to do with it. It wasn't long ago that I would get up sometime around noon on a Sunday morning and still think that was too early because I hadn't returned from partying until after the sun appeared on the horizon. Greek clubs, early morning breakfasts, laughing with friends.

But while I had gotten the wedding gifts, Thomas had gotten the friends. Or, rather, I had given them to him.

So there I was in my kitchen, with Muffy looking at me as if I were insane, making pasticcio, which is essentially Greek lasagna, to take to dinner at my parents' house.

As I added the pasticcio noodles (spaghetti-length macaroni) to a large pot of boiling water, I smiled smugly. I could just imagine my mother's face when I actually turned up bearing food.

Rare was the time when I had cooked growing up. You know, beyond making salad, peeling boiled eggs, or seeing to the other hundred easy jobs that were needed to fill the table with food. I'd made *rizogalo* once (rice pudding), and had burned one of my mother's pans beyond repair. Then there was the incident while making moussaka when I'd caught the stove-top on fire while I was frying slices of eggplant. And never mind the time when I'd grabbed the salt instead of the sugar while making *galaktoboureko*. I shuddered. It would be a long time before I lived that one down.

It was a wonder my mother and paternal grandmother hadn't banned me from the kitchen.

But now that I had my own kitchen, I figured it was long past time I put it to good use.

Besides, I figured I owed Mrs. Nebitz at least a piece of homemade pasticcio after all the food she'd given to me. And give her a plate of mine instead of hoarding all of hers (I'd taken hers back, clean and empty, the morning after she'd asked me for them). Maybe we could start some sort of back-and-forth thing. I'd give her pasticcio on my plate, she'd return my plate bearing some sort of Jewish delicacy, and I would return the favor again with something else.

My hand paused where I stirred the noodles.

Probably I was being just a wee bit ambitious.

I knew that a part of me was trying to avoid thinking about Uncle Tolly and his funeral yesterday. I didn't do funerals well. Especially the Greek idea of what the entire process should include.

There was one memory, in particular, that had given me countless nightmares throughout my childhood. The family had gone to Greece for the funeral of my paternal grandfather (af-terward, we'd brought my grandmother home with us, and she'd lived with my family ever since). I'd been ten and had been ill-prepared for the experience. I suppose because of the laws here, funeral homes like my aunt Sotiria's were necessary. But they didn't have funeral homes in Greece. The deceased were embalmed and then returned to their homes for viewing, the top of the coffin propped outside the front gate indicating the family was accepting those who wished to pay their respects.

And my family had stayed in the house, the makeshift bed I'd slept in mere feet away from my dead grandfather.

I shuddered and tried to focus on what I was doing. But last night, after Uncle Tolly was finally laid to rest, the dreams I'd had as a child had included his face in place of my grandfather's.

I vowed never to attend another funeral in Greece again.

And thanked God that the laws were such in the States that I'd never have to sleep in the same house with the embalmed dead body of a relative again.

It seemed that the whole of Astoria, Greek or otherwise, had attended the services at St. Demetrios' Greek Orthodox Church in honor of Uncle Tolly. A somber service that included the low buzz of speculation on what, exactly, had been the cause of the explosion. While there were surely enough dangerous, flammable chemicals in the dry cleaners, when you factored in what had gone down the month before . . . well, the ultimate conclusion was that the mob had to be involved. It was just too much of a coincidence to believe otherwise.

Me? I wasn't sure what I believed. Probably I was still trying to deal with the shock of his death.

Muffy barked.

"What?" I asked him, happy for the distraction. "Don't look at me like that." I bent so that my face was nearly even with his. "It's called cooking. And, no, you can't have any of it."

Yet.

I turned toward the pan of olive oil I had heating and tossed in finely chopped red onions and garlic, cooking them slightly before adding a choice portion of ground beef, cutting that with some ground pork.

Originally I thought I might make moussaka, you know, just

to prove that I could actually make it. But whenever my mother or grandmother made it at home, the place stank of fried oil for days. So I settled on pasticcio instead.

Anyway, I only bought a small bag of flour and didn't know if it was enough in case I started another grease fire.

I wrote "big bag of flour" on a list I'd stuck to the refrigerator door with a magnet, then stirred the ground beef, setting the timer on the back of the stove for the noodles.

Then I turned toward the counter where I'd placed a new Pyrex pan I'd liberated along with a full set of pans from the wedding gifts in my bedroom. I sprinkled bread crumbs and grated Parmesan on the bottom of it (it should have been *kefalotiri* or *kefalogarvera* but I had forgotten to pick up either of the cheeses from the Greek shops when I bought the pasticcio noodles and farina). After the beef mixture was brown, I added a cup of fresh tomatoes I'd separated from the skin via a shredder and a spoonful of tomato paste and four cloves. I put the cover on and left it to simmer while I drained the noodles, let them cool a bit, then placed a layer in the Pyrex, covering them with Parmesan. The meat done, I spooned a thin layer over the noodles, then repeated the process beginning with the noodles until I had a half inch to spare at the top of the Pyrex dish.

I sang along with a Greek CD I put in. Mitropanos ruled on a Sunday morning. Half the fun of making pasticcio was that there was usually plenty of noodles and beef sauce left over to eat on another occasion. I mixed the two in a bowl, covered it, then put it in the refrigerator. Then I went about making the sauce that would top off the pasticcio.

This is where things got tricky. *Besamel* was hard to get perfect every time. I put butter to melt in a saucepan, got the milk I'd heated up in the microwave, then stirred flour into the butter. I followed with the milk, a bit of farina, forever stirring. I switched the wooden spoon to my left hand and shook my right, remembering another reason why I didn't like making the sauce. Once thick, I added egg yolks, and salt and pepper.

Voilà.

I poured the *besamel* over the top of the noodle mixture.

After I put the casserole into the oven to brown the top, I dropped into a kitchen chair and sighed. I didn't know what it was about the Greeks that they had to cook everything twice. Maybe the women throughout history had had too much time on their hands, I don't know. What I did know was that making the pasticcio had exhausted me. And had completely ruined my appetite, which maybe explained why my mother wasn't as big as a house. I was always curious as to how she managed to keep slim even with so much great food in the house (she and my grandmother had prevented Efi and me from gaining weight by using wooden spoons to swat us away from the stove and out of the kitchen between meals).

Was that the price of making your own food? That once you were done making it, you didn't want it anymore?

Probably that was why Mrs. Nebitz gave me so much food.

Well, that sucked. What was the fun in cooking if you couldn't enjoy eating it?

I picked up my frappé and took the last sip as my cell phone vibrated. Waters.

"Hi, Eugene."

"Hey, yourself. I just lost Venezuela again."

Since I'd upgraded Waters to full agent, and he knew Venezuela probably better than I did, I'd given him the job of following him half the time over the past few days.

I scratched my head, thinking that I still had to take a shower before presenting my perfect pasticcio to my parents. "You think maybe I should send you to PI courses or something? I mean, isn't this like the second time you've lost him?"

"Oh, come on, Metro, even you had to have lost someone in the beginning."

"Where did you lose him?"

"Strangely enough, in Corona. I don't know what in the hell kind of business he'd have there."

I didn't, either, but the fact that Waters had lost Venezuela in the same neighborhood where I'd followed him the other night was interesting.

"Did he have any of his goons with him?"

"No, that's the thing. He was alone in the Mercedes."

"Okay, Waters. Go back to the McMansion. I'm sure you'll pick him up back there."

"By the way," he said, "I may want to buy this car. How much you think your grandfather will want for it?"

"More than you can pay."

I'd talked Grandpa Kosmos into lending me his twenty-year-old Lincoln Town Car for the occasion seeing as Waters didn't have a car and lending him mine was out of the question because Venezuela's security team already had a bead on it.

"Oh, crap. I gotta go."

I rang off and ran for the oven, searching for pot holders and instead finding a towel I doubled up so I could take the pasticcio out.

I smiled. Perfect.

EVERYBODY WAS A CRITIC.

Just as I imagined, my mother and grandmother were surprised and happy that I'd brought the pasticcio. But what I'd left out of the scenario was that Greeks, by nature, were hypercritical. So that when my mother took a fork to one of the pieces I'd piled on top of a serving plate and tasted it, I'd been expecting more praise.

I'd gotten a face instead. "You put *garifalla* in with the beef."

Whole cloves. And, apparently, I'd also forgotten to take the cloves out as I watched her take one from her mouth and toss it in the garbage can.

Cripes.

"Okay, aside from that, do you like it?" I asked, deflated a bit. So my pasticcio wasn't perfect. But it was edible and I had made it. Surely that was a huge plus in the good daughter column.

"You forgot *bahari* in the *besamel*."

I had.

"Bahari" was Greek for spice, in this case nutmeg.

"I couldn't find it at the store," I lied.

She gave me a look that told me she didn't believe me. "It's on the same shelf as the cloves."

And then she smiled. "Very good, Sofia. Very good. I'm very pleased."

I tried not to beam but I couldn't help it, especially when she put her arm around my waist and gave me a squeeze.

"Our guest will enjoy it."

I froze. "Guest? What guest?"

Whenever my mother had a guest over it usually meant a potential groom of one sort or another was being paraded in front of my sister Efi. It wasn't so long ago that they would have been for me. But I'd missed my one shot and was already well into *yerotokori* land, an old maid.

Thalia shrugged and turned the potatoes out of boiling water. "No one special, really."

Which meant that he was.

"Here," Thalia said, pushing a large bowl toward me. "Make the salad while your sister gets ready."

Efi had recently taken over salad duty, but obviously had more important things on her mind right now. Like trying to dodge whatever guest my mother had invited over for Sunday dinner.

Normally Sunday dinner was reserved strictly for family, which gave the visitor special emphasis.

I grimaced. I just hoped whoever it was chewed with his mouth closed and knew how to keep his mouth shut, period, when it came to matters that didn't concern him.

My mother went into the dining room and I stared at my eternally-clad-in-black paternal grandmother, wondering if I could get a clue from her. But she was concentrating on peeling the boiled potatoes. At least she wasn't asking me to bring her any hooch.

The door opened and my mother reentered, saying to an unseen somebody, "Go ahead and join the men in the living room. Dinner will be ready soon."

I looked over my shoulder at her while I methodically cut tomatoes, noticing she held something in her hands. A torte box. Not just any torte box, but one that bore the name of Dino's *zaharoplastio*.

I nearly sliced a piece of my thumb in with the tomatoes.

"Isn't this nice?" Thalia put the box down on the kitchen table and popped open the lid, revealing a chocolate torte not unlike the one Dino had brought for my Name Day. The same one we'd destroyed with our table activities and then ate anyway . . . off each other.

I pretended that I wasn't impressed with the offering as I shrugged and moved from tomatoes to cucumber, sprinkling each layer with sea salt as I went.

Thalia put the box into the refrigerator, took the peeled potatoes from my grandmother and then moved on to mash them with olive oil and garlic.

"Sofie, are you still working on that salad?" she asked me.

I showed her the bowl. "Yep."

"Well, hurry up. I'd like to eat sometime before four."

I didn't know if I was purposely dragging out the process or if I needed extra concentration to prevent me from becoming the attention of a lawsuit like Phoebe Hall's.

Could someone do that? Sue a person for accidentally serving body parts at a private dinner?

I realized the ridiculous direction of my thoughts and winced when the juice from a red onion I was cutting seeped into a small paper cut on my thumb.

At least I wasn't bleeding.

Efi chose then to enter the kitchen from the back steps, coming up behind me to liberate a slice of cucumber and pop it into her mouth. "When do we eat?"

"As soon as you get the table set," my mother said.

Efi gathered the tablecloth and napkins and left the room.

Given her nonchalant behavior, I reasoned that she didn't know a guest had been invited for dinner.

That would change . . .

The door swung inward and Efi glowered at my mother.

. . . soon.

"You invited someone to Sunday dinner?" she asked, incredulous.

Thalia shrugged as if it were an everyday occurrence. "So what if I did?"

"So what?" Efi repeated. "I thought we agreed that Sundays were no-matchmaking zones."

"Who says I'm matchmaking?"

My sister and I shared a look, and then she gave an eye roll and continued gathering the silverware and glasses to set the table.

I looked at my mother.

"What?" she asked. "I'm completely innocent of all charges."

"'Innocent' is not the word that comes to mind."

"Finish the salad, Sofie," she said, brushing by me to get something from the refrigerator.

After drizzling extra-virgin olive oil from a family orchard that a cousin had brought back from his last trip to Greece over the salad, and sprinkling the top with Greek oregano, I swept my hands near the bowl. "Voilà."

"Good," she said. "Now take it and these out to the table."

She filled my arms with trays of freshly-cut bread, feta, and wine carafes. I juggled everything, calling out so that Efi wouldn't open the swinging door while I tried to get through it.

I put everything down on the dining room table and craned my neck, trying to get a gander of whoever Thalia had thought was important enough to break the agreement she and my sister had. I couldn't make out a thing beyond the backs of my father and grandfather's heads.

"I'm going to kill her," Efi said from where she arranged the silverware.

"I'm the eldest. I get first crack."

My brother Kosmos came in from the kitchen empty-handed and picked at the feta. "What's going on?"

"Mom's playing matchmaker again."

"So what else is new?"

"Tell me, why isn't she inviting girls over to meet you?" Efi asked pointedly.

He stared at her and she grinned.

"Kind of puts a whole new spin on things, doesn't it?" I asked.

"Yeah," Efi said. "Actually, maybe we should suggest it to Mom."

"Don't you dare," Koz said, shaking a wedge of crusty bread at her. "Or else I'll give her a list of available Greek men from university to invite over."

Efi scowled at him and disappeared back into the kitchen.

Within minutes, the food was done, the table was full, and everyone but the three men in the other room where ready to sit down.

"Dinner," my mother called.

I stood with my hands on the back of my chair, my sister next to me as my grandfather wandered in first.

Thalia motioned toward me. "No, no, Sofia. Move over one, closer to me, so our guest can sit in the middle."

I looked from her to the man in question coming into the room and nearly fell straight over.

Dino.

Twenty-three

IN THE SCHEME OF THINGS, I supposed I should have seen this one coming, but I hadn't. And midway through dinner I was still in a state of shock.

First, I was so completely aware of Dino sitting next to me that I could barely lift my wineglass without fear of dumping the contents all over the table.

Not that that stopped me, although I was aware of Grandpa Kosmos giving me a couple of odd looks as I sucked back the wine like there was no tomorrow.

I couldn't remember feeling this . . . attracted to Dino before.

Okay, so some would argue that I'd slept with the guy. Indulged in a Sunday one-morning stand. And that, alone, would signify that I was attracted to him. But before then, he'd been a great-looking guy who'd been meant for my sister.

Now . . .

Well now I felt like my body temperature had risen at least a good five degrees—something the wine wasn't helping—and though we weren't touching, I felt like his skin was flush with mine. I couldn't seem to concentrate on a single word of what was being said and the food . . .

Had he just taken another piece of my pasticcio?

I felt my face flush. Of course, Thalia had made a point of telling everyone that I'd made the casserole.

"You don't have to eat another piece," I said. "It's not that good, really."

I fought to keep my jaw from dropping to my plate. Had I really just said that? I felt like I was some blushing girl from the old country who'd just made her first meal for a prospective suitor.

And obviously I wasn't the only one who thought that because conversation ceased as everyone looked at me.

"What?" I said, irritated. "It's not."

"It's excellent," Grandpa Kosmos proclaimed.

"You did a great job," my father said.

Even my grandmother put a piece on her plate, smiling at me. I glowered as I reached for my wineglass.

I hadn't been digging for compliments. Really, I hadn't.

Then why had I acted like I was?

"It's very good, Sofia," Dino said.

And I shivered.

"We need more wine," I said, getting up from the table so quickly that my silverware clattered and everyone reached for their glasses to keep them from falling over.

Once in the kitchen, I put the partially empty carafes on the counter and then leaned both hands against the edge, trying to catch my breath, although I hadn't done anything physical to rob me of the precious commodity.

What was going on? Why was I feeling this way? So my mother had invited Dino for dinner? So what? It wasn't like we were . . . dating or anything. I mean, I wasn't interested in anything beyond what had already happened between us.

I was afraid of being found out.

I hadn't known I had my eyes closed until I realized that was it, the reason I was acting so strangely. I didn't want my family to know that I'd done some really naughty things with such a good Greek boy.

Of course, if I kept acting the way I was, they'd know for sure.

I filled the carafes from large bottles my mother had filled straight from barrels and then went back into the other room to prove that I had nothing to hide. Or pretend that I didn't, anyway. I could handle this. I was a PI who knew her way around a gun, for God's sake. Surely I could manage to get through a meal without blurting out that Dino and I had slept together but had absolutely no plans of dating, much less marrying.

Conversation continued as I entered. I put one of the carafes near my father's elbow, then rounded the table to put the other next to my mother.

Efi leaned forward. "Okay, I've got one for you. A young virgin marries a Greek man and before the wedding her father tells her that, being Greek, her husband may ask her to roll over in bed one day, but that she doesn't have to do it if she doesn't want to.

"Sure enough, after a couple of months, her husband asks her to turn over and she says, 'No, my father said I don't have to do this if I don't want to.' Her husband says, 'Okay, that's fine by me, but I thought you wanted children.'"

The table erupted with laughter as I reseated myself. I glanced at Dino. Only he wasn't looking at me, he was smiling at my sister.

"That was good," he said, wiping his mouth with his napkin and then returning it to his lap. "Let's see if you like this one. There was a Brit, a Frenchman, a Greek, and a Turk on an airplane. The pilot tells them that in order to save the plane from crashing, three of them must jump. The Brit says, 'God Save the Queen!' and jumps. Next comes the Frenchman, who calls, 'Viva la France' as he sails through the air. When it comes time for the Greek, he steps up and says, 'Hail, Greece!' and pushes out the Turk."

Everyone laughed. I reached for the carafe and poured more wine into my glass, while Efi came up with another joke about a couple and a vibrator and Dino followed up with another about two guys from Pyrgos.

I'd never been much good at telling jokes. Somehow I either ended up messing up the beginning so badly that the punch line didn't make sense without explanation, or, worse, I forgot the punch line altogether. I shifted uncomfortably in my chair.

I downed the wine and began to clear the table, wishing I could disappear. . . .

"WHAT ARE YOU DOING HERE?" I whispered fiercely to Dino when he came into the kitchen with a few plates.

"I thought I'd give you a hand."

I gestured blindly. "I don't mean in here, although you bringing in plates while I'm in here is so not a good idea—I mean 'here' as in at my parents' house?"

"Your mother invited me over when she stopped in for a torte this morning."

"And you accepted."

"Of course." He grinned. "I never turn down a home-cooked meal." He drew a little closer to me, and I could nearly feel him pressed against my backside as he put the plates in the sink in front of me. "Or a chance to talk to you."

I turned quickly, nearly causing him to drop the dishes. Not a good idea, but not because of the dishes. But because now I not only felt him, I saw him. And oh what a vision he made.

There's something about a guy looking at you like he wants to eat you alive and that the only thing stopping him is you. While I knew Jake was attracted to me, there was something else going on behind his eyes, something I couldn't pinpoint, and thus couldn't get past.

But with Dino there was no wondering. No playing the "what if" game. I knew that if I crooked my finger into the front of his shirt he was mine.

And what a prize he was.

Tall, dark, and very Greek, with eyes the color of my morning frappé, and a whipcord lean body that practically vibrated with energy, he called out to me on levels I couldn't begin to count.

And I realized how very wrong I had been to think that avoiding him would make everything go away.

My gaze snagged on his mouth and his one-dimple grin and I licked my suddenly parched lips. "You know my mother is trying to fix you up with Efi."

"I know."

I felt the incredible urge to punch him. "And you still came?"

His gaze flicked from my neck to my forehead and then down to my eyes again. "Just being in here with you makes it worth it."

"And if I threatened never to talk to you again?"

His grin widened. "Who said I wanted to talk?"

Then his body was against mine, his hips pressing into my softness, seeming to squeeze every last molecule of air from my body as my heartbeat pulsed loudly in my ears.

"And Efi?"

He lifted a hand and fooled around with a strand of my hair, appearing endlessly fascinated with it. "She's cute."

This time I did punch him.

"Ow. What was that for?" he asked, releasing my hair.

I turned from him and elbowed him out of the way. You know, before I could do something incredibly stupid, like kiss him. "That was to get you away from me before someone comes in and catches us."

"And would that be so bad?"

"Yes!"

"Why?"

"Why?" I turned toward him again, this time making sure there was room between us by using my arm to push him back. "Because I am not interested in my name being mentioned anywhere near a sentence that contains the word 'marriage' in it for a good long time."

"And who said it would?"

I squinted at him. "Are you serious? You are Greek, aren't you? You are aware that in some small towns a kiss is as good as a marriage proposal?"

"I already told you that I'm not proposing."

"Oh, yeah, like that makes a difference. Do you know how many Greek couples are married without there ever having been a question asked?"

"How many?"

"It's a rhetorical question. But I'd guess at least eighty percent of them." I stabbed my finger into his rock-hard chest. "The families catch the couple doing something . . . intimate and wedding invitations are sent out the same night."

"So we tell them we're not interested."

I cocked my head to the side. "And aren't you?"

The smile slipped from his face. "Are you?"

I hit him in the arm again and he looked at me like I was insane. "Go. Get out of here. Now. And don't ever think about calling me again. No tortes, no 'how are you doings,' no . . ."

"No sex?"

I gulped.

The door arced inward and my mother sauntered in with more dishes.

"Oh!" she said. "I didn't know you two were in here."

I moved aside so she could put the dishes in the sink and I gave an eye roll. "Where else would we be, Mama?"

"I thought maybe you went upstairs to the bathroom or something."

Dino waggled his brows as he gestured toward the stairs leading to the second floor and the bedrooms.

I gaped at him.

"I gotta go," I said, wiping my hands on a towel. "Thanks for dinner."

I kissed my mother on both cheeks and then turned to find myself flush with Dino who looked like he expected a kiss as well. I navigated my way around him and into the dining room.

"Aren't you going to stay for torte?" my mother asked.

"No!"

REMEMBER ME SAYING THAT WHENEVER things turned bad, they tended to get even worse? Well, when Dino had shown up for dinner at my parents' place yesterday, I should have braced myself for even more challenging situations to come.

But, of course, I hadn't. I'd been too preoccupied with the memory of Dino's suggestive grin and the fact that I'd spent all of last night dreaming about our time together.

Scratch that. That would have meant I had relived that morning. Rather my overactive subconscious had created new scenarios that included the gorgeous Greek. Like having sex with him in my childhood bedroom at my parents' while everyone was downstairs having dinner. Going at it at his bakery where all the sugary confections gave us the energy to go for hours. His hands had been everywhere. His mouth even more places.

So that when I woke up hot and bothered, I'd barked at Muffy instead of him barking at me.

And now that I was at the agency, and Rosie had reported that some of the new surveillance equipment I had purchased had come up missing, I was loaded for bear.

The first person that came to mind was Eugene. So sue me if you think I'm being racist. The guy had a rap sheet as long as my arm and had talked about surveillance equipment and being plugged into the five-finger discount underworld in the same sentence. It wasn't too far-fetched for me to think of him first.

But when I called him and he denied taking the high-end items, I believed him.

"Pete," I said into my cell, my cousin's name the next to pop to mind. "I need to see you at the agency. Stat."

I hung up only to find Rosie staring at me.

"What?" I asked.

"Venezuela's wife is on line three for you."

I raised my brows and then turned toward my desk, staring at the blinking light on my phone. I picked up. "Hi, Gisela. What's up?"

"I need to meet you. Now. At the Top Tomato."

She hung up.

Great.

I remembered our last meeting at the drugstore that hadn't exactly gone according to plan.

I took my purse out of my drawer and moved toward the door.

"What should I do about Pete?"

"Make him wait for me."

"I can't make him do anything."

I took a twenty out of my purse and handed it to her. "Stash this somewhere in Spyros' office and tell him to wait in there."

I figured once Pete was inside he would go on his regular money hunt. And once he found the twenty he'd assume there was more money to be found. That should keep him occupied for at least an hour.

An hour that I ended up not needing.

I got to the Top Tomato to find no goons I had to hide from. Gisela was inside by herself . . . and looked happier than I had certainly ever seen her.

"What's going on?" I asked, sidling up next to her and pretending interest in Fuji apples.

"What are you doing?"

I gave her a sidelong glance. "What do you mean, what am I doing?"

"You look like a moron."

I gave a long sigh and turned to stare openly at her. "I thought we were supposed to be keeping a low profile."

She smiled at me and waggled the fingers on her left hand. "Not anymore."

On her ring finger sat the biggest rock I'd ever seen in my life cuddled up against her wedding band. It was at least the size of my five-year-old niece's hand when she made a fist. And easily eclipsed three of Gisela's slender fingers.

"Jesus, tell me that's not real." I grabbed her hand so that I could get a better look.

"Oh, it's real all right," she said, staring at it. "I just came from old man Bachman's now. That's where I called you from. He says I should insure it and lock it in a safe somewhere. But I told him what was the point in having a diamond like this if you couldn't wear it, you know?"

I couldn't stop myself from gawking. I hadn't known they sold diamonds that big. "How are you holding your hand up without dragging it on the ground?"

"I know. Isn't it enormous?" Her smile nearly rivaled the shine of the precious jewel. "That's why I asked you here to tell you face-to-face what I have to say."

I was still jewel-struck. I'd been surprised by how much my grandmother's diamond had been worth. This . . . well, the money that had gone to pay for this could easily feed all the inhabitants in a third-world country for at least a year.

I finally moved my gaze from Gisela's hand to her face to find her waiting.

"What did you want to tell me?" I asked.

She smiled. "You're fired."

Twenty-four

I BLINKED AT GISELA.

Had she just said what I thought she had?

I could count the times I'd been fired on one finger. My aunt Sotiria, the funeral home owner. And then it had been because I'd ralphed all over a deceased's family member. The old woman had been dead for a week in her apartment before anyone had figured out they hadn't seen her in a while and decay had set in. The daughter had wanted an open casket. And I had tossed my cookies all over the front of her nice new black suit.

Aunt Sotiria had finally figured out I probably wasn't meant for the funeral biz and fired me.

And that had been a good ten years ago.

"You're what?"

"I said I'm firing you." She took an envelope out of her purse that was a twin to the first one she had given me two weeks ago. "Here. For your trouble."

I looked inside the envelope and then handed it back. "I haven't used all of the first envelope yet."

She pressed it into my hand. "You brought my Reni back to me. That's worth that and more."

I looked around. It was worth noting that there were no goons and that Gisela was obviously happy. Very happy. And who wouldn't be, with a make-up rock that big on her finger?

"So . . . ," I said, looking at her. "I take it that means everything's back to normal in the, um, bedroom?"

Gisela's smile widened. "Not just back to normal. Better." She licked her bloodred lips. "God, the things he did to me last night. I swear I could barely get out of bed this morning, much less walk."

I turned my palm in her direction. "A little more information than I was looking for."

So Reni had found passion for his wife again. That was a good thing, no? I mean, whenever a family could find a way to stay together it was good thing, diamond or no.

Then why was I not feeling good about this whole thing?

"What kind of things?" I asked, bracing myself for the answer.

Gisela laughed. "Wouldn't you like to know."

"So these . . . things were things he'd never done before?"

She waved me off. "Of course we've done everything. We've been married for four years and were a couple for a year before that. It's just that last night . . . well, it was almost like the first time all over again."

Her cell phone chirped and she fished it out of her Gucci bag. It was him.

"Hey, baby," she answered.

I made a face and moved farther down the aisle to stare at Gisela. I picked up a squash while I waited for her to finish.

"Sure, sweetie. I'll be right home."

I looked around. Was it me or was that one of Reni's goons

at the end of the next aisle? I stared harder. Was he looking at pie filling? Maybe I should go recommend a brand to him.

"He can't go a minute without me," Gisela said, finishing up and coming to stand closer to me.

"Mmm."

"So, I guess we're done, then," she said.

"I guess we are."

"I'll see what other business I can send your way."

"Thanks."

And with that she waggled her fingers at me in a way that showed off the Hope diamond in all its glory, swaying her silk-clad hips as she walked away.

Interesting . . .

I THINK TO SOME DEGREE we're all creatures of habit. That's why I wasn't surprised to find Pete still in my uncle Spyros' office when I got back to the agency.

"Where'd you stash the twenty?" I asked Rosie.

"Under that cheap statue he has of Bogart on his shelf, you know, next to the plant." She popped her gum. "Probably he already found it. Probably it's in his pocket."

Probably.

I handed her the envelope Gisela had given me and then headed for Spyros' office to confront Pete.

Rosie gasped. "Oh my God. Just what I was wishing for. Thank you, Sofie."

"Log it in under the Venezuela account."

I should have told her to also close the account, since I had been fired, but for some reason I wasn't ready to do that just yet.

"Can you ask Gisela if she wants to adopt me?"

I grimaced at Rosie, knocked on the office door, and then let myself in. Pete snapped upright from where he was going through one of my uncle's filing cabinets. I caught Rosie craning her neck to see what was going on. I closed the door.

"Hey, Pete," I said, taking a seat in one of the visitor's chairs. I propped my feet on the desk, crossing them at the ankles. "I think you and I need to have a little talk."

"Whatever's in my father's office is fair game," he said.

"I don't care about the twenty you palmed," I said. "Although I do plan to take it out of your paycheck since it was my twenty."

He grimaced and sat down behind the desk. I noticed he didn't offer the money back. Probably his mother was bugging him for rent. Probably he would give the twenty to her when he got home.

"How's everything going?" I asked.

"How do you mean?"

"Are you finding everything okay on the job?"

"Sure. Fine. Why?"

"I want to know what you needed the equipment you lifted from here for."

"Equipment?"

I was coming to hate when people answered my questions with questions. It made for slow headway in any conversation.

I took my feet from the desk and leaned forward. "Come on, Pete, I know you took it. You have a long history of lifting things that aren't yours around here."

"What things are you talking about?"

"The new surveillance equipment I bought."

"I don't know nothing about any of that."

Sure he didn't. Probably he'd known the minute I'd bought it and had planned to steal it the minute I turned my back.

"I'm telling you the truth, Sofie," he said. "Look, I know I'm bad with cash. Put a twenty in front of me and I won't sleep until I find a way to relieve you of it. But stolen property isn't my thing."

"Not your thing."

"Nope."

"Which pawnshop did you take it to? Antypas?"

"I didn't take it."

"Well, someone did."

"Why does that someone have to be me?"

"You tell me."

"Maybe it was that old man Nash who took it."

I stared at him.

"Okay, maybe not." He held up his hands. "All I know is that I didn't touch the stuff. That's not my style."

"And you consider lifting cash style?"

He grinned at me.

"You're fired."

I got up and left the room.

He followed me out. "You can't fire me."

"I hired you, I can fire you."

I expected to feel better about firing someone rather than being fired, but I found little joy in giving my cousin the boot.

"My father owns this place. You can't fire me."

"Your father didn't hire you."

Pete visibly winced, which inspired a frown of my own.

He pointed his finger at me. "You shouldn't even be working here. I should be the one running this agency."

"Yes, well, if you'd showed your father an ounce of honest integrity instead of stealing from him whenever the opportunity arose, maybe you would be the one running this agency."

He stared at me and I tried to size him up, wondering if he was a physical threat. He looked angry enough to hit something. Or someone. I just hoped it wouldn't be me.

He reached into his pocket and I backed up.

"Omigawd, he's got a gun!" Rosie shouted, crouching down on the other side of her desk.

"I don't have a goddamn gun," Pete said, taking his hand out of his pocket and then slapping something onto my desk.

"I didn't take any equipment, Sofie."

He turned and fumed out of the agency, nearly taking the front door off its hinges.

I looked to find the twenty he'd lifted sitting on my desk.

"SO WHEN ARE YOU GOING to make it permanent?"

I took a long pull off my frappé and considered my sister sitting next to me at the counter of Grandpa Kosmos' café. I nearly choked as I realized she could be talking about Dino. Had I given something away at dinner Sunday? "Make what permanent?"

She motioned toward my ankle. "The tat. Are you going to go with the lizard? Or the unicorn?"

I looked down. Truth was, the novelty of having a tattoo had worn off along with the fading temporary tattoo. Of course, I probably wouldn't have gone as far as I had without Efi's involvement.

"I don't know," I said. "I'm thinking that I might sit on it for a while."

"You're going to wuss out, aren't you?"

"Wuss out? I'm not wussing out."

"Yes, you are." She fiddled with the straw in her water with lemon. "God, and to think I used to look up to you."

"And you're not going to anymore because I won't get a tattoo?"

She smiled at me.

I said, "Hey, even Bruno told me that if I have a shadow of a doubt I shouldn't make it permanent."

"Yes, well, maybe that's the problem. Ever since Thomas-the-Toad, you're having a major problem with anything permanent."

I gaped at her. "Am not."

"Are too."

I gave her an eye roll. "Name one thing I've waffled on."

"The tattoo."

"Two things."

"Dino."

I nearly fell from my stool.

I looked around the café to check out who might be within hearing distance. Thankfully, no one fell into that category. Grandpa Kosmos had gone back to sit with his friends, the counter waitress was waiting on someone at the other end, and no customers sat near us.

"What in the hell are you talking about?"

"Oh, come off it, Sof. I saw the way the two of you were look-ing at each other the other day." She batted her eyes dramatically.

"Stop it. We were not . . . looking at each other." My con-stricted throat nearly didn't let the sip of frappé through. "Any-way, Mom invited Dino over for you. Not me."

"Yeah, and if I was even minutely interested in him I'd be majorly pissed right now."

"Why?"

"Because you stole a guy from your own sister."

"I didn't steal anything."

"I know, because he wasn't mine to steal." She shifted on her stool to better face me. "What I want to know is whether or not you've knocked boots with him yet."

I was pretty sure my mouth was open to make some sort of reply, but nothing was coming out.

"Oh my God! You have, haven't you?"

I turned to face the counter. "I don't know what you're talk-ing about."

"Oh yes you do. Just look at your face. You're redder than *batsaria.*"

"I am not redder than beets."

She thankfully fell silent, probably as shocked as I felt by the news that I'd slept with Dino.

She leaned into me. "Was it good?"

I couldn't help myself. I meant to protest her question, deny that anything had happened.

Instead I smiled at her.

Efi looked satisfied as she straightened her shoulders and took a sip from her water. "You've just elevated yourself back to hero status. Slut."

I threw back my head and laughed.

"Just wait until I tell Mom."

I grabbed her arm so tightly she made a sound. "You had better not breathe a word to Mom. Or Dad. Or Pappou. Anyone, do you hear me?"

"Why not?" she asked teasingly.

"Because . . . well, because it's not going to happen again."

She stared at me unblinkingly. "Why not? I mean, if it was that good . . ."

"Because it's just not going to, that's why."

She *tsk*ed. "See. The whole permanent thing again."

"This has absolutely nothing to do with Thomas."

"Then what does it have to do with?"

"The fact that I'm not interested in a serious relationship with anyone right now."

"Uh-huh."

I'd learned that when it came to my siblings, sometimes the best defense was a great offense. "And you? Have you told Mom that you and Jeremy are dating yet?"

The extreme focus on me had left her unprotected and she averted her gaze.

"Uh-huh."

"That was a low blow," she said.

"Yes, well, I had to knock you off track somehow."

"Well, congratulations. You achieved your objective." She glowered. "I wouldn't have said anything anyway. You know that."

I did, but that hadn't stopped me from being terrified that she might.

We sat sipping our beverages of choice for a few minutes in silence. Then I leaned into her.

"Truce?"

She made a face. "Truce." She shook her finger. "But don't think this is anywhere near finished."

That's exactly what I was afraid of. In more ways than I could count. . . .

Twenty-five

MY REFLECTION ON ALL OF us being creatures of habit ended up being the theme for the day. It was midnight and I was sitting in my car parked up the street from the McMansion, working a case that was officially closed.

I don't know. There was just something about the entire Venezuela thing that wasn't settling well with me. Fine, the couple's sex life was back to normal and then some. And Gisela had gotten one hell of an apology for his behavior via the rock the size of a city block. But somehow I got the impression that that's not all that she wrote in this case.

A black Mercedes passed and I slid down in my seat. Not that it mattered. Lucille was as inconspicuous as a house marked-up for demolition. Call it a reflex action.

Much like my continuing to work on a case that had nowhere else to go.

I watched the gates to the property open and the Mercedes drive inside. I tried to get a gander at who was driving, but didn't have any luck because it disappeared into the garage and the door closed before I could catch a glimpse of the driver.

I sighed and settled back more comfortably in my seat. Muffy whined from where he was sitting next to me.

"I know, boy. I know." I gave his ears a scratch then reached into my glove box where I'd put a stash of biscuits for just such occasions. His stubby tail slapped against the leather seat as he sat up for the treat. I fed it to him, along with another.

"Okay, that's enough," I said, putting the rest of the treats back inside the glove box alongside my Glock. "We don't want to ruin our appetites."

After all, we had leftover pasticcio noodles and sauce to snack on when we got back home.

God, was I that pathetic?

I reached over to the passenger seat, feeling under Muffy's furry butt for my cell phone. He nipped at my hand.

"Ow."

I took it as a warning against goosing him again anytime soon or else the nip might be a bite.

I scrolled through my recent call log until I came across the number I wanted. I pushed the call button, not much caring that it was the middle of the night.

"Christ, Metro, do you know what time it is?" Fowler answered after seven rings.

"Oh, I'm sorry. You weren't sleeping, were you?"

"Yes, I was."

"Alone, I presume."

"If that's a proposition, you can forget about it."

Eeew. The mere reference to sex with the icky sports reporter would be enough to give me nightmares for days. "Not a chance."

"What do you want, Sofie?"

I twisted my lips. What did I want? "I don't know. I guess I just wanted to make sure that I wasn't the only one up this late at night."

"You working the Venezuela case?"

"Something like that." I scratched my head. "Actually, I guess you can't say that I'm working it. I got fired today."

His chuckle got under my skin. "Shocker."

"Hey, I'm good at what I do."

"They why'd you get fired?"

"Because Venezuela gave his wife a 'make-up' diamond the size of Long Island."

"Really?"

He seemed abnormally surprised by this.

"So . . . ," I said. "What's going on from your end?"

"Read my column in the morning."

And then he hung up on me.

I sighed and tossed the phone back to the passenger seat where Muffy got up so he could sit back down on it. I didn't even want to think about putting the thing to my face again. Much less what the vibrate option did for him.

I sat for another ten minutes watching as the interior lights went out in the Venezuela house. Then I started my car and headed for home, thinking that my life was pretty pathetic indeed.

THE FOLLOWING MORNING, I STOOD in line waiting my turn for an open booth at the shooting range. Much to my chagrin, I'd woken up at around 5:00 A.M. sweaty and restless and unable to get back to sleep again. Not because I'd had a wet dream about Dino or Porter. Rather, images of Gisela and Reni Venezuela kept rolling through my mind, as I subconsciously investigated every angle that my conscious mind could not.

Unfortunately the lesson in futility left me with no answers but more than a little sleep-deprived.

I looked around. I'd never seen the range this packed. Who knew so many people hit the range early in the morning?

"Hey, Sofie."

I looked to where Pamela Coe had stepped up next to me. "Hey, yourself." I motioned toward the line. "Is it always this busy this early?"

"Yeah. A lot of the boys in blue stop in either before their shift begins or after it ends. You know, to wake themselves up or help them relax."

"Ah."

So essentially I was surrounded by cops. I don't know why that surprised me, but it did. Didn't the department have some sort of shooting range? I would have thought they would.

"So . . . I hear you've been flashing a press badge around town with my name on it."

I stared at Pamela as if she'd just told me someone had dyed my hair blue while I slept. "What?"

Okay, so I'd completely forgotten that I'd borrowed her identity for a couple of days. Not so much her identity as her name attached to a made-up identity.

"Oh, yeah," I said, checking to make sure my gun was on safety and hoping hers was, too. "Sorry about that. I found myself in a jam and, well, I'd just seen you that day and your name was the first that came to mind."

Her gaze narrowed on me. "You done with it?"

"Yeah, pretty much. I'm not working the case I was using it for anymore."

"Can I have the ID?"

"Sure. I'll give it to you at back at the agency. Why? Think you can get some use out of it?"

"It's not so much that than making sure you're not tempted to use it again."

I squinted at her. "How did you hear about that, anyway?"

She shrugged. "Word gets around."

"Where? I'm always the last to know about anything."

She smiled at me. "Maybe you're not listening in the right places."

"Maybe." I wondered where those places were and whether she might tell me if I asked in the right way.

Truth was the first minute I'd laid eyes on Pamela Coe I'd felt there was far more going on beneath the surface of her polished blond good looks than most suspected. I knew she was a great process server and she'd handled a couple of cheating spouse cases. That was about it.

At another place of business I could take a look at her employment application to get more information. But I suspected that there weren't any official forms at the agency bearing her name beyond the checks she received.

"Can I see your weapon?" she asked.

I lifted the Glock.

She handed me her Beretta and I watched as she looked down the nose of my firearm, released the clip, considered it, and then slid it back home. We exchanged guns again.

"You may want to think about cleaning it."

I remembered the little pamphlet that had come with the gun along with a small container of what had looked like WD-40 and small pads and a pipe cleaner thing. "How often do you think I should do it?"

"It wouldn't be a bad idea to give her a quick once over every time you fire it. Keeps her in good working order. Target on. Something as small as a snowflake in the barrel could affect firing."

I stared at her. "How do you know so much about this stuff?"

She gestured to where the booth down the way had cleared out. "You're up."

I shuffled toward the booth, watching as another opened down the way for Pamela, meaning I couldn't follow up on my question.

Exactly how and why did she seem to know so much about guns and shooting? And how had she found out I'd been using her name?

I put on my headphones and safety goggles and then attached the target and pushed the button to extend it fifty feet. I didn't know, but I determined to find out. . . .

"YOU GOT FIRED, DIDN'T YOU?" Rosie asked.

I nearly broke the tip off the pencil I was using to draw circles around the map I'd taken from Rosie's desk when I'd come in earlier that morning. It was the one she'd made outlining all the reports of missing pets that had been pouring into the agency for the past three weeks.

"What?" I asked, although I'd heard her just fine.

"The Venezuela case. You got fired."

I motioned at her with the pencil without looking at her. "I didn't get fired . . . I was let go."

You say tomato, I say tomato . . . The old song taunted me as I tried to concentrate on the matter at hand.

"Uh-huh. You were fired. When Phoebe told me that at the restaurant this morning, I thought it couldn't be true and I told her so. Only by the time I got to the office with my bear claw, I wondered if it was. I mean, you got that envelope and everything when you hadn't used the first of the money yet. . . ."

My head snapped up. "Is there somewhere you're going with this? Because if there is, I wish you'd hurry up and get there."

"Whoa. We're snappy this morning, aren't we?"

"I'm not snappy," I snapped. "I'm just PMSing, that's all."

"Ah. That time of the month. My sister Lupe says that's what she's going to miss most after she has the baby, you know? No periods. Then again, I told her that she won't have to go to the bathroom every five minutes neither. I mean, she went before we left for the movies last night and I had to stop at a Key Food so she could go again before we even got there." She shook her head. "I'd have soiled myself before going in there."

"When you've gotta go, you gotta go."

"Whatever."

"You're chatty this morning."

"That's because today is Lupe's due date."

I looked at her. I'd been hearing so much about Lupe's pregnancy that I had half-expected she would stay pregnant forever. "She having a C-section?"

"No. She's going natural. But this is her due date, you know, the one set by the doctor when he told her she was pregnant."

"You know that most women never deliver on their due date."

"Yeah, I know. But Lupe thinks it's going to happen." She tapped her cell phone sitting on her desk. "That's why I'm on call."

"Oh." I tried to sound interested, I really did. But I'd heard so much about Lupe this, Yolanda-the-coming-baby that, that I felt like I was the one having morning sickness.

Which, of course, I wasn't. Thank God for sparing me that one at that particular point in my life.

The door opened, letting in a burst of cool air. I idly wondered if there was something we could do about that. It must be a bitch in the winter.

"Hey, guys," Debbie Matenopoulos said, her white-blond hair perfectly framing her perfectly made-up face. She was wearing a clingy purple dress that barely covered her delicate areas both north and south of the border. And those shoes . . . how did she walk around in six-inch stilettos without getting blisters or twisting her ankle? Or, at the very least, without getting fined for looking like a call girl?

"Whatcha got for me?" Debbie asked Rosie, on whom I'd placed the responsibility of handling her. Half the work she did still involved process serving, but she was doing such a good job on the cheating spouse angle that I was pushing more of those cases her way.

"Oh, Sof, I forgot to tell you, I picked up some of that equipment the other day. It's great. Thank you."

I felt like that aforementioned winter wind had just hit me full in the face. "What?"

"You know. That surveillance stuff. Mr. Nash was nice enough to let me in the other day when I came by to find the agency closed. It was only four thirty so I knocked and he let me in. I found the stuff on your desk."

She'd taken the surveillance equipment. . . .

I stared at Rosie who shrugged. "I had to take Lupe to a doctor's appointment so I closed up early."

Debbie said, "I haven't figured out how to use it all yet, but—"

I held my hand out palm up. "Give it to me."

She popped her gum and shrugged. "Sure." She dug inside her knockoff Fendi bag and came out with all the items that I'd accused my cousin Pete of stealing.

I winced even as Rosie *tsk-tsk*ed me.

I glared at her. "I don't even want to hear it."

"I didn't say anything."

"Good. Just keep it that way."

Debbie said, "What don't you want to hear?"

"Never mind," Rosie and I said in unison.

I didn't even bother to ask Debbie why she'd felt the equipment was for her. She was one of those types that passed a store and thought a blouse had her name all over it—literally.

The important part was that I had the equipment back . . . and that I knew I had an apology to make.

Twenty-six

SO I FELT LIKE A heel. I'd accused my cousin Pete of a crime he hadn't committed.

Figured. He takes over a hundred out of my purse and I don't say anything. Something comes up missing and I finger him for it and he hadn't even done it.

Cripes.

I wasn't looking forward to that particular apology.

I'd taken off from the agency shortly after Debbie had left, deciding I couldn't really handle any more Lupe bathroom stories, and picked up Muffy from my apartment before driving around, hitting all the points on the map I'd drawn up from Rosie's outline.

Okay, so I didn't like the thought that I was working a missing pet case. But this whole firing thing had really gotten to me. And sitting around obsessing over it—or, worse, working a case that was no longer open—wasn't an option. So I had to do something until the next big thing rolled in (and this, I knew, was no guarantee; big things in my biz were few and far between, if at all).

So there I was, cruising around Astoria, glad it was warm enough to put down the top of the Mustang. Muffy was in full agreement as he sat with his paws leaning against the top of his door, his tongue catching a breeze as he cased the other side of the street.

I didn't know what I was looking for. A sign maybe? A handwritten one would be nice: "Missing Pets This Way." Of course, I wasn't going to find one of those. And even if I did, it would be highly suspect.

No, any signs I saw would be of the subtle variety. Little clues, arrows, pointing to what was probably a simple solution. Kids, maybe, playing a practical joke by cutting holes into containing fences so the pets could get out.

It was said that animals could sense an oncoming earthquake or impending natural disaster long before we humans could. As I battled with a crosswind to spread the map out on the steering wheel, I thought that the pattern looked suspiciously like the diagram of an earthquake, the shocks moving outward like little waves.

Could a tremor be in the offing? Had the animals predicted it and run from the relative safety of their homes toward higher ground?

If so, then this thing was bigger than even I could handle.

Muffy barked and I looked up just in time to slam on the brakes to keep from hitting a white toy poodle that was crossing the street in front of me. It had a tuft of fur on its head that bore a dirty pink ribbon, and a puff on its tail. A puff that jerked every time the little mongrel barked at me from its now safe position on the side of the sidewalk. Stupid little dog. Muffy crossed my lap in order to get a closer look from my side of the car.

Wait a minute. I knew this dog . . .

I pushed Muffy aside and grabbed the folder in the passenger's seat. Ah, yes. The guy I'd ignored who had come in about his wife's missing eight-year-old poodle named . . . I searched the page even as my brain produced the answer: Tiffany.

Gone missing a little over two weeks ago. I stared at the Tiffany look-alike. She didn't look none the worse for wear, which meant if it was her, she was getting fed.

A car honked behind me. I put up my hand and then clicked on my hazard lights. I only hoped the dog wasn't too well fed to turn down one of Muffy's favorite snacks.

I reached into the glove box as the driver gave another honk. I freed a dog treat just as the driver appeared beside my car.

"What in the hell are you doing, blocking the friggin' road?" he asked.

He spotted my Glock in the glove box, probably thinking that's what I was reaching for. He lifted his hands up.

"Whoa. That's fine. The street's all yours. I'll back up."

And that's exactly what he did in a squeal of tires as I closed the glove box, rolled up the windows to prevent Muffy from getting out (a futile attempt because unless I put the top up, he could always jump out via the trunk), and then did a fast open-jump-close move to prevent him from exiting with me. He barked and scratched at the closed window.

"Here, Tiffany, Tiffany, Tiffany," I said, calling the dog by her name.

I received a head cock in return as the poodle apparently recognized her name.

"Do you want a treat?" I crouched down even as I drew nearer, holding out the biscuit.

I got close enough for her to sniff, but when I tried to reach out for her, she barked and ran a couple feet away, trembling from head to toenail before turning back to face me, barking again.

I stood upright and stretched my neck. This was so not how

I envisioned myself when I hired on as a detective at my uncle's agency.

"Come on, Tiffany," I said to the dog. "I'm trying to help you, not hurt you."

I held out the treat again and she edged closer. I dropped the biscuit and she ran to it, hungrily going to work on it as her tail wagged a million miles a minute.

I easily scooped her up and held her a few inches away from my face. Close enough to inspect her, but not for any nips she might want to throw my way. She wore a collar with an ID in the shape of a heart. I flipped it over. TIFFANY, it read, a phone number listed under it that matched the one in my file.

Bingo.

I smiled.

"Hey, Tiffany. My name's Sofie. I'm going to take you home."

I was afraid the small dog might vibrate straight out of my hand as I opened my car door, put her down on the backseat, and then climbed in, quickly closing the door to prevent Muffy or Tiffany from getting out.

Hey, I had skills.

And I found out fairly quickly that Muffy wasn't discriminatory when it came to age or breed as he buried his nose in the poodle's fluffy white butt.

Eeew.

I put the car into gear and drove slowly onward.

Coming across Tiffany was an unexpected setback. Yes, I'd said setback. Because I had a sneaking suspicion that while one or two of the missing pet incidents were the result of simple runaways (or breakouts, depending on the pets' living conditions), there was something more going on here, something more than what met the eye.

Something that wouldn't result in finding each missing pet one-by-one crossing the street.

So I navigated around the locations on my maps, drawing a tighter circle each time I went. Muffy and Tiff were still busy getting acquainted in the back of the car, so I didn't have to worry about them. I got so comfortable, in fact, that I rolled the windows back down.

And the instant I did, they both made a jump for it.

For the second time in so many minutes, I jammed on the brakes. Tiffany had gone sailing over the passenger's side door, and Muffy had followed, chasing the wildly barking poodle up the block until they disappeared between two houses.

Aw, hell.

See. It was just my luck that the instant I decided to look into a missing pet case that I ended up with a missing pet of my own.

Rather than leaving my car in the middle of the street like last time, I found a spot nearer the driveway they had run up and then gave chase myself.

Only there wasn't far for me to go, because both dogs were outside a beat-up, closed garage, barking their heads off.

Or, rather, the poodle was barking her head off and digging at the bottom of the garage door, while Muffy was barking at her.

I verified that the poodle's owners, the Kaufmans, didn't live at this address.

"Muffy, come here," I ordered the Jack Russell terrier.

He spared me a look, but kept on barking at his new friend, nipping at her small back legs when he didn't receive the attention he wanted.

"Hey, what the hell you doing back there?"

I turned to find a woman standing in the back door of a matching run-down house, a half-burned cigarette with the ash still attached was not so much hanging from her mouth as it appeared glued to her bottom lip.

"I'm sorry. My dogs jumped from my car and I'm just trying to catch them before they run off again."

"Those aren't your dogs. They're mine."

I raised my brows. Okay, so maybe there was a Tiffany look-alike somewhere. But I knew that Muffy was, indeed, my dog.

"Pardon me?" I asked.

The woman yelled over her shoulder. "Josh. Johnny. Get out here. Looks like we've got a problem. Somebody's trying to break into our garage."

Two teenage boys who were maybe fourteen and fifteen but a foot taller than I was, appeared in the door behind her.

"Aw, Mom, what is it? I'm in the middle of a game."

The poodle spotted the guys and gave a small whine before ducking behind my legs. Muffy stopped barking, gave her a sniff, and then looked up at me as if to say, "What did you do to her?"

It was during the momentary lull in the barking that I heard other barking. A lot of it. Coming from the direction of the garage.

"You don't mind if I take a look in here, do you?" I asked.

I was five feet closer to the garage than the guys and their mother were to me.

"Hey, that's private property!" the woman shouted. "Get out of here before I call the police."

I tried to lift the garage door but it stuck somewhere. I gave it a kick and then it went up on its own.

And inside I found ten dog cages of various sizes holding dogs of various sizes. And I suspected that each and every one of them would match the descriptions of the missing pets in my file.

Bingo.

The woman and her two sons were advancing on me.

I pulled the cell phone from my jeans pocket. "Don't worry about the police. I'll call them."

One of the kids made a move for the phone. Muffy immediately attached himself to his ankle and growled like the dickens. The other kid moved to grab Muffy and I used his hunched over position to my advantage by shoving my foot against his shoulder. He landed on his behind with a loud thud and groaned. The poodle bit at his hand, and then the other when he snatched them back.

I held out a finger toward the mother. "One more step, ma'am, and I won't be responsible for what I'll do."

A couple of the neighbors gathered on the sidewalk at the end of the drive. I looked toward them even as I gave 911 my location and told them I was being physically assaulted.

"Any of you guys in on this?" I called to the neighbors.

"In on what?" a guy in his forties answered.

"This pet-napping scheme."

"Scheme? Hell, lady, they told me they were breeding the noisy bastards."

I was pretty sure that no one was going to try anything now that the police were on their way. And since I was fairly certain the mother and her two sons lived in the house, even if they ran, they wouldn't get far. For all I knew, they probably thought they could talk their way out of what was an obvious attempt at extortion.

Swipe the dogs. Lock them up. And then wait for the worried owners to offer a reward for the return of their beloved pets, no questions asked.

I called off Muffy and picked up Tiffany, who repeatedly licked my face, her little body trembling with what could have been joy.

I turned toward the dogs in the cages and shook my head. What some people called a living . . .

WHAT SOME PEOPLE CALLED NEWS.

I was at home later that night watching the Mets game on channel eleven, enjoying a celebratory souvlaki with Muffy, when I received at least three calls from people telling me that they'd seen my mug on the ten o'clock.

Yes, a local television station had been monitoring the police scanner, picked up on the goings-on, and had showed up at what I learned was the Cummings' house, the pet-napped dogs making good filler, I guess.

There had been sixteen of them all told. Dogs taken from the safety of their yards and locked up in the Cummings' garage, waiting until the owners offered up a reward of some merit before they would conveniently "find" the dog and collect the money with no one the wiser.

No paper routes for the Cummings kids. It seemed Mom had bigger things in mind for them.

My cell vibrated again. I nudged it with the side of my hand that didn't have cucumber sauce running down it so I could see the display. Rosie. I wiped my hand on a napkin.

"Why didn't you stop by the office to tell me?" she demanded. "I could have used some good news while I was doing all that waiting."

"I did stop by, but by the time everything was finished up, it was past closing time and you were gone." I used the napkin to wipe my mouth and moved Muffy away from where he was poised to gobble up the rest of my pita sandwich. "I take it Lupe hasn't delivered yet?"

Rosie gave an exaggerated sigh. "No. I'm at her house still, but she's not even gassy, much less anywhere near labor."

"I told you."

I imagined her sticking her tongue out to the phone.

"Anyway, I just wanted to tell you that I think it's great, you know, what you did finding all those peoples' pets like that."

"Sheer coincidence."

Actually Tiffany and Muffy had done the finding. All I did was follow their canine noses.

"Oh, and I wanted to tell you that you looked good on TV. Does that poodle belong to anyone? I was thinking I'd like to adopt it."

"Tiffany is home with her owners, safe and sound," I told her.

I'd taken her home, personally. Partly because she was a hero of sorts in my eyes. Mostly because Muffy wouldn't let the Humane Society people take her, where they would hold the dogs until their owners picked them up.

"Oh. Okay. That's all I wanted to say."

I rang off and shook my head, more than happy to return to my dinner.

Reni was warming up in the bullpen at the beginning of the fourth inning. Were they considering putting him in as relief? I watched the way his tattoo rippled even as my cell phone vibrated again.

Now what?

I looked at the display to find that it read, "Elmhurst Hospital."

Rosie couldn't have gotten from her sister's house to the hospital that quickly, could she?

I wiped my hands again and picked up.

"Ms. Metropolis?" a woman's voice asked.

"This is she."

"What's your relationship to George Fowler?"

What was my relationship to Fowler? Nothing. "Why do you ask?"

"Because Mr. Fowler was just brought into the hospital, unconscious and with multiple contusions that probably got him that way. And your contact information was all we found on him.

"When can you come down?"

Twenty-seven

I NEVER QUITE UNDERSTOOD WHERE the saying "What am I, chopped liver?" came from. I mean, beyond the fact that most people didn't like liver. (I was an exception. I always enjoyed the liver Mom made. Of course, the key was eating it straight out of the frying pan with lots of fresh lemon juice squeezed over the top along with a small plate of greens drizzled with olive oil and lemon.) At any rate, after visiting Fowler at the hospital, I now understood what chopped liver looked like in relationship to people. The guy was little more than a big, dark bruise with countless slashes across his swollen skin, some of which were left uncovered.

My God, who would do this to him?

Unfortunately, I hadn't been able to ask him because he had been unconscious.

Still, that didn't stop me from bending over and whispering, "Fowler, who should I call? Do you have family or friends or someone I should let know? Should I call the newspaper?"

He hadn't answered.

I wasn't sure how I felt about being the closest thing to the next living relative to a guy I barely knew and didn't even like.

What I did like, however, was that my status gave me access to his personal items. A nurse easily handed over a large Ziploc baggie that held his cell phone, wallet, and notepad, one of which I hoped would help me help him. And if it helped me help myself, too, well, all the better.

The first thing I did was call information to track down his ex-wife. How long had he said he'd been divorced? Six years? And, call me clairvoyant, it was my guess that things probably hadn't gone very well.

To my surprise, however, finding his ex had been relatively easy, and she not only took my call and listened to me without hanging up, she said she'd come to the hospital to visit him first thing in the morning.

Which wasn't that far off at this point.

I didn't know how Fowler would feel about that. But probably hearing his ex's voice would snap him back to the land of the living posthaste so maybe I could get some answers.

The police were little help. The reporting officer told me that they'd received a call that there was a gang fight of some sort. When they arrived at the fringes of Corona, there was Fowler, alone, lying in a pool of his own blood in the middle of the street.

Yeah, there had been a gang fight, all right. There had been a gang, and Fowler. And Fowler had lost.

I scratched my head and flipped through his notepad, which had been found a couple of feet from where he was lying. It was damp and some of the ink had run. I had never been any good at deciphering shorthand, especially sloppy shorthand such as Fowler's, but it seemed most of the notations referred in some way or another to Venezuela. Which wouldn't be unusual, really, since he was a New York reporter and the Mets were heading straight for the pennant, do not pass go, do not collect $200. But given the nebulous connection between Fowler and I, and our collective interest in the latest celebrity pitcher, I pored over the pad looking for something I might use to assuage my own curiosity.

Nothing.

I flipped back to the end to see the last thing he had written. The page held a number that looked like a Queens cross-street address.

Which helped me not at all without some sort of precise street reference; not in a borough that had a Forty-third Street that met at Forty-third Avenue.

At any rate, all of this made it doubly important to ensure Fowler made it safely back over to this side of the fence. Because there was little doubt in my mind that this hadn't been just some random beating. This had been either a warning attempt gone wrong, or an out-and-out murder attempt.

AT THE AGENCY THE FOLLOWING afternoon, I was having a hard time ducking the media that wanted a follow-up on the Dog-napping Caper, as it was being called, and phone calls and visits from the owners who wanted to express their thanks and offer up money. I talked to the press when I could, declined the money since I hadn't officially taken any of the cases on, and accepted the thanks.

And during all this Rosie stared at me as if I were some sort of saint.

"What is it now?" I grumbled for the third time in as many minutes when I caught her staring at me again.

"I don't want nothing. I was just wondering how it felt to be a hero and all."

"I'm not a hero. I was bored and took a drive through the neighborhood. What's the big deal?"

"The big deal is that there are a dozen people out there happy as clams to have their children back."

"They were pets, Rosie."

"Pets are like children. They're so helpless. They need you to feed them and bathe them and take care of them and love them."

It was a leap for me, but who was I to argue?

At any rate, I'd asked Rosie to call in my cousin Pete so I could offer up my apology and he'd said that he would try to stop in some time today. He hadn't shown up yet. And while Fowler's ex-wife was reported to be holding vigil at his bedside, he had yet to regain full consciousness, making me wonder if calling her had been a good idea, you know, beyond getting me off the hook for looking after him.

Between Rosie looking at me like I sported a halo and rattling on about her sister's being a day past her due date and how that wasn't good, I all but jumped on Waters when he walked through the door after his morning process-serving rounds.

"Thank God," I said, grabbing him and taking him inside my uncle's office. I soundly closed the door.

He looked from it, to me, then grinned, his big brown eyes and gold teeth flashing suggestively. "Hey, baby, all you gotta do is say the word and Uncle Eugene will take care of whatever ails you."

I gave him an eye roll. "Is that all men ever think about?"

"What else is there?"

I crossed my arms, not up to arguing the point just then.

"Good showing on the tube, by the way. Rescuing dogs ought to be good for business."

"Yeah, as in drumming up more missing pet cases."

"Could be worse."

I supposed it could. "Look, the reason I brought you in here is that you've heard the Venezuela case is closed, right?"

"I heard you got fired."

Rosie and her big mouth. "Whatever. Anyway, I wanted to ask you if you've had a chance to visit the ballpark recently."

"All the time. I went to the game yesterday and," he dug in his front shirt pocket, "I got tickets to today's game."

I tried to snatch them from his hand but I wasn't fast enough.

"Uh-uh. Do you know what markers I had to cash in to get these?"

"I don't want to know. I just want those tickets."

"Why? You're not officially on the case anymore. And with Mrs. Venezuela back to acting like a dutiful wife, I'd recommend you let sleeping dogs lie."

"She's acting dutiful? What does that entail, exactly?"

He shrugged. "She's attending all the games and sitting in the family box pretending to support her husband while looking like a million bucks. Fawning all over him after the game, et cetera, et cetera."

"More like she has a million bucks on her ring finger."

"Then there's that. A lot of sports wives have an extensive jewelry collection."

"I bet. Anyway, what's it going to take?"

He stared at the tickets as if trying to come up with an amount. "I suppose I might be able to sell you one of them . . ."

A LITTLE WHILE LATER, I sat in my car up the block from Dino's *zaharoplastio*, the ticket for tonight's Mets game in my pocket, hoping I wouldn't live to regret having given Waters an interesting chunk of my personal savings account in order to get it.

You know, like I was coming to regret having slept with Dino.

I'm not sure if "regret" was the right word in the case of the latter. I suppose it was if you looked at it one way, but not in the way you might automatically think. You see, I didn't regret sleeping with him, meaning he was "what in the hell was I thinking?" one-night stand material. Rather the regret I was coming to understand was that I couldn't pursue something with him. Maybe a date or two. A night out at one of the Greek restaurants or clubs, see how he danced, what kind of food he liked that didn't come out of Thalia's kitchen—where he was pretty much required to say he liked everything if he hoped to be invited back and not find a hot dish dumped into his lap—to distinguish if my attraction to him was but a momentary, yet significant, blip on the radar, or if there was a firm foundation on which to build.

Take a closer look at him as a man rather than as a threat to my independence—not only as a Greek my parents might try to railroad me into marrying, but to my new career.

That caught me up short.

While there were quite a number of things I didn't like about my job (the paperwork, the enraged or crying wives that found out their suspicions were right and their spouses were cheating or, worse, caught husbands that sent me dead flowers), but there were a lot of things I did like.

The dogs, for example.

Don't get me wrong. I don't think Dino or my parents are threatening to chain me to the kitchen sink and make me have little Greek baby after little Greek baby. But since my breakup with Thomas, I'd done my best to run as far as fast as I could away from my previous beliefs on what life had in store for me. I'd gone from dreamy-eyed predictions of picture-perfect holidays and family trips to Greece to throwing myself headlong into my new career as a PI. And I hadn't looked back, hadn't had a reason to.

Until now.

A part of me wished I had met Dino before Thomas. Another scoffed at that because that would have meant giving up the past six months. A period that had opened me to new experiences and helped me develop new skills. I no longer looked at the world in the same way.

Simply, there was no going back.

And then there was Porter . . .

The car filled with the sound of my deep sigh.

I wondered if I would still be pining after him if we had slept together.

But we hadn't, so that question would remain forever unanswered.

So while the future had been gaping out in front of me like a wide desert waiting to be crossed on the day of my would-be wedding, now I was noticing little lush side roads and routes I had been blind to before merely because of the newness of the vista. And I needed a while to examine them, see which ones I might be interested in traveling.

Right now, the old routes appealed to me not at all.

I blinked, not realizing I'd been staring until movement jostled me out of my reverie. Dino had come out of his shop and stood on the sidewalk looking up and down the street, rubbing the back of his neck, almost as if he sensed someone's attention but couldn't put his finger on the source. Boy, did I ever know that feeling.

Damn but he looked good. Better than the sweet concoctions that filled the front window of his shop. Well, okay, just as good, perhaps. I didn't know if any man had what it took to beat out a great chocolate torte. But if anyone could, it would be Dino.

I watched as he fished a cigarette out of the front pocket of his snow-white apron and lit it, inhaling deeply.

I smiled. I hadn't known he smoked. Had never detected the smell on his clothes. Then again, I hadn't exactly been paying attention to anything other than the roar of my own hormones at the time.

My cell phone chirped. I picked it up.

"You'll never guess what I just found out," Rosie said.

"I give up. What did you find out?" Truth was, I'd given up trying to figure out Rosie logic sometime during my first day at the agency. The woman was brilliant, but the way she arrived at the final destination was nothing if not a little convoluted.

"That couple that says they found that ear in their soup at Phoebe's? Well, since I couldn't find anything more by looking up their names and Social Security numbers, I decided to do a search on body parts found in food. And guess what I discovered? It looks like the same couple, using aliases, may have 'accidentally' found what could be a different part of that same ear floating in their minestrone soup in Memphis."

"That's fantastic."

"I think it's sick."

"Not the incident, but the fact that we have what we need to save Phoebe's bacon."

"In more ways than one."

"Yeah. In more ways than one." I watched as Dino put his cigarette out on the bottom of his shoe, taking the butt back inside with him, probably to throw it out. I started Lucille and pulled away from the curb. "Give me the complete lowdown . . ."

Twenty-eight

I WAS COMING TO UNDERSTAND that there were two very distinct types of people in the world: The ones that worked their asses off trying to make an honest living; and the ones that endeavored to prove those people were idiots as they took advantage of that honesty.

Phoebe Hall had been genuinely afraid that the ear had ended up in the soup through some fault of her own. Perhaps it had been in the jar of chicken stock she'd canned herself. Maybe when she'd made the stock she hadn't checked the chicken well and had ended up accidentally canning the piece of ear that could have come from the butcher's. Or the chicken ranch.

Yeah, and maybe the ear fairy had paid her a visit and dropped the piece into her soup when she wasn't looking so she might pay up on some sort of outstanding cosmic debt.

I'd had Rosie give me the address to the accusing couple, Susan and Tom Miller—also known as Suzie and Thomas Jones—and I walked up to the panel of mailboxes and doorbells now. They lived in a maze-like complex, auspiciously called the Acropolis Gardens, in the northern part of Astoria. Not more than eight blocks away from the Venezuela McMansion, as luck would have it, but worlds away. I located the couple's doorbell and rang it.

"What?" a man's voice shouted through the speaker.

"I'm Sofie Metropolis. I'd like to speak to Tom and/or Susan Miller please."

"Speaking."

"Face to face."

Silence.

And then the door lock gave.

I walked inside the building, detecting the immediate smell of boiled cabbage. (I swear, there must be some unwritten contract that apartment dwellers had to boil cabbage at least once a week so that the halls reeked of it. Or maybe it was some sort of twisted attempt to keep others from loitering in the halls. Whatever it was, the stink made me remember Muffy's bout with gas a month or so ago. Not a happy time.)

Normally, I didn't like going into apartment buildings like these that I wasn't familiar with. But I'd been here before, had a friend who'd lived there a few years back.

Still, I found my hand going into my purse where I had stowed my pepper spray. Just in case.

I double-checked that I had the right apartment and then knocked.

"Who is it?"

Hadn't we just had this exchange?

"Sofie Metropolis."

The door opened on a security chain. "Aren't you that woman who found all those dogs?" A woman openly eyed me.

"That would be me."

"We don't have any pets."

"That's good. Because that's not why I'm here." I looked

down the hall to where a neighbor had cracked open their door, an eyeball peering out at me. "I'm here about the restaurant matter."

The woman disappeared and a man's head popped into the crack. I had to look up to meet his gaze. "What's she offering?"

Now that was a question. "Well, let's see, how should I put this? She's offering that she won't put your sorry asses in jail for attempted grand theft if you leave town within the month." I held up a printout I'd picked up from Rosie that bore their mugs and also listed the crime for which they'd been arrested in Memphis.

The door slammed.

I took out the adhesive I'd brought along with me and taped the page to their door, info and pics facing out. I figured the neighbor watching me would be the first to come see what this was about.

"I take it I'm understood?" I called through the wood to where I'm sure they both still stood.

No answer. Not that I expected one. I'd made my point. If they tried to contact Phoebe again, I'd call Pino, see what my options were on having them arrested and possibly extradited back to Memphis.

The reason I hadn't called him straight out is Phoebe was the only one who knew what the couple looked like, so Rosie had her come by the agency to positively ID their mug shots. And she'd asked that we not contact the authorities. She was just glad that she wouldn't have to close her doors and didn't want to cause any trouble for them.

Actually, I thought I might give Pino a call anyway. Probably the couple already had their next move planned out, their next target a small diner in Ohio or something. If Phoebe found out that I'd called the police, I could explain it to her in a language even her generous heart could understand.

After all, she didn't want to be responsible for allowing what had happened to her to happen to somebody else, did she? I knew I didn't.

A part of me wanted to find out where they'd gotten their body parts, and probably I could have found out if I applied a little elbow grease. But I'd accomplished my goal of getting the couple to back away from Phoebe and her restaurant, and would have to be happy with that for now.

Besides, I reasoned that I probably really didn't want to know.

So I decided I would file the information solidly in the "all's well that ends well" column and move on.

At any rate, it seemed Rosie's interest in her new computer had expanded her ability to search for information that might have otherwise gone undiscovered. I just wish she could have dug up something useful on one wily Reni Bastardo Venezuela.

Actually, that reminded me of something . . .

I leaned closer to the door, unable to resist getting in one last jab. "Oh, and I've included the number to a good plastic surgeon. You know, for whoever you know that keeps volunteering body parts for your little schemes. And one last piece of advice: Get a job."

"STOW IT, METRO," WATERS MUMBLED next to me.

I grinned at him, oblivious to the fans cheering around me, the Mets vs. Reds game playing out on the field on the other side of the fence from our exclusive Home Plate Club Gold seats.

"So *that's* how you get such exclusive access."

I looked at the black woman walking away from us up the aisle in a uniform like those of others that worked at Shea Stadium, probably going back to work. I recognized her. More specifically, I remembered her shouting at me when I'd tried to deliver landlord dispute papers to Eugene a month ago. The encounter had resulted in my landing butt-first in the mud outside her apartment door. Not one of my most stellar moments. Even if it did ultimately result in hiring Waters.

At any rate, five minutes ago she'd come up to Eugene, said, "Hey, baby," planted a big wet one on him, and then handed over a pass of sorts that I suspected would get him access to the press level.

I looked back at Eugene. "And here I thought you might be a scalper. But then again, ticket-scalping wouldn't get you access to the players now, would it?"

He puffed out his skinny chest under his leather jacket. "I have connections. I used to work at the Long Island Islanders stadium." He patted his Afro. "It's how Dolores and I met."

I laughed and he scowled.

For some reason I couldn't define, I was a little disappointed that Eugene's connections weren't of the more nefarious variety. While I suspected that Dolores could get in some major trouble for giving her lover such exclusive access to the Mets, somehow it didn't rank up there with supplying steroids or weed or another equally illegal substance to the players.

"Don't ask, don't tell, indeed," I said, turning my attention back to the game.

Another mystery solved.

"Shut up, Metro." He waggled a finger at me. "And don't go telling anybody about this, you hear?" He pulled on the hem of his jacket to straighten it. "A man's got to uphold his reputation."

I cleared my throat. "Don't worry. Your secret's safe with me." I eyed him. "For now."

At least until I needed more tickets. Possibly to the World Series.

Of course, knowing that he'd gotten the seats free and had made me pay—big—this time around rankled in a way my conscience wouldn't let me ignore.

Not that it had mattered. I'd wanted the access and would have paid for it anyway. I needed to get to the bottom of this Venezuela case. And I needed to get to it now.

I checked my cell phone to see if Rosie had called me back while I was otherwise occupied. She hadn't.

Of course, it only stood to reason that now that I had my hands around a line which could pull up the winning fish, Rosie's sister probably would go into labor.

It was the top of the eighth and the Mets were down by two runs. Only one inning to go. Things didn't get any more exciting than this. And we all knew what I did at ball games when I got excited.

I shouted at the ump.

"If you don't settle down, I'm going to escort you out myself," Waters said.

I gave him a double take. "You couldn't take down a baby goat with two helpers."

"Try me."

I decided to contain myself. Not so much because of Waters' threat, but because—the Venezuela case aside—I really wanted to see this game. Hey, this was sports and Queens' history in the making. And I wanted to be able to tell my grandchildren I'd been there, instead of mumbling about how I got kicked out of the game.

I looked toward the team family box seats to see what Gisela was doing, but halfway there, my gaze caught and held on someone a few rows above them. Funny that the instant I should think about grandchildren I would spot Dino.

How, in this sea of people, was it that I would see him?

Hmm. Had I known he was coming, I could have asked to use his ticket. And with a little shameless flirting I could have gotten it without the use of money.

Then again, what price could I put on my freedom?

I purposely glanced toward the family boxes, instantly finding Gisela Venezuela. She looked at least as good as the ring that flashed in the overhead lights as she clapped.

Dutiful wife, indeed.

But I had to admit that she did look happy. And for the first time I spotted the two Venezuela children, no older than two and three, as she bent down and pointed for them to wave at their daddy.

I grimaced and looked to the left. It's then that I spotted what looked like a cowboy hat on a man who was walking away from me toward the mezzanine level. I squinted, and then grabbed for the small binoculars hanging on a cord around Waters' neck.

"Ow. What in the hell are you trying to do, Metro? Kill me?"

I ignored him and lifted the glasses to my eyes. But just as I focused on the cowboy hat, it disappeared into the exit well leading to the concession stands.

Damn.

Waters tugged and I had to release the cord.

Was it Porter? I hadn't pegged him as the baseball type. They didn't even have baseball in Australia, did they? I think the closest they came was cricket.

No. It couldn't have been Porter. Probably my mind was playing tricks on me, what with making out Dino in the crowd. Dino, who was from a place that didn't have baseball, either.

I looked to see him cheering on Venezuela as he took the mound for the last inning. I smiled.

"You know, you're a real pain in the ass," Waters said,

straightening his binoculars. "I knew I'd regret selling you that ticket."

I stared at him.

"What's that look mean?" he asked.

"What look?"

"That one, right there. It looks like you're thinking about something that means harm for me."

I shrugged. "I'm not thinking anything."

"Sure you aren't. You know, sometimes you scare me, Metro."

"Sometimes I scare myself."

Venezuela struck out the first two batters, relying entirely on his left hand.

The fact inspired thoughts of Fowler, who was still laid up in a hospital bed, unconscious, his ex-wife still holding vigil. I'd actually stopped by in person earlier, but I hadn't stayed long. He'd looked even worse in the light of day and I was pretty sure his ex had seen me wince when I stepped into the room.

Still, not even that could compare to his ex's quietly asked question after I'd said I'd check in again later as I'd been heading for the door: "So you and George . . . you're a couple, then?"

I would have passed out straightaway if I hadn't been so afraid they'd put me in the bed next to Fowler's.

Fowler's ex reminded me of the quiet girls in school. You know the type. The smart ones that sat in the middle of the room trying not to draw attention to themselves, the ones that usually had stringy hair they didn't wash nearly often enough and wore eyeglasses that were two decades out of style? The type that when they had a makeover they came out looking va-va-voom gorgeous, like a female version of Superman without the red tights and cape?

At any rate, I still wasn't sure what I had said to her, only knew that I couldn't have gotten out of that room fast enough.

Me and Fowler . . . cripes.

The crack of a bat whacking a ball sounded, yanking me back to the game. Up and up the ball went. And the catcher and Venezuela made a run for it even as the fans in the box to my right fell over each other trying to catch it. Venezuela didn't reach over the wall with his mitt, but with his left, pitching hand, giving me a great view of his tattoo as he grabbed the ball in midair and away from the outstretched fans' hands.

I cheered along with the other fifty thousand fans in the stadium, the roar deafening.

My cell phone vibrated in my pocket. Rosie.

My heart beat a million miles a minute as I watched Venezuela walk back to the mound, waving the ball in the air.

"Whatcha got, Rosie, girl?" I asked.

"You're never going to believe it . . ."

A minute later I rang off and then put the cell back into my pocket.

"Where are you going?" Waters asked me as I picked up my purse and turned toward the aisle.

"Not me," I said, grabbing his hand, "us."

He stared at me and the way I held him. "I'm not going anywhere."

I smiled at him and yanked.

He came.

AS I STOOD IN THE packed press area waiting for the players to emerge from the locker room after their latest victory, I held my spot at the front of the crowd even as I considered the picture I had pieced together. Was it possible? As farfetched as it seemed, could I have stumbled onto what was really happening in the Venezuela household without even trying?

Six months. That's how long I'd been a private investigator. And while I didn't consider myself a master PI by any means—but it's definitely what I was aiming for—I was coming to understand that much of the job had to do with instinct and flat-out luck. Not luck that the answers would fall into your lap, but rather that you'd be able to figure out everything before you got fired or someone got away with doing something really bad.

I shivered despite the warm press of bodies around me.

"Hey, lady, you here again?"

I eyed the reporter who had pegged me as the "broad" who'd been ejected from the game a couple of weeks back. "Yeah. You got a problem with it?"

I looked at where Waters had hung back and was talking to what looked like another reporter and then returned my attention to the entryway. The players were just beginning to trickle out. I noticed that Gisela was waiting on the other side of the long hall nearer the exit to walk her husband out. I cleared my throat, readying myself for the moment of truth. I didn't know if my ruse would pay off, but if it did . . .

Venezuela finally came out, grinning like a champion and the crowd of reporters cheered. He caught his wife in a bear hug and kissed her, her make-up ring outshining the bright camera lights illuminating the area.

Finally, he turned toward the press.

"Reni, Reni!" Everyone wanted his attention as he approached to my left. My throat tightened as I watched him. If I was right, this meant that I'd just cracked my biggest case to date. Forget being known for rescuing dogs. This . . . this had the potential to launch me straight into the stratosphere of Master PI Land.

He neared me and I held out my notepad. "Your autograph, please."

His grin froze as he looked into my face.

"Oh, and could you please sign your real name, Santos?"

Just like that I found his hand around my neck, cutting off all air.

And I discovered how ill conceived my idea had been . . .

Twenty-nine

JUST AS QUICKLY THE HAND disappeared, and so did Santos Bastardo, with only those in the immediate vicinity having witnessed his physical attack, and apparently dismissing it as either a figment of their imagination or convincing themselves that I had deserved it.

If they believed the latter, they would have been right. I had deserved it, because I'd been dumb enough to test out a theory without thinking it through first, believing myself safe in public.

And completely ignoring what I had just put at risk: namely, my life.

Not only mine, but that of the real Reni Venezuela.

You see, after having sorted through the aliases in order to finger the ear soup couple for the frauds that they were, I'd gone back to my car and looked through all my notes and files on Reni. I'd come across the poor copy of the Spanish language newspaper that Rosie had downloaded but that I'd been unable to read because she'd shrunk it to fit on the page. I'd called Rosie to ask her to read the original she'd accessed online to me. Where I had thought the photo and piece was on Reni Bastardo during his pre-Venezuela days (or post-Venezuela, depending on the way you looked at it), instead it had been on his older brother, Santos Bastardo. The piece was dated last year, and had mentioned Reni as going under the name "Venezuela" now and playing AAA in New York.

It seemed both of them had been pitchers through elementary and high school in South America. And both of them had been very good.

They also looked enough alike that they could have been twins.

And then a thought had occurred to me. Up until now, Rosie had been searching for items on Reni under the name Venezuela. So I'd asked her to get anything she could find on Bastardo, both Reni and his brother Santos. She'd balked at working from home at first, especially since she was on baby watch, but I'd reminded her that the entire reason we'd gotten her the laptop instead of a regular desktop computer was so that she could work anywhere. And since she had it with her, she could easily do the search I was asking for. And I even helped her narrow it, asking her to concentrate on Pittsburgh around the time it was said Reni had changed his demeanor according to his wife and his ex-security detail, and giving her the cross-street address I'd found in Fowler's notepad.

She'd gotten back to me during the game.

"You're never going to believe this, but at the team hotel in Pittsburgh not only was there a room reserved for Venezuela, but another under the name Bastardo. Santos Bastardo."

My skin had absolutely tingled at the news.

"And, get this. Those cross streets you gave me? It's in Corona. I called the company that manages the apartment building and guess what I found out? They rented an apartment to none other than Santos Bastardo the same day the team returned home from Pittsburgh."

I fought my way back to the press level of the stadium and out to the parking area, hoping to make it there before Santos could drive off. I nearly tripped over a box of popcorn someone had dropped in the aisle. I took the stairs instead of waiting for the elevator. I made it to Lot B just in time to watch Santos drive out of the players' lot in the Mercedes by himself. He squealed off, nearly hitting a group of waiting fans as he went.

Damn!

I ran full out for my own car, which was parked at the end of a long aisle, my reasoning when I arrived being that it would be easier to get out once the game ended. Of course, I hadn't taken into consideration that I'd actually have to reach the car first. Or that I would need to give chase to someone.

I finally reached Lucille and backed her out, nearly slamming into the Hummer limo that probably held Gisela and her children along with Santos' security detail. The driver laid on the horn as I threw the car into drive and sped off, trying like hell to spot the Mercedes.

I couldn't see it anywhere.

I turned out of the parking lot, frantically trying to figure out where he might go.

I remembered Gisela's telling me that first day when she hired me that she felt her husband had changed. I never in a million years would have guessed that he had. Quite literally.

And that it had been done so seamlessly that not even Gisela had noticed the difference. Oh, she had. In the beginning. But after two weeks of being afraid her marriage might be over, her mind had probably started playing tricks on her. I mean, who would ever suspect that the brother of your husband had traded places with him? Both had played baseball coming up, so there would be little difference there. (I had little doubt that when I looked into it, I'd find that Santos wasn't a switch pitcher like his younger brother, but rather a leftie, thus the reason why "Reni" suddenly stopped switching hands.)

But shouldn't Gisela have noticed the difference in bed?

Then I remembered what she'd said, "It was just like the first time all over again."

It hadn't been *like* the first time, it had been the first time. And I supposed that the rock had distracted her so much that she might not have noticed any other physical differences. So that quicker than you could blink the abnormal began to become normal.

Christ.

I banged on the steering wheel at the intersection of Forty-first and 108th. Where would he go, where would he go?

Then it occurred to me: The only place he ever went without his security team, when he thought that no one was looking. The apartment building was not too far from the stadium in Corona. The same one that had been rented in his name.

Could his brother Reni still be alive? Maybe hiding out there?

And what? I asked myself. He'd given up a primo position pitching for a major league team he'd worked so hard to achieve because he couldn't handle the celebrity? Handed over his mitt to his brother to give him a shot in the spotlight?

No. I suspected that if Reni were alive, it wasn't due to any of those reasons. Rather, Santos hadn't had the guts to kill him.

Yet.

I turned left and stepped on the gas, hoping I wouldn't be too late. . . .

FIVE MINUTES LATER I SQUEALED onto the street where the apartment was located, double-parked, and got out of the car, my heart leaping into my throat when I discovered the Mercedes was parked across the sidewalk in front of the building.

He was already there.

I reached into my purse for my pepper spray and then stared at it. Using this for protection against a Major League Baseball player would be like trying to use a stop sign against a herd of elephants. I backtracked to my car and reached into the glove compartment, only then I realized my gun wasn't there. The Glock was sitting on my kitchen table where I'd taken it to clean it last night (damn, Pamela Coe). If I'd also been a little creeped out about what happened to Fowler, I wasn't saying. Although I could probably safely admit to fear now without concern of coming off as a way off base conspiracy theorist.

Double crap.

I looked around the car, spotting the end of the souvenir wood baseball bat that I'd bought and had Reni—rather Santos impersonating Reni—sign. I pulled it out, gripping the wood tightly, and then headed for the building again.

I didn't know what I expected to do with the bat. I mean, didn't it veer toward stupidity to try to use a bat—as a weapon or otherwise—against someone who was a literal pro when it came to the same? But forced to choose between my pepper spray and the bat, well, the heavy stick came out way ahead.

I reached the front of the building. The front door hung open about a foot, indicating the hinges were either broken or Santos had left it open. I used the bat to open it farther and hold it as I peeked inside the hallway. Only a dim bulb on the second floor illuminated the stairwell. The place smelled of urine and mold and was littered with toys and garbage and other items I didn't want to try to identify (was that a used syringe in the corner?). I looked up the stairs, then down into the inky blackness that led to the basement apartments. My heart beat so heavily that I was afraid it might punch a hole through my chest.

Probably I should have asked Rosie for the apartment number.

Where was he?

I heard the unmistakable sound of glass breaking.

The basement.

I ran down into the darkness before I could think twice about my actions, finding the door behind the steps cracked open an inch. As a result of someone just going in? Grabbing the bat tightly in both hands and lifting it to hang over my shoulder, I neared the crack, peering inside. Diffused yellow light from an old lamp that sat on the floor brightened what appeared to be an otherwise unfurnished apartment. I listened intently for another sound. Muffled noises came from some-where behind the door. With the toe of my shoe, I edged the door open slightly, cringing when it squeaked.

Silence.

Then the door began to close as if someone had quickly pushed it.

I caught it with my shoe and then gave it a kick, staring wide-eyed as it arced open, revealing a man tied to a heavy chair (Reni? I figured it was a pretty safe bet at this point), Santos poised over him with a knife.

Yikes!

The door hit the wall and then slammed closed, shutting me out in the dark hallway.

The image of Reni tied to a chair brought a memory crash-ing back. The day I'd gone to see Gisela at the McMansion she'd told me that last year Santos had been denied a tourist visa to the States because he'd kept his estranged wife tied to a chair for a week.

Given the situation inside the apartment, I suspected that he was perfecting his technique with his brother.

I was forced to release the bat in order to try the door handle. It was unlocked. But I wasn't sure that was a good thing or a bad thing considering that Santos had seen me standing in the hall. I opened the door and moved to grip the bat again, only to find a hand snaking out from inside the apartment and grabbing me and yanking me inside. The bat flew from my left hand, landing with a clatter on the floor even as I was thrown across the room. My head hit the wall with a sickening thud and I crumpled to a heap on the floor. I scrambled to all fours and turned around as quickly as I could, rapid-fire Spanish filling my ears.

I didn't understand it all, but I understood enough. Santos was unhappy with me being there. And judging by the knife he held, he intended to remedy that.

I slid a glance toward Reni. He was bound to a heavy oak chair in four places, chest, ankles, hands, and waist. A bucket had been placed under the chair and the stench threatened to choke me. Fast-food wrappers littered the place and duct tape wasn't just fastened to his lips, it appeared an entire roll had been wound around his head to cover his mouth to make sure he couldn't get a peep out.

"Santos, look," I said, getting to my feet with help from my left hand against the wall as I held out my right to ward off any attack. "I wasn't even sure until fifteen minutes ago that you had done what you had. I'm sure no one else knows about it." Was that bright? Letting him know that I was the only one that had figured everything out? I gulped. "What I'm trying to say is that no one else needs to know. Ever."

He was sweating profusely, his eyes two burning black coals as he glared at me. He looked more dangerous than anyone I'd ever encountered in my life. Including the incident on Hell Gate Bridge with Tony DiPiazza and his goons. While I'd been fitted with cement boots then, the mere act of being out in the open had allowed for the possibility for escape, however remote.

Here . . .

Well, here I experienced a dread that probably mirrored what those caged dogs must have felt. Santos stood between me and the door. A wall was behind me. And Reni would be of no help at all.

"Come on, Santos," I said, continuing to use his name. Over the past two weeks he had probably done a pretty good job of convincing himself that he'd become his brother. I needed to remind him of who he really was. Because it was that man that had tied his brother up rather than killing him straight off, which revealed my only chance of talking any sense into him.

"That's your baby brother over there. The kid you grew up with. Family. Probably you taught him how to play baseball—"

"That's why it should have been me who had been picked up by the teams in Venezuela," he shouted in such a thick accent I had trouble making out the words. "Me, who should have been brought to the States to play for Triple A. Me, who got the multimillion dollar contract with the Mets."

Okay, so I'd touched a nerve I hadn't expected to. But I did get the motivation behind his actions.

"I was the better player," he said, jabbing his thumb against the impressive wall of his chest. "Me. I was the better pitcher, the better hitter. But they wanted him. They wanted my brother because he was nicer. Because he got along better with everyone. Because he was ambidextrous. They wanted a brand, something different that was marketable. And they got that in him."

I held up my hands. "I'm sure you're right. I know it's been you who's nabbed the team the pennant." At this point I was capable of saying he was a shoo-in for the position of New York City mayor. Anything to get him to put that knife down and stop looking at me like I was all that stood between him and a roast beef dinner. And he appeared to be very, very hungry. "You're the man, Santos. You're the man."

I ordered my brain to come up with something clever to say. Something that would convince him that killing me, killing his brother, was so the wrong thing to do. But someone appeared to have pulled the plug to my head, cutting off electricity to the only thing that could save me.

Reni was trying to say something through the tape. I looked to see him beseeching his brother, a man who looked so much like him it was eerie, with his eyes. Trying to talk to the man who had stolen his life, slept with his wife, played father to his children, all while he'd been tied to a chair and forced to do his business in a bucket.

"I don't think he can breathe," I said, edging toward the chair.

"Where are you going?" Santos shouted, waving the knife a little too close to me.

"He can't breathe! We've got to get the tape off."

I stared at Reni, trying to communicate with him without words.

Finally, he appeared to catch on to what I was saying. He held his breath and thrashed against his bindings as if he couldn't get air into his lungs.

"Help me!" I said to Santos. "Help me get the tape off before he dies."

Of course, I was purposely leaving out that probably Santos' intention was to kill his brother. To finally and completely step into his shoes. Forever.

But he was operating on pure adrenaline, and he didn't seem to connect those dots.

Either that or he had exactly how he was going to take his brother's life planned out and this wasn't it.

"Give me the knife!"

Santos looked at me as if I'd lost a few gumdrops on the way to the game.

"Give me the goddamn knife so I can cut the tape!" I said again, as if it was the most natural demand for me to make.

He gave me the knife.

I couldn't believe it.

So there I stood, with the only weapon in the room. And I didn't have a clue what to do with it. . . .

Thirty

THERE ARE TIMES WHEN A knife comes in handy. Cutting tags from new clothes comes to mind. And it didn't suck to have one when jewelry snagged your favorite sweater. But when it came to protecting myself, well, the weapon rated low on the list if only because there was something messy about it. And because if you were going to use it, well, then, you'd better be prepared to kill the other person.

I'd used my gun three times to protect myself. But kill someone?

I don't know. I wasn't sure I had it in me. Death was permanent. And I didn't relish the thought of playing the role of judge, jury, and executioner.

Hell, I couldn't even commit to the permanency of a tattoo.

Which brought me back to the knife I now held in my hands. A gun I could aim at his foot and effectively stop him. A knife . . . well, a knife I'd have to make damn sure I hit something important like an artery, or else I risked certain death myself. Because I had little doubt that he would slam me against the wall and take the knife back unless I incapacitated him somehow.

And how did I do that? Did I go for the neck? I eyed his, wondering if I'd be able to hit an artery, it was so thick. The chest? Again, he was in such good shape that I pondered if I'd do any real damage. And then there was the whole bone issue to deal with. How about the eyes?

That one made me shudder as I thought of how many lamb eyes my grandmother had tried to make me eat over the years. And I had eaten one. Once. And the juicy way it had exploded in my mouth made bile rise in my throat even now, many years later.

So that left me with what, exactly?

Reni made a sound and I realized that I was taking far too long to do what I'd said I was going to do, namely remove the tape from his mouth so he could breathe. By now, he certainly would have died from asphyxiation had his struggling been real.

"Hold on, Reni," I said loudly, trying to appear like I didn't have any other agenda than to cut the tape from him. "I'll have this off in a minute. You need to be real still for me."

I stared at him meaningfully as I positioned myself so that Santos couldn't see what I was doing. I reached for the tape with my left hand even as with my right I tried to slide the blade under the bindings on his left hand. I figured if I could free one of his hands, then he would be able to get loose. But the thick rope was resistant.

"Let me do it," Santos said, stepping up to my side.

I ditched my cutting attempts and smiled shakily at him. "I've got it. See, I'm almost there."

I redirected the blade toward the duct tape. Reni's eyes widened. Yes, yes, I knew that one slip and I might end up getting myself an eyeball yet.

Finally I cut through the tape and yanked a swatch from in front of his mouth. He feigned fighting for breath, his chin hanging low and his chest heaving even as I desperately sought for a way to go back to work on the bindings.

"Give me back the knife." Santos' large hand appeared before me.

The last thing I wanted to do was give him back the knife.

"I don't think that's such a good idea," I said. And then I threw the knife over a counter and into the kitchen. It hit something then clattered to the floor.

Santos grabbed me. "What in the hell did you have to go and do a fool thing like that for?"

His fingers bit into my arms and my teeth rattled where he shook me.

"Let her go," Reni rasped.

We both looked at him, surprised to hear a third voice in the room.

Santos cursed. "I shouldn't have let you cut the tape."

"Goddamn your soul to hell, Santos," Reni said between clenched teeth, his every muscle straining against the bindings. I stared at his left hand where I'd managed to cut partially through the rope. "Did you think you'd really get away with this? Mama always said you were the dumbest out of her kids. That you knew more about baseball than you did the alphabet. And I always stuck up for you. But not now. Now you've gone too far."

Santos wasn't looking too good. Big, thick veins bulged in his neck and his hands tightened on my arms.

I made a little sound and he released me, his attention on his brother.

"You ungrateful little fuck," Santos said, concentrating completely on his brother. "If it weren't for me, you would have tossed the baseball bat onto the fire for warmth."

"Considering where we are now, I wish I would have. We'd all have been the better for it."

"What? Freezing and going hungry?"

"No, we would still be a family."

I followed the exchange, trying to make sense out of what was being said. The best I could figure was that while Santos had been the better player, Reni had been the better person. (Go figure. Hell, I didn't even know either of them well, and I preferred Reni.) And while I was in no condition to think clearly, and was definitely no psychologist, I suspected that when Santos' wife had left him a year ago, and he'd tied her to a chair in an attempt to force her to stay, something in him had snapped. The something that keeps us all from crossing an invisible line between what we wanted and what we couldn't have.

After that, he'd decided to make a full-out attempt at what he saw had been denied him.

I began backing away from the brothers, searching for a way out of the situation.

That's when something my grandfather once said echoed in my mind. "Always remember, and never forget, that it's not a person's size or strength that matters, Sofie. It's their brains."

He'd tapped a gnarled finger against his temple.

At the time I thought he was taking a pacifist, nonviolence stance. But as I stood there looking at a man that was easily twice my size, and who could choke the life out of me with two fingers, I understood that Grandpa Kosmos hadn't been talking about not hitting someone. Rather, he'd been referring to hitting them right.

Much like with the knife.

But what I was thinking about wouldn't kill Santos. It would only incapacitate him so I could get out of there and get some help.

The problem was that I'd never taken any self-defense courses, and beyond what I'd seen on TV or in action movies, I didn't have a clue how to attack Santos in a way that would incapacitate him.

Something about the solar plexus. And, again, the eyes. And, of course, there was always my personal favorite, aiming a hit straight for the gonads.

"Hey, Santos," I said.

He snapped upright and looked at me.

I punched him in the chest, and then brought my foot up right between his legs.

The problem was that my hit seemed to bounce off and I'd probably done more damage to my knuckles than his chest, and by the time I'd gotten my foot halfway up, he had a hand down to block the kick.

Oh, shit.

His hand went directly around my neck again and he shoved me the few feet to the wall, holding me there.

I coughed, and clawed at his arm.

"*Puta*. When I first found out Gisela had hired you, I thought that you were too stupid to figure everything out. I should have known better. I should have killed you straight off the bat."

Bat . . .

My mind caught and held on to the fact that the baseball bat was on the floor across the room.

Of course, I'd actually have to be able to get to it in order for it to make any difference. And it didn't look like I was going to get that chance. Not with the iron vice around my neck pinning me to the wall.

I coughed again, my throat burning.

Movement behind me caught my attention and I looked to see Reni freeing his left hand from the bindings. He frantically pushed at the rope around his chest and shrugged it up over his right shoulder and then went to work on his right hand.

Please, hurry, I thought, my sight beginning to dim.

Every bit of air I managed to suck in scorched my lungs and my clawing and kicking stopped. Simply, I didn't have the energy beyond that required to stare at my attacker in shock.

This was really happening, wasn't it?

I was on the verge of passing out when suddenly the hand moved from my neck. I collapsed to the floor like a rag doll, gasping for air as a partially freed Reni pounced on his brother, knocking him away from me. His right leg was still attached to the chair, but he had enough leverage to get Santos away from me.

But he didn't have enough leverage, or enough power after having been tied to a chair for two weeks, to be any kind of a match against his brother.

Even as I regained some control over my breathing, and a good number of my wits, I pushed myself up with the help of the wall, watching as Santos landed punch after punch on Reni's face and chest. I winced every time bone hit flesh. I looked toward the kitchen. Would I be able to get in there and find the knife before Santos could catch up with me?

Not a chance in hell.

But I could get to the bat . . .

I limped toward the opposite side of the room, curious as to the lethargy in my limbs as I rasped for a normal intake of breath. I curved my fingers around the bat in one smooth move, ordering my body to cooperate. I barely had to adjust my hold before I pulled it back and let one rip against the man who would have taken my life.

The bat caught Santos across the shoulders and he fell against Reni. I swung again, this time catching him across the back of the legs. He went down to his knees, his attempt to stop his fall bringing him to face me.

I swallowed hard, staring into his surprised face.

"Yeah, I don't think you exactly saw things going down this way, did you?" I said, my voice sounding like sandpaper scratching against cement.

He roared and tried to get to his feet again to lunge at me.

I gripped the bat snugly in both hands and swung it harder yet, aiming straight for his left upper arm near the shoulder. The crack of wood against bone filled the room. His roar turned to a howl of pain. He gripped the area with his opposite hand and went all the way down.

"Uh-huh. Try impersonating your brother again, you bastard. Actually, I don't think you'll be throwing a ball again, or swinging a bat again, anytime soon."

And just like that, with a little help from Reni, I had faced down my most frightening opponent to date. And won.

I'D LEARNED A LONG TIME ago that what my mother didn't know, wouldn't hurt her.

Of course, that applied to the current situation not at all. Or did it?

At any rate, as I let myself into my apartment to find my very happy dog Muffy waiting for me, I figured I'd find out soon enough. And I would be the only one to find out.

First, since Santos was deemed a nonissue, Reni had taken it upon himself to transfer the bindings he'd worn to his brother, just in case. Then Reni and I had stood there staring at each other, speechless.

Santos would need medical attention, that much was obvious. But how and where and under what name seemed to be the question.

At first I didn't catch on to what Reni was saying. Mostly because I couldn't seem to get beyond the similarities between him and his brother. Although the more time I spent around them, the more I counted out the differences. Reni's face was a little fuller, Santos' build just a little stockier. Where Santos' regularly wore an intense expression, Reni's eyes were softer and warmer.

"What do you mean, under which name?" I'd asked him.

Reni had shared a look with his incapacitated brother even as he shuffled over to the chair he had been tied to for the past two weeks.

"I don't want my brother arrested," he'd said.

I'd stared at him, gobsmacked. "What do you mean you don't want him arrested? Don't you want him to pay for what he's done to you?" I'd gestured with my hands. "He wore your cleats, pitched your balls . . ." What I was saying didn't seem to be hitting home so I pulled out the big guns. "He slept with your wife."

"Once," Santos said quickly, taking a moment out from groaning to defend himself. "I slept with her once."

Reni looked a breath away from slugging his brother. "I don't ever want her to know that. I don't want her to know that she lived with a stranger for two weeks. That she . . . shared a bed with him. It would destroy her. And it's not her fault."

I agreed with him there. "No, it's not her fault. She hired me straight off because she knew there was something strange going on. And she wanted me to find out what it was, without knowing exactly what she was looking for." I cleared my throat. "Oh, and by the way, she's seen pictures of you sleeping with three women in Florida."

"You son of a bitch!" Reni advanced on his brother and lifted his arm. I played interference by standing in between them, although by all rights, I should have let him have at him. If anyone had reason to dole out a beating, it was Reni.

That's when what he'd said about not wanting Gisela to know the truth or having his brother arrested began to make a strange kind of sense.

Since it didn't look like Santos was going to be picking up a baseball again unless he was showing a kid how to throw, well, no one would have to worry about him doing something like this again, no matter the crime he'd committed. So what was the point in letting everyone know?

And then you had the whole team angle. What would happen if the press found out the Mets' prize pitcher had been replaced by his brother for a couple of weeks? Would the wins still be valid? What would happen to Reni? I'd seen countless sports celebrities built up only to be torn right back down. Would this end his major league career before it had even really begun?

It was then I realized that when all was said and done, it always came back to the game. And I wasn't talking about just baseball, either. I was referring to the game of life. Not so much the outcome, but how it was played. The strategy that Reni was proposing by keeping everything quiet wouldn't have been my first choice. But considering everything riding on the outcome, it might just have been the best play, if not the only play, to make.

Thirty-one

I WOKE UP THE FOLLOWING morning feeling like I'd swallowed the contents of my down pillow. I reached for the glass of water I'd left on my nightstand only to find it empty from having drunk from it throughout the night.

So, there I was, feeling beaten and battered, and I had nothing to show for it other than the knowledge that I'd saved a guy's life. And my own. And that I'd done it with extraordinary flair.

Not exactly a bad day at work. Except that I couldn't tell anybody about it.

I disengaged my legs from where Muffy was lying on them so I could go to the bathroom.

I finished my business, took a shower, got dressed, and then wandered into the kitchen to make my frappé, Muffy having roused himself and following me, getting a bit of breakfast of his own via his dog bowl. I got the paper from the hall and then sat down and spread it out on the coffee table. It wasn't all that difficult to imagine my name on the front page of the sports section, if not the front page, period.

As it stood, Santos had been admitted to Elmhurst Hospital under his real name, Santos Bastardo, and had a broken collarbone and shoulder thanks to me and the souvenir bat he'd signed. Following his recovery, he promised to go back home to Venezuela where he'd remain. Reni had contacted his sports agent who had discreetly brought in a private doctor for him (Reni had told the agent and Gisela that he'd been mugged by a stranger after last night's game and didn't want police involvement). The physician had visited him at home and reported that aside from dehydration and some muscle strain—injuries not consistent with a mugging, but no one had questioned it—he was fine. While he wouldn't be playing baseball for the next couple of days, he could easily return to the game in time to get us to, and then win us, the World Series.

All in all, I guessed that would make Fowler and most of New York happy.

Speaking of which, I'd called Elmhurst this morning to find that Fowler had not only regained consciousness, but that it looked like he and his ex might have a chance at reconciliation. The latter I'd worked out during a brief conversation with the crusty reporter, who'd pretended anger at my contacting his ex, even though I could tell he was pleased.

His recovery and our conversation had taken a bit of the sting out of my decision not to let him in on last night's happenings, no matter how much I wanted tell him that we'd both been right. There had been something amiss with Venezuela.

But I figured that he'd find another hunch to follow soon enough. Hopefully next time I wouldn't be along for the ride.

And hopefully it wouldn't come as a result of his passing Santos' room at the hospital.

Muffy put his right paw on the paper in front of me, his tongue lolling out of the side of his mouth.

"What do you want, boy?" I gave his ears a scratch.

He barked once, looking at me expectantly.

"Sorry, I don't know dog speak," I told him.

A moment later, a knock sounded at the door. Muffy remained where he was, staring at me.

Could it be that he'd been trying to tell me a visitor was imminent?

Nah.

I closed the paper and went to answer it, expecting Mrs. Nebitz or someone else as familiar to both Muffy and me since he hadn't barked.

I got Dino.

"*Kalimera,* Sofie," he said, "good morning" in Greek.

I looked to where Muffy silently wagged his tail next to me. Why hadn't he barked? Was this his way of giving Dino his stamp of approval? And how did I feel about that? The fact that everybody seemed to like Dino, including my no good mutt?

"What are you doing here?" I blurted out.

Dino's grin slipped, but not by much. "You asked to borrow my car."

I rubbed the heel of my hand against my forehead. I'd completely forgotten that I'd run out of cars that Venezuela's goons wouldn't recognize and had called Dino for his yesterday.

I could easily forgive myself the memory lapse if merely because of everything that had gone down last night. If only I didn't suspect that I'd forgotten on purpose so that I would be faced with Dino and nothing but time on my hands this morning.

He held up his keys. "I need you to drop me back at the shop."

My cell phone buzzed on the coffee table behind me and I held up a finger. "Give me a sec."

Rosie.

"To what do I owe the pleasure?"

Rosie shrieked more than said, "Yolanda's on the way!"

AS I SAT IN THE waiting area of St. John's Hospital, watching where Dino paced opposite me, I wondered why I hadn't just told him the truth—that I no longer needed his car—rather than ask him to drive me to the hospital. My gaze flicked over his manly frame. Okay, so I didn't have to think hard. A situation like this was just what the doctor ordered. I could look my fill without worrying about having to talk to him, fight him off, or otherwise come up with excuses why he and I shouldn't date.

"My cousin was in labor for forty hours with her first," Dino quietly said.

I pretended interest in the neonatal magazine I was flipping through. "Really?"

I couldn't imagine being in labor an hour, much less forty of them.

"This baby wouldn't dare take that long," I told him. "Or else she'd have to deal with her aunt Rosie."

Just then, Rosie entered the room like a shot, looking sweaty and tired, as if she were the one giving birth. Her smile was as big as the borough. "It's a boy."

I got up to give her a hug as Dino looked at his watch and slid his hands into the pockets of Dockers.

"And Lupe?"

"Worn out but happy." Rosie drew back. "But we don't know what we're going to name him. I mean, they told us it was going to be a girl. We even bought everything in pink."

"I'm sure they'll let you exchange it."

"Probably." She chewed on the inside of her cheek. "But I'm

going to have to repaint the walls. Even though Ricky thinks it's kismet and that probably we should leave everything the way it is."

Ricky was Rosie's openly gay brother who'd also been in the private delivery suite with his sisters and what, I suspected, was the entire Rodriguez family, extended and otherwise.

"Do you want to see the baby?" Rosie asked excitedly. "They're cleaning him up now, but they should be bringing him back soon. Come on. Both of you."

She took my hand and started leading me from the room. "This is really a family event," I said.

"Don't be ridiculous. You are family."

Her words warmed me as I allowed myself to be led, Dino following after me, into the private suite. Dino and I congratulated the new mother, who looked like Rosie—sweaty and tired, but happy—and the family welcomed us.

A nurse brought the baby back in as Dino and I donned the face masks we were given. Everyone awwed and cooed at the notably quiet and curious newborn as he was handed around the room.

It came my turn and I hesitated. He was so small. And appeared to weigh nothing as I took him into my arms and looked down into his open birth-blue eyes. Beautiful.

"You're a natural," Dino said next to me.

I quickly handed the baby back to his aunt Rosie and she handed him to a surprised Dino.

"With his father being gone and all, he'll need all the male influences he can get," she explained.

I melted back to the fringes of the group, watching Dino handle the newborn with ease. The Rodriguez family gushed with happiness. Rosie looked as proud as a mother.

In one way, I felt like I didn't belong there. In another, my presence felt completely natural.

Life was funny sometimes, wasn't it?

I reflected on the past few weeks, on the baseball games I'd attended, the cases I'd worked, everything that happened, expected or otherwise.

I think from time to time, we all hit a few foul balls. Or were thrown pitches we had no chance of hitting. What mattered was that when you stepped up to the plate you always aimed for that home run. That one perfect moment when your bat hit the ball at just the right angle and you knocked it straight out of the park.

You wouldn't hit it every time. But oh when you did . . .

But if straight out of the dugout you aimed for a foul, as was the case with Santos' underhanded plan to take his brother Reni's place, then you shouldn't be surprised if what you got didn't turn out the way you planned.

Then again, you didn't have to be behind the plate to get hit by a foul ball. Was it fair that Rosie's sister Lupe faced a challenging life as a single mother because of a cad of an exhusband? Or that I had to stoop to Thomas' level in order to keep him from seeking prosecution against my elderly grandfather? That Uncle Tolly had died in an explosion when he'd finally found peace with his wife?

Was it fair that I got a peek beyond the bright lights of celebrity? Understood that my icons, sports heroes, were human beings prone to making human mistakes?

This job was expanding my awareness on myriad topics.

It was also my job on a personal level to assimilate it all, accept it, and still find a way to achieve joy without compromising myself or my beliefs.

As I watched the easy way Dino talked to the tiny baby in his large hands, I squinted. Had I committed a foul with him? Had I taken a half-assed swing at the inside fast ball life had thrown at me that I had no chance of hitting right?

I remembered thinking that I'd given Dino Jake's sex. That all the pent-up sexual desire I held for the sexy Australian had erupted on one hot Sunday morning with the sexy Greek. I now saw that wasn't the case. Dino had gotten Dino's sex, period. What I felt for Porter was still tucked away in a neat little box, untouched.

But what I felt for Dino had begun to take on a life of its own. In a way I couldn't hope to contain, either in a box or otherwise.

So maybe, I reflected, I'd made a two-base hit with him, with the potential of an earned run. But I wouldn't know that unless I played out the rest of the game.

"Sofie?"

I blinked at where Rosie had taken the baby from Dino's arms. The newborn began crying like the dickens, signaling that he'd been handled enough for one day. The guests began breaking up, saying their final good-byes to the new mom and baby.

And Dino stood directly in front of me, looking at me curiously.

I smiled at him, deciding in that one moment that this was a game that I wanted to play, that I had to play, no matter the outcome.

And if Jake Porter showed up again, wanting to tinker with both me and my Sheila? Well, I'd consider that ball when it was thrown my way. . . .

Recipes

Dear Reader,

Food plays such a huge role in Greek and Greek-American life. It's more than the source of fuel for the body, it's a salve for the soul, an excuse to bring family and friends together. A brief stop can easily turn into a long visit, usually resulting in empty plates, laughter, and happy memories. Below are a few recipes of Greek dishes mentioned in this book. You can find more on our Web site at www.sofiemetro.com. *Kali Orexi!*

TRADITIONAL GREEK COFFEE

1 teaspoon Greek coffee powder (found at any Greek shop)
1 teaspoon sugar (to taste)
1 cup water (measure using the cup you plan to serve the coffee in, increasing the above ingredients for a larger cup)

Add coffee and sugar to water in a *briki* (small coffee pan). Stir over low heat until mixed. Let rise to the top. Serve. *Stin eyeia sas!*

GALAKTOBOUREKO—GREEK CUSTARD DESSERT

1 cup fine semolina (farina)
1½ cups sugar
1 tablespoon flour
1 teaspoon vanilla
6 cups whole milk
1 stick unsalted butter (½ cup)
6 egg yolks
25 phyllo sheets, thawed
¾ cup melted butter (to brush phyllo sheets)

Syrup:
2 cups sugar
1 cup water
1 teaspoon vanilla
1 teaspoon fresh lemon juice
2 thin strips of lemon peel

Combine semolina, sugar, and vanilla in a bowl. In a saucepan, bring milk to a boil, stirring to prevent scorching. Slowly add semolina mixture to the boiling milk. Cook over medium heat, stirring constantly, until the mixture thickens and comes to a full boil. Remove from heat.

In a small bowl, beat the egg yolks with a fork, and then stir into the hot custard mixture.

Butter a 9×13-inch Pyrex baking pan and cover bottom with 10 sheets of the phyllo, brushing melted butter on each sheet as you go (sheets should extend up the sides of the pan). Pour the custard mixture on top. Cover with remaining phyllo sheets, brushing each with butter as you go.

Score the top phyllo sheets into square or diamond shapes, being careful not to score as deeply as the custard. Bake on the center rack of a 375-degree oven for 35 to 40 minutes, until golden. Cut pieces all the way through.

Syrup: Boil sugar with water, vanilla, lemon juice, and peel for 5 minutes. Ladle the hot syrup over the top.

Cool thoroughly before serving. Refrigerate in hot weather. *Opa!*

PASTICCIO (Greek Lasagna)

Beef Mixture:
1 tablespoon olive oil
2 pounds ground chuck or beef
1 small, finely chopped onion
2 finely chopped garlic cloves (to taste)
6 whole cloves

2 teaspoons salt
1/2 teaspoon pepper
1 14.5-ounce can diced tomatoes

Noodles:
1 pound pasticcio noodles (found at any Greek or Italian
store)
1 tablespoon salt
1 cup grated *kefalotiri* cheese (or Parmesan)

Besamel:
1/2 cup butter (one stick)
3/4 cup flour
4 hot cups milk
Salt
Pepper
Dash of nutmeg (optional)
1 cup grated *kefalotiri* cheese (or Parmesan)
4 egg yolks

Beef mixture: Heat the olive oil in a large frying pan and
sauté the ground beef and onion and garlic until slightly
browned. Add remaining ingredients, cover, and cook
over medium heat for approximately 20 minutes.

Noodles: Cook the pasticcio in salted boiling water until soft but firm. Drain and return to the pan.

Besamel: Melt the butter in a heavy saucepan; add the
flour and cook, stirring constantly for 1 minute. Add the
milk and stir until the sauce is smooth. Add salt, pepper,
and nutmeg. Remove from heat and stir in the cheese and
egg yolks.

Sprinkle a 9×13-inch Pyrex pan with grated cheese
and put in half the pasticcio. Sprinkle with cheese and

cover with half the beef mixture. Repeat with the rest of the pasticcio and beef mixture and cheese. Spoon besamel over the top and sprinkle that with the rest of the cheese and cook in 350-degree oven for about 45 minutes or until golden brown. Let settle for 20 minutes and then cut into square pieces and serve. *Kali Orixi!*

TOR

Award-winning authors
Compelling stories

Please join us at the website
below for more information
about this author and other great
Tor selections, and to sign up for
our monthly newsletter!